Praise for the Kindred Ties series

Praise for Convergence

"This book has all you could possibly want:
betrayal, animals, action, adventure, and a
peculiar love triangle... I couldn't put it down.
This is definitely a series to get behind."
Jess, Book Bonding Independent Bookstore

"An action packed, sci-fi novel with real
contemporary issues."
Rob, Lamont Books

"Smith blends the spiritual, scientific and
environmental elements together well
among a cast of authentic characters. I
would recommend for people twelve and up
with an interest in science fiction and the
environment."
Kayla Gaskell, Read Plus

"Marita Smith's debut novel, Convergence,
carefully explores genes and more, with
scientific precision and an engaging plot...
Convergence will have readers travelling on
an adventure that will capture and entertain
their minds for hours."
Natasha Tambiah, Aurealis #112

Praise for Emergence

"An action-packed race against the clock where found family is championed. I couldn't put it down, I was desperate to know what happened next."
Alison Evans, YA author

"Smith has created an intriguing world in which animals and humans share a remarkable – and potentially lethal – bond. Enhanced by a diverse cast of characters, Emergence is a high-stakes tale that explores the frontiers of science, the depths of treachery in the pursuit of power, and the potency of love."
Erin Gough, YA author

"Emergence is full of surprises. Never holding back, Marita Smith's second novel continues the high stakes adventure that readers were introduced to in her debut, Convergence. Emergence definitely lives up to its namesake and reveals more than its fair share of twists and turns… It's an excellent sequel to Convergence and well worth reading."
Natasha Tambiah, Aurealis #113

RESILIENCE

First published in Australia by Marita Smith 2022

www.maritasmithauthor.com

Text Copyright © Marita Smith

This is a work of fiction.

Design by Fritz & Christie Design and Illustration: fritzandchristie.com

Cataloguing-in-Publication entry is available from the National Library of Australia
catalogue.nla.gov.au

Author: Marita Smith
Book Title: Resilience
Series: Kindred Ties
Number: Book Three
ISBN: 978-0-646-85790-9
Subject: Science Fiction

KINDRED TIES
BOOK THREE

RESILIENCE

MARITA SMITH

To the mind that is still, the whole universe surrenders.

– Lao Tzu

For Garry: publisher, mentor and friend.

1

Return

Robyn pressed her hand against the rock face, tracing the veins of glittering crystal revealed by the dancing sunlight. The wooden ruin of the walker temple protruded from the mountain's highest point, as if reaching for the stars. Uncrossing her legs, Robyn pushed herself onto her knees. Her head spun and she swayed for a moment until she felt the familiar push and pull of energy through her spine, the gentle pressure of the walkers' tethers. The quartz at her fingertips seemed to ground her, sharpening her awareness.

It shouldn't be possible. In the blink of an eye, she'd somehow travelled from the farmhouse to Laos through the spirit world. Energy coursed through her body as she stood on shaky legs, taking in the line of canvas tents just below the temple ruins.

"Laos," Robyn rasped. "I'm in *Laos?*"

"Each solstice feels more powerful than the last." The strange woman – Miranda – stepped forward.

"How do you know about the solstice? What are you doing here?" Robyn said in bewilderment.

Miranda removed her sunglasses and slowly wiped each lens with a cloth before placing them in a case in her jacket pocket. "You'll be pleased to know that I may be able to provide some answers." She turned and picked her way up the steep slope toward the encampment where a satellite dish suspended from a long pole swung in the breeze. Desperate for answers, Robyn followed, the stone firm against her bare feet, her mind awash with questions.

"Robyn?" called a familiar voice.

She shielded her eyes and looked to the line of tents. A skinny boy dressed in jeans and a t-shirt waved frantically. Without his robes, it took her a second to recognise him. And he had *hair.* "Lenti?"

As she crested the mountain top, the monk raced toward her and dropped to his knees, bowing to the ground. "It is an honour to serve you."

Curious faces peeked out from the tents. Cheeks burning, Robyn crouched and pulled Lenti to his feet. "You don't need to serve me, you've already done so much." Robyn stifled her exasperation. Lenti knew more about the spirit world and the walkers' abilities than most, but he wasn't her servant, nor did she want him to be. He was just a monk plucked from another era trying to live as a kid in the new. "You don't need to bow to me."

"Of course." Lenti bowed his head in deference, and then quickly straightened. "Apologies."

"But maybe you could tell me what the hell is going on here?"

Pleased to be given a task, Lenti bowed again and led her toward the largest of the tents where Miranda waited.

"When you first entered the spirit world," he said, "I felt something change. Everything started to fade, and I ended up back here at the temple. You are the true guide, finally returned." Lenti glanced reverently at the temple ruins then ducked inside the tent, beckoning for Robyn to follow him.

A huge desk covered in papers dominated the centre of the tent. Against one wall a hammock hung above a rug. Low cushions filled the remaining space.

Fear filled Robyn's guts. She spun around and confronted Miranda. "You're MRI."

Miranda simply smiled.

Lenti looked at Robyn in confusion. "Miranda is here to help us. She knows all about my order, about the walkers, and Nyx."

The pieces fell into place. "I know who you are. You're the Chief Director. Fang's supervisor. You're supposed to be dead." Here she stood, face to face with the woman responsible for the Beijing testing facility and the deaths of countless innocent kids. Robyn glanced at the tent entrance. She could run for it, but where would she go?

Miranda's smile morphed into a laugh. "Therefore, why should you trust me?" She walked around the table and began sorting through a stack of files. "I understand how you might feel about Fang, but I think you underestimate her abilities. I blame myself. She has a brilliant mind but needed a mentor stronger than me to guide her." Miranda pushed the papers aside. "But where were we. Ah, yes – reasons you should trust me. For one, I am a scientist like you. Two, I faked my own death when I realised the direction the program was taking." Miranda glanced up as the tent flap rustled and a figure entered. "And right on cue comes reason number three. I've been working with a close friend of yours."

Robyn frowned, turned around and gasped. Brock, the supervisor she'd once trusted so implicitly, stood in the entryway, eyes locked on hers. He looked older, thinner. A wiry white beard clung to his face. For a ridiculous moment, Robyn wondered who was feeding his cats. "You're … you're dead. I saw Fang shoot you."

Brock gave Miranda a 'told you so' look and she rolled her eyes. "I really didn't think she'd go that far."

"It still hurt like a mother," Brock said, rubbing his chest. Seeing Robyn's confusion, he added, "Bulletproof vest."

He stepped forward with his arms up, as if to hug her. "We're on the same side, Robyn."

In Bulgaria, he'd risked his life to save them. He'd always been so supportive of her research, academically and emotionally. Robyn had struggled to believe him to be capable of the atrocities perpetrated by the Mitochondrial Research Institute. "I think I need to sit down."

Lenti led her over to the cushions and crouched on his haunches by her side. Brock and Miranda joined her, sitting on the geometric-patterned rug. They looked at

Robyn as if she were the strange one in this equation. She glanced at Lenti. The boy monk seemed completely at ease, gazing at her with his open smile.

Robyn shifted her gaze between Brock and Miranda, searching for answers. In Bulgaria, Brock had taken a bullet for her. Miranda had disappeared right when the MRI was on the brink of a major breakthrough, allowing Vulcan to take control of the organisation. Why had she done that? Surely Miranda, of all people, knew what Vulcan was capable of.

"Are you telling me that you've been collaborating against Fang? Against Vulcan?"

Brock nodded at Miranda as if to say, *you start*.

Miranda hesitated then reached for a bulky walkie-talkie that looked like it had never left the 1980s. "First, I think refreshments are in order." A burst of static rippled through the air. "Tea and sandwiches to my tent, please."

Robyn's stomach rumbled at the idea of food. She blushed – she hadn't realised how ravenous she was.

Miranda raised an eyebrow. "And something more substantial, if you would. Thank you." She put down the walkie-talkie and resettled herself against a bright cushion. "I've been studying this temple for decades. I never expected to stumble upon something so big or so ancient. It proves the walkers are an irreplaceable component of our shared humanity."

Robyn saw the fragments of tile in her mind's eye, glittering shards painting the story of Ariana, Eli and Fletcher. "The mosaics?"

"Exactly. Records of each walker lineage, extending back thousands of years. The temple was in much better condition thirty years ago. But to conduct an in-depth examination required financing beyond my means as a young anthropologist, and a remote Laotian temple crumbling to dust meant time was not on my side. So I approached my four most trusted friends and shared my theory."

The pieces slotted into place. *The other supervisors. Weaving, Deckker, Vulcan and ... Brock.*

"They shared a mutual interest. They jumped at the chance to help finance the initial dig. Then, after what we found, we committed to the construction of the institute."

Robyn found it so easy to imagine the four young researchers, high on the thrill of discovery and eager to share their findings with the world. Had she, Catherine,

Terence, Derek and Fang been any different? The thought unsettled her – look at how the discovery had changed Derek and Fang. A sudden shiver ran down her spine. "What did you find?"

Miranda clasped her hands and brought them to her chin, her eyes sombre. "Around a thousand years ago, there was a massacre. A dark spirit killed hundreds of monks, worshippers and villagers. The temple has remained empty ever since."

"My people were killed. The last guide – Liro – saved my life so that our work would not be forgotten, so that I could instruct the next guide." Lenti's voice was wrought with emotion. Soft, reverential.

Fragments of Liro's memory floated through Robyn's consciousness, and for a heartbeat she was back at the temple, powerless to stop the swirling dark force of destruction that rose from the ground to envelop the monks who once lived and meditated there. "Nyx," she whispered.

Brock's eyes widened. "You know about Nyx?"

Robyn nodded, forcing her fear aside.

"Then we now share the same fear," Miranda said. "But at the time, all we could see was how the evidence of the event was seared into the very foundations of the temple – the ruins are ablaze with radioactivity. Here, on a remote mountain in rural Laos, centuries before Villard discovered gamma radiation, we found the remains of what was essentially an ancient nuclear reactor. Can you imagine the importance of our discovery? An extra-terrestrial, high-energy event akin to the asteroid impact that wiped the dinosaurs from the face of the earth."

The words echoed in Robyn's mind. Nyx was an ancient cosmic entity, a being beyond humanity's physical perception. In her spirit world conversation with Liro, the old monk had called Nyx a planet killer. Anger bubbled to the surface. "Not a nuclear reactor," she said. "Nyx is hellbent on wiping out humanity. What happened to the dinosaurs is nothing compared to what Nyx can unleash. We'd be nothing but a blip on the cosmic radar."

Miranda's eyes bore into her. "Across the globe, Nyx is depicted as an incorporeal, intergalactic, living organism. A being unconstrained by time or space like we mere humans. Every civilisation in recorded history has feared and revered Nyx in equal measure. Feared by those who understood her power and revered by those who wish to own it."

Lenti bumped his fists together and began chanting softly, as if weaving a spell of protection against Nyx. Robyn didn't blame him. With powers so far beyond humanity's own, Nyx instilled terror. The spirit was the darkness that seeped between worlds, consuming all in her wake. Robyn shivered. The mosaics lining the temple walls ended with three walkers from the land, air and sea – Fletcher, Eli and Ariana. Were they really the last walkers? If Liro hadn't been able to stop Nyx, what chance did she stand?

A young scientist pushed a trolley laden with food through the tent flap. Miranda rose and thanked him and the scientist nodded and disappeared. She took a tray from the trolley and placed it between them on the rug. "Tea?" she asked, pouring four steaming mugs. Lenti ignored the plates of scones and sandwiches and passed Robyn a bowl of steaming vegetable soup. She nodded her thanks and inhaled the delicious aroma. It was hard not to simply shove her entire face in the bowl.

Miranda passed Brock a mug and sipped her tea. "I came to realise that the mosaics lining the temple walls illustrated an energy boundary between our world and a world beyond. If we could understand the bonds depicted in the temple, the energy ties binding humans and animals, then we held the future of technology in our hands."

Robyn slurped another mouthful of broth, feeling its nourishment slowly restore her from within.

Miranda continued. "Even a fraction of the energy the walkers wield could provide clean energy to the entire planet. If we could figure out how to control it, we could steer the world in a new direction and re-create humanity's respect and care for the environment."

Robyn lowered her bowl and glared at the woman who had faked her own death, who left the MRI at the mercy of Vulcan and Fang. Under Vulcan's directorship, the MRI was only interested in one thing – controlling the convergence gene and forcing convergent teenagers and animals to fight. "Since when has the MRI had any interest in the environment?"

"We did, in the beginning. Our first objective was to find the current incarnation of the three walkers. When we found Eli, we were over the moon. We thought we'd found the answer to everything." Miranda set her mug down and rubbed the bridge of her nose. "Once we figured out how to unlock the convergence sequence in two other subjects, we thought we'd found the key."

Robyn stared at Miranda in disbelief. Her anger spilled over. "Sara and Jacob are real people, not test subjects. They are the only survivors of the initial testing program in Beijing. You, the MRI, held those two convergers against their will, pumped them full of a cocktail of dangerous drugs in an attempt to activate their convergence genes. How can you call them *subjects?*"

Brock opened his mouth as if to say something, but Miranda glared at him before turning back to Robyn. "Real breakthroughs aren't made within the realms of ethics approval. You have to *push* the barriers of what we know to get the kind of results we did. Fang understood."

Robyn swallowed thickly. "Push the barriers? How dare you justify what you did in the name of scientific research. People have died."

"Including by your own hand. Nothing happens in a vacuum, Robyn. Your research far surpassed our own. We didn't find the key – it was *you*." She smiled at Robyn and held out the plate of sandwiches, as if they were enjoying nothing more than a spot of afternoon tea rather than discussing the painful death of so many innocent people.

Robyn waved away the plate. Miranda was right. Her research had led to the creation of the activation dose, which was now in the hands of the MRI. Their application of that research – the teenagers recruited to fight tooth and claw, the countless dead around the world, and the scars on Ariana's back. The warm, comforting soup turned to acid in her throat. She pushed away her half-empty bowl.

Brock sprang to Miranda's defence. "We didn't set out to cause such chaos. We only wanted to understand the convergence genetic sequence." His voice wavered with emotion as he paced the narrow confines of the tent. "We went too far in Beijing. We thought we understood what we were working with, but we didn't."

"I was a fool," Miranda confessed. She ran her finger around the rim of her mug. "I wanted results. I didn't think about where those results might take us in the wrong hands, but Vulcan did. He immediately saw the potential for a military-grade application. Vulcan swayed Deckker and Weaving. I realised I had lost control of the program. I wasn't the mentor Fang

13

needed. I failed her too – I'd crafted her in my own image. She was even hungrier, more driven than me."

Brock stopped beside Robyn. For a moment, his hand hovered near her shoulder then dropped. "I always knew you'd crack it."

Robyn turned away. None of them were innocent. Each had contributed to the monster the MRI had become, whether willingly or not. Tears pricked her eyelids. She *had* cracked it, together with Terence, Catherine and Derek. They'd been caught up in the excitement of learning the secrets of the convergence sequence, of helping the walkers and convergers in their care. Had any of them been less hungry or driven? "You're right. Nothing happens in a vacuum."

Miranda joined Brock and squeezed his hand. "None of us hold the moral high ground," she said. "I thought I could control Vulcan, but I was wrong. Once he'd convinced Weaving and Deckker to join him, I knew there was nothing more I could achieve on the inside. The attack in Beijing presented the perfect opportunity to disappear before Vulcan arranged a less pleasant alternative for me."

"And now we are running out of time." Brock turned

to Robyn, his voice filled with sorrow. "The world has been out of balance for nearly a thousand years. We've surpassed the environmental tipping point. The human population has skyrocketed, as has our dependency on natural resources. The planet has never been stretched so thin. Loss of ice cover, rising sea levels, extreme weather events, carbon dioxide thresholds." Something of his old energy returned. Robyn remembered how he could once walk into a lecture theatre filled with students and hold their attention in the palm of his hand. "When the two worlds diverged, we lost the ability to communicate with animals and with it, access to a vast amount of energy. For centuries, an ancient part of ourselves has been dormant. Now that power is reawakening."

Liro's words came back to Robyn. *Humankind woke up as if from a long slumber, the gifts of the spirit world stripped from their grasp.*

Lenti's chanting rose and fell, weaving a soft blanket of sound around them, drawing the circle closer. Miranda knelt, hands clasped in her lap. Brock wore a path around the inner confines of the tent. "We've been asleep at the wheel. No longer able to understand and care for the planet, or each other. And in the intervening centuries, our weakness has allowed Nyx to grow stronger."

Maybe it was the meditative power of Lenti's chant, Brock's passion or Miranda's reflection, but the threads were drawing together. "And now the solar storm is coming, Nyx will have the energy she needs to escape." Robyn scrambled to her feet, desperate to act before it was too late. She crossed to the tent entrance, parting the flaps to gaze up at the temple ruins. "I've dreamt about this place for so long," she murmured. "Visited it in the spirit world. I never thought I'd see it in our world."

"If we are to have any chance of stopping Nyx, we need to work together. We've already lost too much time," Brock said.

Robyn turned around. Lenti's chanting stopped. Miranda studied her upturned palms. Only Brock would meet her eye. "What do you mean?"

Brock and Miranda shared an awkward glance but neither seemed prepared to answer her question.

"Time passes differently in the spirit world," said Lenti.

Robyn looked at the young monk. His hair. Last time she had seen him, his head had been shaved, as was the tradition. Now it curled and wisped around the bony knobs of his spine. "How long was I there?"

"Three months," Brock said.

"But that means …"

"That's right. We only have three months before the solar storm." In one fluid movement, Miranda was on her feet. In two steps, she was standing by the desk. "There's an enormous amount still to do."

Robyn reeled and clutched the tent flap to steady herself. *I've been missing for three months? How was that possible?* She turned to the one person who could answer her. "Lenti?"

The boy monk nodded. "It is true. You have been gone three moons."

Gripping the canvas for dear life, Robyn blinked rapidly to focus her vision. "I need to contact my friends," Robyn choked out. "They need to know …"

"That you're alive and safe. I understand." Miranda searched under the stack of papers for her mobile phone. "In your absence, your friends have spearheaded a resistance operation."

"We've been keeping a close eye on them," Brock added, joining Robyn at the tent entrance. "Since you left, the situation has deteriorated."

"Define deteriorated."

Brock squeezed her shoulder. "Don't worry. The walkers are safe. Your friends are based at Ariana's farm in Wales."

Robyn remembered sitting in the field of wildflowers on the day of the solstice when she slipped into the spirit world. *Three whole months ago.* She'd left her friends Kate and Kara protecting the carriers of the ancient convergence gene sequence – the walkers, the bridge between the physical and spirit worlds, and the rescued convergers. God, it felt like it was only hours ago that she sat beside the twins plotting how to stay one step ahead of the MRI.

A shock of icy fear gripped Robyn. The last time she had seen Catherine, Fang had a gun pressed into her girlfriend's back. Was she okay? Had she been rescued? If not, that meant the MRI had held Catherine prisoner for three long months. "Catherine?"

Miranda clutched the mobile phone to her chest. "That I don't know. I've lost my inside man."

Before Catherine, Fang had kidnapped and tortured Ariana. Even though the teen was the sea walker, she'd barely survived. Compared to Ariana, Catherine was defenceless. Tears blurred Robyn's view of the temple. "I wasn't there for her. For any of them."

So many innocent children dead. So many animals slaughtered. Eva's final ragged breath, the bear's heart still beneath her bloodstained fur. When he lost Eva, Fletcher, the earth walker, had lost his link with the spirit world. Liro's words came back to Robyn. About the threat the earth spirit posed. How, over her long imprisonment, Nyx had slowly infected the gentle earth spirit. How she had made Fletcher a vessel through which she could unleash her terrible power. "Nyx has Fletcher."

Brock cleared his throat. "Unfortunately, yes. Without his bear, Eva, the earth walker is vulnerable."

It took a few seconds before the full meaning of Brock's words sank in. "The earth spirit, Gaia. The sea spirit, Atlantis. The air spirit, Notos," Robyn said, the realisation dawning.

"Since Nyx has infected Gaia, she has twisted the relationship between the earth walker and his earth spirit."

It all made sense. When the walkers trained, Eli and Ariana had instantly felt the pull of the air and sea spirits. Had easily reached the walker state, that delicate space between the physical and spirit worlds where they became awash with energy. Yet for Fletcher, it had been a constant struggle to connect to the earth spirit. He'd never been able to reach the walker state. Now they knew why. Nyx.

Miranda straightened a stack of papers, then moved them to the other side of her desk. "There's a complication."

Robyn pivoted to face Miranda. "You said the walkers were all safe." Every time she got an answer, it seemed to raise more questions. "Didn't you say the walkers were all in Wales?"

"Not quite." Miranda abandoned the papers but only to wring her hands. "We have absolutely no idea where Fletcher is."

2

Extraction

Radiocarbon dating has enabled us to pinpoint the exact time of the high-energy event recorded at the Laotian temple. Between the sixteenth and seventeenth centuries, Earth experienced an unprecedented glaciation event, commonly termed the 'Little Ice Age'. The high-energy event at the temple falls smack bang in the middle of the Little Ice Age, and may even have extended the glaciation due to radioactive fallout. Comparative ice cores from Greenland and the Antarctic share the same high-energy residue, albeit in lower concentrations. What happened here has never been recorded before. I believe this high-energy event at the Laotian temple site altered the trajectory of the Earth and its inhabitants. Miranda's anthropological work in the temple itself points to the emergence of a dark spirit, an entity of terrible power that threatens to unbalance our biological equilibrium: Nyx.

Brock Williams, Working Notes.

Inside the chopper was a maelstrom of noise, but Eli still heard his heartbeat over the whirring blades and staccato of the earbud comms. His fingers trembled against the railing, and the band of pressure across his chest made it hard to breathe. *Concentrate. You've done this plenty of times now. In and out. Simple extraction.* He rolled his shoulders and his carbon polymer chest armour adjusted to the movement. His osprey, Una, fluttered on his shoulder as she regained her balance. *Sorry girl*, Eli projected.

"Landing now." The pilot's voice crackled in his ear. Eli surveyed the others, hunched in their seats with their animals. Lucy's knees jiggled, shaking the vampire bat that hung from her collar. Sara nodded at him, her leopard, Ming, winding through her legs. Chris clutched his polar bear's flank as the chopper banked through the clouds, heading downwards fast. Eli tried to remember a time when Chris and the other convergers were still strangers but couldn't. They'd become battle-hardened – a team bonded by blood and pain.

Dust billowed inside as Eli swung the huge cargo door open. Una dug her claws into the padded grip on his shoulder to avoid the updraft from the blades. He leapt from the hovering aircraft onto the grass below, his resistance unit right behind him. Eli braced himself as the helicopter peeled away. The convergers stepped out from the dust like wraiths, dark and menacing in their armour. Eli surveyed their surroundings. They stood in the middle of an athletics field, a row of empty stands on one side.

"Are you sure we're in the right place?" Sara said, joining him. "This is a school."

Eli took in the quadrangle of buildings beyond the

field and pointed. "This is the twins' co-ordinates. Two convergers are supposed to meet us here."

Sara signalled back 'okay' and gestured to the unit to form a wedge behind Eli. The team ran toward the quadrangle, Una and Lucy's vampire bat flying above them.

There's no-one outside, Una projected. *But the air tastes sour, like cold metal.*

When they reached the courtyard, there were faces plastered at every window.

"So much for the element of surprise," Lucy said.

"It's like they knew we were coming," Sara murmured. By her side, Ming's tail whipped through the air in a nervous arc.

"Kate and Kara double check every distress call. We're not leaving until we find the convergers. They're in danger here," Eli said, motioning for the unit to fan out.

Sara hesitated. "But there's no cover."

"Shit," said Lucy.

Sara pivoted, the words 'what's wrong?' dying on her lips.

Kids spilled into the courtyard, a fluid mass of navy blazers, screaming insults.

"Freaks!"

"Get out of here, you mutants!"

"They're killers! Terrorists!"

In moments, hundreds of students surrounded the unit. Faces filled with loathing and anger. Eli wanted to yell, *We're not like the convergers you've seen on TV. We're here to help you.* But it would make no difference. The MRI had made sure of that. Everyone knew that convergers were being rounded up, tortured, or worse. Execution videos floated around the web, picked up by global media. Teenagers with bags over their heads, trembling where they stood in the firing line, their anonymous bodies falling with blossoming red flowers. *If only Robyn was here*, he thought for the millionth time. *She could fix this.*

"I've called the chopper in," Sara urged, touching his arm. "It's a trap."

"Look!" Lucy shouted, pointing at a tall boy sprinting toward them. "See? There are convergers here."

A sickening crack echoed around the quadrangle. The boy sank to his knees, a dog keening by his side.

No! Panic flared low in Eli's stomach. Sara's warning echoed through his mind. *Trap trap trap.*

An explosion. The windows around the courtyard splintering, showering the students in jagged fragments. The air filled with shrieks. Teenagers ran for cover, shielding their faces with bloody arms. Gun muzzles pointing from empty windows. Above the screaming, Eli swore he heard the staggered clicks of dozens of firearms. Time slowed. The shot converger lay immobile, his dog sprawled beside him, surrounded by a crimson halo. Eli spotted the distant speck of a chopper; slow, too slow. The courtyard filled with stampeding students desperate to escape this killing field.

Eli closed his eyes, calmed his breathing then slipped into the in-between. His arms moved around his body and the familiar flare of his aura bathed his limbs in red light. The red energy formed a sphere around him and his feet left the ground. Eli expanded his energy aura, aware of the bullets pinging against his defence shield. He tuned into the string of minds around him. In a heartbeat, the air filled with birds. He rose into their soaring consciousnesses, flitting between minds filled with outrage.

We will protect you, air walker, they chorused.

In an instant, the sky darkened. The storm of birds

descended – a swirling mass of feathers and fury raking the attackers with their claws. A man in dark fatigues fell from a second-storey window with a bone-splintering thud.

Another mind skimmed Eli's consciousness. *We're coming. Wait for us.*

He saw a girl pushing through the knot of students, her expression tight, desperate. Out of the throng, a dark crow swooped and landed on her shoulder. The girl ran at Eli, her dark braids flying. "We're coming with you," she screamed above the noise of the approaching chopper.

Eli descended, lessening his connection with the airborne birds as the helicopter loomed above their heads. The birds retreated from its deadly blades. Una flew to him, digging her claws deep into the faded leather shoulder pad as she landed.

Sara grabbed the girl and pulled her to safety behind Eli. Bullets peppered the chopper. Most ricocheted off the reinforced glass but some pierced metal, sending smoke billowing upwards.

"Are they local militia or MRI?" Sara yelled at Eli over the noise. An explosion of bloody feathers billowed over them as a soldier's bullets found its mark.

Eli shook his head, shuddering as he skimmed the dying bird's consciousness. From this distance, it was impossible to tell who the soldiers fought for. Whirling his arms, he extended his aura, red energy flaring outwards to form a solid sphere of energy that encased the chopper. Eli strained to maintain the force field, aware of the wave of soldiers descending upon Chris and Lucy. Chris jabbed his finger at something to their left, mouthing words Eli couldn't discern in the chaos. Eli looked for what Chris was pointing at. He recognised two soldiers. Correction. Mercenaries. A streak of sadism ran through the pair as wide as he was high. Mikey and Daniel. They strode through the chaos straight toward Eli and his team.

Sara pressed the new converger to the ground. "Shit! Looks like it's time to go!"

Eli funnelled tendrils of red energy toward Chris and Lucy, dividing them from the onslaught. The pair sprinted toward them, leaping over bodies scattered across the ground, through air heavy with the smell of iron. Bullets kicked up flecks of stone among the dead. Birds dived in and out of the fray, talons and beaks stained red, their shrieks bloodcurdling.

Mikey pulled a sleek blaster from his shoulder holster and aimed it straight at Eli. The crackling yellow electricity arced against his energy aura. Eli smelled ozone. Scowling, Mikey primed his weapon and shot again but Eli's energy barrier held.

"We have to go," Chris screamed, signalling toward the chopper, which had landed under the protection of Eli's aura. Maintaining the energy field sapped his strength, but there was no way he could leave yet.

"Go!" he yelled. Chris hesitated, prepared to argue, but Eli repeated his command. Chris shrugged and joined the others sprinting to the chopper. Sara urged the new girl to her feet. She covered her as they ran for the chopper, Ming snarling and slashing as soldiers erupted from around the quadrangle. Flashes of gunfire flickered from the darkness of the broken windows as they hurdled bodies and dived into the cargo bay. Gritting his teeth, Eli pushed his aura out further and ran through the red haze rippling around the chopper. He jumped inside and braced himself against the door. A litany of voices sang in his mind. *Thank you*, he projected back to the birds who had flown to their aid.

Dropping to the floor, Eli slowly left the in-between,

relinquishing his hold on the energy as the chopper gained altitude. His arms trembled with fatigue. He pressed his forehead to the cool metal to quell the nausea washing over him.

"Chris?" Lucy yelled, accidentally elbowing Eli as she scrambled over the tangled limbs of the exhausted convergers.

Eli turned around. Chris lay on the floor, his armour stained crimson. Lucy ripped off her vest and yanked her t-shirt over her head, pressing it against Chris' shoulder. Wind whipped through the open cargo bay, grasping at her hair, forcing her to brace against the seat. Eli wrenched the door shut and leaned against it, fighting the exhaustion threatening to overwhelm him.

Sara knelt in front of him. "Are you hurt?" she said, her words piercing the veil of fatigue.

Eli shook his head and pointed to the pale girl with the crow huddled in the corner. The unspoken question passed between them.

Sara leapt across the cargo bay and grabbed the girl by her shirt. "Did you know this was an ambush?" she demanded, dragging the child to her feet.

"No! You have to believe me. Please," the girl pleaded, her eyes wide with fear.

Sara stared at her for a long moment. Knowing her desire for retribution was frightening the child, she let her go and turned back to Eli. She pressed her earbud. "Get us back to base. Asap."

Eli heard the pilot's reply in his own link. "Roger that."

The grandfather clock chimed ten times. Kara rubbed her eyes and pushed away from the keyboard. Out the window, the golden fields of wheat shimmered in a light breeze. A pinging noise interrupted the peace. Her sister's laptop. Kate had almost a dozen open screens. She was working on Hypatia's latest column about the impending catastrophe and the need for international government co-operation. Another tab was a spreadsheet of confirmed converger sightings and distress calls. Another a box of flickering code – a reminder of how much work they still had left to do. Kara's headache ratcheted up a notch and she rubbed circles around her temples.

Kate appeared in the doorway carrying two mugs. She handed one to Kara, who sipped the scalding hot coffee, marvelling at the brown fuzz covering Kate's scalp. The trademark pink mohawk went the day they lost five convergers. Kara had found her sister braced over the bathroom sink, eyes red from crying, a razor in one hand and snakes of pink hair writhing in the sink. Kara still wasn't used to her sister's new vulnerability.

"Enjoy that coffee. It might be our last. I had to raid Bry's emergency stash."

Kara swallowed past the lump in her throat. Two months ago, Bry and Fletcher had disappeared, leaving only a hastily scrawled note on the kitchen table. *I have to do this.* "I miss them."

"Hey – we've talked about this. We'll keep looking. Hack more satellites to send on recon missions between solar flares, check the fragmentary news reports still circulating." Kate rubbed her sister's arm then leaned against the doorjamb. "I wish Fletcher had talked to us, about whatever it was he felt he had to do."

"He would have talked to Robyn," Kara replied, sinking into Bry's big old leather executive office chair. She'd claimed it as her own the moment she clapped eyes on its cracked baby vomit yellow leather.

"Maybe. But she's not here, is she?" Kate snapped, carefully balancing her weight on her sorry excuse for a desk chair with its wonky wheel. She sighed. "I'm sorry. I'm worried about her too. At least Fletcher has Ariana's father to keep him safe. Bry is a bloody capable adventurer, used to long stints of fieldwork in unforgiving conditions."

Kara surveyed Bry's study, her gaze flitting between heavy fossils and chunky quartz crystals. None of them held the answers she sought. Kara turned back to her computer. No point dwelling in the past, they had so much work to do *now*.

Kate tapped on her keyboard, refreshing screens. "Aster's going over the rest of the inventory the UN gifted us. We still have a lot of resources, and our renegade hacker is the man for the job."

After the breakdown of the UN, the Secretary General, Ester Akintola, had smuggled them several military helicopters and a metric shit tonne of communications equipment and weaponry. More importantly, she'd sent them a small contingent of key military personnel – pilots, soldiers, doctors. The twins had wasted no time putting them to good use. Over the last twelve weeks, they'd extracted stranded convergers and smuggled them to safe houses dotted across the globe. The farmhouse and outbuildings hid the comings and goings of soldiers and convergers alike.

It was real now. People relied on Kate and Kara. Before the UN collapsed, it had still felt like a game. Hypatia's articles, the comment threads pulling in politicians and business leaders, were a simulation compared to this. Offline, in the real world, there were no second chances. In the real world, people died.

Beside her, Kate rubbed her new hair as she hunched over her computer, checking Aster's spreadsheets. *They thought they knew everything, but really they knew nothing.* Thank God Aster had arrived on the first UN chopper, goggles pushed up on his head, waving like a madman. The task before them was too much for two people. No, too much *power*, too much *responsibility*. Even between the three of them, the workload was barely manageable. She didn't need a mirror to know she'd lost weight. Kate's gaunt figure, the dark shadows etched under her eyes told her everything she needed to know. They couldn't keep this up forever. *Damn it, Robyn, where are you?*

Kara flicked to the MRI feed. She refused to believe her best friend was dead. Ariana and Eli had searched the spirit world to no avail. Somehow Robyn had disappeared off the face of the earth leaving behind everyone who loved and respected her. It made no sense. Kara pulled up a video feed of a small cell showing a thin figure curled on the mattress. During the attack on the MRI compound in Bulgaria, Kara had hacked into the MRI's network and could do whatever she liked, go wherever she wanted. Not now. The MRI had an army of tech monitoring every ingoing and outgoing packet of data, leaving Kara floating around the network like a ghost. Kara kissed her fingertips and pressed them against the onscreen image. As if in response to the touch, the girl rolled over and drew her knees to her chest. Catherine was alive, but they were no closer to saving her. Meddling with the network would alert the MRI techs and Kara would lose all access. Instead, she forced herself to witness Catherine's brutal torture because not witnessing it would be worse. Catherine lifted her gaze to the camera. It felt like she was staring right at Kara. Pleading.

"Aster to Head Command," vibrated in Kara's

earbud. She jolted upright.

"You've got us," she replied, closing the video feed.

"Last extraction should have returned by now. Can you reach Eli?"

Beside her, Kate pulled up another window of code and began punching away. "Encrypted line is up."

"Thanks, Aster. We're on it," Kara said, clicking the earbud over to the more secure line. "Eli? Report."

Static crackled in her ear then a girl's voice said her name.

"Is that you, Sara?"

"They knew … coming. I've been trying to … through for the last half hour, but I guess … Another flare."

Panic rose in Kara's gut. "Is everyone all right?"

"Chris … not critical. On track … twenty minutes."

"Roger. We'll be ready." Kara turned to her sister. "Sara said the MRI knew they were coming."

"Shit." Kate paled. "How the fuck did the MRI find them?"

"I don't know. We've been so damn careful." Kara switched back to the local comms line. "Aster. They're coming in hot. One confirmed wounded. Not sure what shape the chopper will be in."

"Got it. I'll get a team ready."

Kate pulled up her records. "Benjamin Sakamoto, age 14. Partnered with a wolfhound. Kat Miller, 15, crow." Kate's leg jiggled, her fingers raced across the keyboard, struggling to keep up with her thoughts. "Did they get them out?"

"There's so many unaccounted for," Kara replied.

Although the MRI had seized most of the convergers, many had slipped through their net.

Kara reached for her cold mug of coffee and a blister pack of pain relief. "We'll know soon enough."

"I miss Robyn and Catherine. We can't keep this up much longer," Kate muttered.

"That's what I'm afraid of," Kara replied, swallowing the bitter pills.

From its perch on the girl's shoulder, the crow cocked its head and stared right at him. Eli looked into its dark eyes, aware the chopper had begun to spin around him. Nausea rose in his gut. When the floor finally stopped moving, the chopper had gone and Eli was standing in the middle of a dusty playing field. A girl in a bright sari sat cross-legged in the dirt, watching him.

"Clara," he managed, his throat tight and dry.

Red light rippled around the last air walker's body. Clara stroked her raven as it nuzzled her face. "Everyone is hunting the convergers. Too few have been saved."

Eli sank to his knees opposite her. Clara was right. "What else can we do? Convergers are either being rounded up by the MRI or killed by people who don't understand what they are. I can't sit back and watch it happen."

Clara spread her sari around her feet. "Landing in a metal bird in a crowded place is not particularly subtle. You need a new strategy."

Eli pressed his palms into the red dust with a sigh. "Like what? They keep slipping through our grasp."

"Rendezvous points hidden deep in the wilderness. Use the underground network to reach as many convergers as possible. That way you can rescue them away from prying eyes." Clara flickered, the red glow on her skin fading. As if in response, red light flared around Eli's skin. "And be careful," she added as she began to disappear. "The world can't lose you. Not now."

"No! Don't go, Clara. I need your help. The MRI, Nyx – it's too much. Please …"

An eddy of dust swirled around him and Eli was thrown back into the sickening darkness. When he opened his eyes, he was sprawled on the floor of the chopper, cold metal against his cheek.

Sara shook his shoulder. "Eli, are you okay?"

He pushed himself upright. "I'm fine."

The chopper's engines started whining as the pilot began the descent. The nausea returned and Eli slumped back down.

Sara poked him in the chest. "You're going to medical as soon as we land – no arguments."

Eli leaned back against the chopper door, the sound of bullets puncturing flesh seared into his memory. Clara was right. They had to find a better way.

As soon as the chopper touched down and its blades had slowed, Ariana sprinted over and wrenched open the door. A group of medics in faded khaki ducked inside ahead of her. Strong hands took the stretcher, jolting Chris across the field, carving a path through the wildflowers. Ariana ran alongside, his polar bear,

Iki, roaring in distress as she loped next to the stretcher. Skirting the farmhouse, they entered the barn. Ariana slowed to a stop, letting the medics do their job. She rested her hand on Iki's snow-white flank to reassure her as the medics lifted Chris onto a bed and began removing his armour and clothes. Iki's tension churned through Ariana's stomach. The polar bear had left bloody prints on the floor. She stared at the sticky trail and swallowed against the horror of all this carnage. Once the family barn was filled with straw bales, her mother's gardening supplies, and her brother Terence's potato vodka distillation setup. Now the new concrete floor supported a line of bunks. Stainless-steel benches held an array of medical supplies and deconstructed weapons. Two more helicopters concealed a camouflage jeep parked on the other side. Peace had given way to war.

Her salamander, Jericho, climbed her neck and perched behind her ear. *A war we must fight and win*, he projected.

The sound of familiar voices arguing drew Ariana's attention.

"You're not going anywhere," Sara said, pushing Eli down onto a spare bed.

"Says who?" he snapped and while he glowered at Sara, he stayed put. A medic raced over and strapped a blood pressure cuff to his arm.

Ariana joined them at the medical bay. "What happened?"

"Ambush. The MRI knew about the extraction." Sara grabbed a protein bar and a bottle of water from a passing medic who was taking supplies out to the rest of the resistance unit. "It wouldn't take a genius to figure out we're picking up stranded convergers. We've been doing this for months."

"I've been worried about the possibility," Eli said, ignoring the medic taking a blood sample. "Clara says we have to change tactics."

Sara twisted the cap off the bottle of water and passed it to Eli. "Meaning?"

"Rendezvous points away from major cities," Eli said. He swigged water and reached for Sara's half-eaten protein bar. "Getting the convergers to meet us instead of the other way around."

Chris hissed in pain and Iki knocked over an IV trolley trying to reach him. The bear wailed in apology as Ariana and a medic attempted to untangle her, the frightened medic trembling at the closeness of an enormous, bloodied polar bear.

"Get that chopper under cover asap – let's move, people!" Kara's voice thundered through the barn. Several soldiers organising materials rushed out to the field.

Having freed Iki, Ariana returned to Eli's suggestion. "On the surface it sounds like a good idea, but we'd better run it past the twins to be sure." Ariana examined Eli's bullet-pocked, blood-streaked armour and recalled the gentle boy he once was. In his place sat a warrior. "I wish I could have been there with you."

"You know that's not possible," Kara said, sipping an energy drink. "We can't afford for both of you to get captured. One walker per mission. Like the damn royal family."

Especially now there's only two of us, Ariana thought. She missed Fletcher; his stupid smile, how neatly his fingers entwined with hers, the way his stupid lips tasted. Hated his stupid plan that risked his life, her father's life, doing who knows what. When Fletcher came back to training and started laughing and contributing ideas again, she'd thought he was getting better. But in reality, he'd been planning this ridiculous adventure. *I'm fine,*

Fletcher had kept telling her. *Thanks to you*. Only it wasn't true.

Kara rubbed the bridge of her nose. "Sorry. I didn't mean ..."

"I'm fine," Ariana snapped, swiping away the tears. She ignored the pain around her heart. Fletcher had betrayed her trust.

Cursing her insensitivity, Kara turned her attention to the air walker. "Eli – you okay?"

"Yeah, but the extraction didn't go to plan."

Sara nodded and tapped Ariana's arm. "You need to talk to her," she said, pointing to a girl with a crow who sat wrapped in a blanket on the other side of the barn. "She's the only surviving extraction target. Maybe she can tell you what went wrong."

Kara drained the can and crushed it beneath her boot. "If we'd known the MRI had got wind of our plans, we'd never have sent you in there."

Eli removed the blood pressure cuff and passed it to the medic. "The question is, how do they keep finding us?"

Una flew through the barn door and landed on his shoulder, buffeting them all with air. Eli's skin rippled with red light.

At the momentary flare of energy, the entire base went quiet. "They just – they have the resources, the reach." Kara stretched out her arms. "All of this? It's nothing compared to the MRI. We're doing our best."

Sara rubbed her leopard Ming's ears, trying to stay calm. "What I want to know is why is everyone out to kill us convergers? We're not the terrorists."

Ariana surveyed the barn. Chris sedated in the hospital bed, Iki slumped by his side. Convergers straggled in, looking for something to eat, somewhere to sleep, or both. Others sat with their arms around their partner animals, trying to find solace in their shared bond. How had it come to this? The ever-present knot of fear expanded in her stomach. "Because the convergers scare them," Ariana murmured. In the corner of the barn, the crow on the girl's shoulder cawed.

3

Prisoner

The high-energy event at the temple reveals the existence of a powerful energy source that must be contained within those individuals with the extraordinary ability to communicate with animals. The spherical energy auras of red, green and blue are repeated throughout the mosaic-work that survives in the temple. The artwork indicates that in the past, people worshipped beings of pure energy from the major biomes of land, air and sea – Gaia, Notos and Atlantis. This in turn suggests that humans have a connection of such magnitude it is beyond our comprehension. Consider a limitless source of cosmic energy. Imagine the potential of an energy system derived from such a connection. Humanity could move toward a golden age of harmonious coexistence with all species. An age of balance, of equilibrium. Conversely, whoever controls such power could unleash absolute and total annihilation.

Brock Williams, Working Notes.

"Is a little co-operation really too much to ask?" Vulcan rapped his cane against the floor as he paced the cell. "I've been patient with you thus far, but I have my limits."

Catherine sagged against the chair, trying to ease the cramping in her arms. She glanced at the two soldiers standing either side, their eyes glued on the Director of the MRI. *I'm not sure how starvation and torture count as patience*, she thought. "I'm sure your protégé, Derek, has told you everything there is to know. You have the activation vector."

Despite her efforts to find relief, the metal restraints dug into her wrists, agony against last week's bruises. How long had she been the MRI's prisoner? The days blurred together, punctuated by meals on trays and Vulcan's interrogations. The only thoughts keeping her sane were of Robyn and ensuring the walkers and convergers were safe. Her only joy was knowing that as long as Vulcan stood in her cell asking questions, it proved he had no idea where the walkers were. Or what they were capable of.

At Vulcan's signal, one of the soldiers stepped forward and tugged her restraints. Catherine bit her lip, the cry dying in her throat.

"Well, if you refuse to give me the answers I seek, you leave me no option but to alter my approach." Vulcan placed both hands on his cane and smiled. "It took some time for the chamber to be built to my satisfaction, but it's been operational for several weeks now. It's based on the original design from our facility at Bulgaria. I'm sure you'll be most impressed."

The two soldiers wrenched Catherine to her feet and dragged her toward the door. After the half-light of her cell, the brightness of the corridor temporarily blinded her. Vulcan shuffled several paces ahead, the soldiers pulling her along in his wake. Too soon, they shoved her inside a stark white room. The handcuffs clanked to the floor, but her relief was short-lived. A soldier wrenched her arms upwards and secured them above her head. Catherine's muscles screamed. Flicking her hair from her face, she watched the soldiers retreat, closing the heavy door behind them with a sickening thud. Above, Vulcan scrutinised her through a thick glass window, then his hand moved.

Before she had time to wonder why, stabbing bursts of current ripped through her. Her awareness narrowed to one thought; surviving the next moment. After an eternity, it stopped. Catherine sobbed in relief.

Vulcan's voice invaded the chamber. "Unpleasant, isn't it? Now, I'll ask you again. Where are Robyn and the others?"

Catherine squeezed her eyes shut and shook her head. Another burst shuddered through her body. She felt dislocated from her own musculature, her skeleton; everything fragmented by the pain.

"Did you know that this chamber is designed to withstand extraordinarily high currents and to mitigate high-energy diffusions?" Vulcan continued, as if she were a visiting academic touring the facilities. "We've made some improvements since your friend Ariana was our guest in the original shock chamber in Bulgaria. I wonder if you'll last as long as she did."

Catherine's head snapped up. She stared at Vulcan's smug face, searing every detail into her memory. Despite the walker's healing abilities, Ariana's back was scribbled with mycelial-like scars.

"Weeks and weeks and weeks she lasted, her and her little salamander. I confess, it was impressive how long it took to break her."

Catherine clenched her jaw. *One day soon, I'm going to wipe that grin off your damn face.*

"I'll find your friends eventually, Catherine. The world order is crumbling and they'll soon run out of places to hide." Vulcan tapped his cane against the glass wall. "Everything I need to know about the walkers' energy auras I learned in that original chamber in Bulgaria. Poor Ariana couldn't prevent her energy aura activating when exposed to that much current. It's a type of self-defence mechanism, if you will. It is what the walkers do when their lives are in danger. Fletcher was most impressive. He stopped a squad of elite soldiers, brought down a helicopter. Eli destroyed our facility in Beijing. And little Ariana glowed exactly on cue. They are agents of destruction."

"No! They bring balance," Catherine shouted as she struggled against her restraints, her mind reeling at Vulcan's words. Surely, he can't have figured out how to harness the walkers' energy aura? The destruction he would cause with such power was terrifying.

"Balance? You are mistaken, Catherine. Chaos is the natural order. Balance is only ever temporary." Vulcan's voice echoed through the chamber. "So you see, I don't particularly need your co-operation. I am merely demonstrating the fruits of our labour. This chamber was built to test our latest invention. It amplifies the convergers' energy capacity and converts it into something ... shall we say, useful. Let me show you."

The chamber door opened. In stepped Mikey, his lion at his side. The sight of the sadistic converger sent a chill down Catherine's spine. With a sickening grin, he raised a sleek metal blaster. Under the harsh lights, something shiny glinted at the base of his skull.

"You, of all people, will appreciate the sophistication

of this weapon," Vulcan continued as if he were demonstrating nothing more exciting than the latest model food processor. "It draws on the enhanced mitochondrial regenerative capacity of the convergers as a form of bioelectricity. The strength of this prototype is a fraction of what the real weapon can do. That is on an entirely different scale."

The blaster lit up in Mikey's hands and yellow light cascaded over his fingers. His lion growled.

"So, here we are. One last chance. Where are your friends?"

"You and the MRI can go to hell," Catherine spat.

Vulcan chuckled, safe on the other side of the glass. "Oh my dear, why do you insist on putting yourself through this?" He raised a finger then slowly pointed it at Mikey. "You may proceed."

Mikey raised the blaster and sent yellow electricity arcing through the air. The electroshock hit Catherine's chest. Current ripped through her neurons; hot and cold. The taste of iron hit the back of her throat, hope dissipating as darkness crushed her vision.

Moving was a mistake. As Catherine woke up, pain

lanced her spine, sending shuddering spasms through her limbs. Bruises snaked up her wrists and ankles, those telltale mycelial-like imprints of the electroshock chamber. She staggered to the toilet and retched until she was empty. Catherine collapsed against the cool tiles and searched her memory. Had she broken in the chamber and spilled the location of the walkers? She drew a blank. Hopefully, she'd passed out before she betrayed her friends. Catherine crawled back to bed and curled up into the foetal position. A vision of Mikey's blaster brought a wave of pain; Catherine forced herself to breathe. Never, in all her years as a researcher, had she imagined weaponising the convergers' enhanced energy production. The blaster was an abomination, a monstrosity. Robyn and the walkers stood no chance against it.

Catherine shuddered and pulled the thin blanket around her. Her only hope was that Robyn and the resistance had hatched some brilliant plan. They'd come for her, Robyn would insist. Catherine rolled up her shirt and pressed a shaky palm over the dark bruise on her sternum where she'd been shot. Tendrils of bruised tissue writhed across her chest, her shoulders, and coiled down to her hips. Vulcan had stood at the glass, relishing her agony, that she did remember. A man assured by the proven power of his weapon. A weapon that wouldn't exist if not for her research. Rage filled her with its fiery warmth and pushed away the pain. *They'll pay for this.*

4

Unity

Throughout history, humans have sought enlightenment and unity with the cosmos. In every culture, this process involves meditation and a focus on the breath. Why? Because the air we breathe is laced with energy. Plants release pollen, fungi radiate spores. We inhale an elixir of life with each expansion of our lungs, distilling this energy with each exhalation. Perhaps this ancient process reveals a truth: equilibrium can be found amidst all forms of life, united as one.

Brock Williams, Working Notes.

Robyn woke to find Lenti sitting cross-legged in the middle of her tent. Eyes shut, his head dropped a little toward his chest. She knew better than to assume he was asleep. "What the heck are you doing here, Lenti?"

The boy raised his head, opened his eyes and smiled. "Good morning."

Robyn brought her knees to her chest, discomfited by the fact that Lenti might have been watching over her while she slept. "You don't have to serve me, you know. You can just be you."

The young monk's grin widened. "This *is* who I am. I chose this life when I entered the order. I am blessed to have a guide to serve." He unfolded his limbs and pointed to a pile of clothes. "These are for you. I hope they fit. You will find the amenities block at the end of this row of tents. If you go now, there will still be hot water. It's very nice."

"Thank you," Robyn managed, unsettled by his attentiveness and determination. "That's really thoughtful of you."

Lenti bowed and padded over to the corner of the tent. Robyn heard liquid being poured and, when he returned, he passed her a steaming cup of herbal tea.

Maybe I could get used to this, she thought, shimmying out of her sleeping bag. Robyn joined the monk on the stone floor, inhaling the earthy scent.

"Nettle and Echinacea," he said, sipping his own tea with a blissful smile.

Robyn blew on her tea. Steam spiralled into the air caught by the light caressing the edges of the canvas. She gave voice to what she had been dreaming about only moments ago. "What do you think of my supervisor and the ex-Chief Director?"

Lenti wrapped his fingers around the warmth of his mug, letting her question linger. "They are sincere in their intentions. Maybe they truly can help you."

Robyn sipped her tea. If only things were that simple.

Lenti was right about one thing though, the camp shower was heaven. Robyn washed her hair twice and scrubbed the dust from her skin until the water ran clear. Once dry, she put on the clean jeans and oversized t-shirt Lenti had picked. No shoes. She smiled; he'd chosen well. Barefoot, she padded down the line of tents, hearing the sound of people beginning to stir.

At the edge of the mountain, below the temple, Lenti moved fluidly through a series of tai chi poses. Robyn joined him, feeling energy well in her abdomen and spread through her limbs as the sun rose. By the time she finished her practice, it was full daylight. Lenti had already left but Brock sat nearby, enthralled. Self-conscious, Robyn waved at him. Her supervisor stood and said, "I have something to show you."

Robyn never expected to see a fully functional laboratory inside a tent. Yet, it felt strangely *normal* following Brock between the lab benches, the air sweet with swirling solvents and starched lab coats. Back to the days when she traipsed after her former supervisor, hanging off his every word. In fact, in pretty much the same way the scientists were looking at her now – acknowledging her with brief, wide-eyed nods, then continuing with their work.

Propped against a lab fridge was a whiteboard with a familiar chromatogram pinned to it. Robyn studied the two unique peaks that represented the very compounds that had started her search and led her to Fletcher. The compounds she still couldn't identify.

Brock stopped beside her. "Whatever they are, it's

not a product of human biochemistry. We were hoping you might be able to enlighten us."

Robyn shook her head. "Each of the walkers has them. *I* have them. But as to what they are, or what they do? Sorry, I know as much as you."

"Don't be. You've more than exceeded my expectations." Brock's proud smile was too much for her. As a young student, she'd looked up to Brock, yearning for his praise. Now she had it, she wasn't sure she wanted it. Everything had changed.

Brock indicated the pristine lab bench next to where they stood. "This is yours, if you'd like it."

Robyn surveyed the racks of test tubes, the starched white lab coat folded neatly on the stool. All this could be hers once more – the recognition, the sense of control her work gave her. Robyn's face fell. "I can't. I need to get back to my friends." She felt for the reassuring bulge of the mobile phone in her pocket. She needed to try and reach Kara again soon.

Brock rubbed his chin, a poor attempt at hiding his disappointment. "But you could do so much good here. And sorry to state the obvious, but time is not on our side."

"I know," Robyn murmured. She thought of Ariana's brother, Terence, of all the convergers she couldn't save, of Catherine. Her throat tightened as she glanced back at the lab bench, at the possibilities it represented. *It's not like I'm any closer to figuring this out on my own.* "You're right. I'll stay. Just until I can figure out how to get back."

Brock could not conceal his gratitude. "Thank you."

Robyn looked at her lab bench, then through the tent flap to the rocky mountain peak. "But I'll do it my way."

No service. Robyn fought the urge to dash the phone against the rocks, instead shoving it in her jacket pocket. She'd climbed all over this mountain top but still the damn phone didn't work. She sat in the shadow of the temple walls and rested her head on her knees. For three whole months, her friends thought her missing, likely dead, leaving them to continue the fight.

"It's because the sun is starting to sing," said a voice behind her.

Robyn started. There stood Lenti, eyes on the horizon, hands resting by his side. Even when dressed as a teenager he stood like a monk.

She looked up at the sky and imagined multitudes of invisible energy threads coiling earthwards from the cosmos. "Of course. The solar flares." The increased solar activity in the lead-up to the solar storm would be creating havoc with global communications.

Lenti knelt beside her, the wind pulling at his dark hair. He placed a hand on a stone cairn, and Robyn couldn't help thinking of Terence, buried beneath a similar cairn in a clearing in the Cobalt Valley. It seemed a lifetime ago that she sat beside him in the shade of the trees. Tears pricking her eyes, she focused instead on the activity in the village below.

Oxen pulled ploughs and children played in the street while women washed clothes in the river. Faint metallic glints pinpointed a few satellite dishes rigged up against the tiny huts. The odd rumble betrayed the existence of generators, but otherwise, life continued on as it had for centuries.

"Miranda showed me pictures – I think she called them photographs? – from her archaeological dig here. All my order are buried here on this mountain, including Liro, the guide before you. I'm truly the last of my order." Lenti bowed his head.

Robyn observed the boy. She wasn't the only one burdened by history. "Without you, we'd never have made it this far," Robyn said. "Liro would be proud of you. I'm proud of you."

Lenti straightened. "Thank you. But I am the fortunate one; I have a guide to serve." The boy rose and pointed toward the temple. "Come with me."

Robyn padded across the cool temple stones and sat in the middle of the floor. She looked up. Once there was a golden ceiling where a skylight flooded the temple with light and warmth. Now only a few beams remained and the temple's roof was the sky. The temple had been reduced to a ruin; scattered mosaics interspersed with rotting wood and mountain air. Yet, she still felt the jittery, powerful surge coiling through her toes, relaxing her shoulders and calming her mind. Robyn closed her eyes and slowed her breathing, light dancing behind her eyelids. Liro was right – something about this temple amplified the available electromagnetic energy to the guide. To her. Despite Lenti's reverential stare and the deferential gaze of the scientists in the tent, she still felt like an imposter. *I'm not special*, she wanted to shout. *I've only made everything worse.* The activation dose she'd helped to create had resulted in so many deaths. Then she'd disappeared for three whole months when everyone needed her. The energy in her body tightened like a spring, and white light fuzzed at the edges of her vision.

Lenti squeaked in alarm.

Robyn opened her eyes. The white light danced around the temple walls, making the mosaic tiles pulsate.

Lenti turned in circles, mesmerised by the tiles illuminating in sequence; red, green, blue. "I've never seen this before," he whispered. "I thought meditating here would give you access to the spirit energy but not this."

Entranced by the rhythm of the tiles, Robyn stood and pressed her palm against a glowing tile. Light flooded her vision and the tug of the spirit world suddenly stopped. She found herself surrounded by darkness. Distant lights flickered like stars and a deep hum reverberated through her, filling her mind with images as energy rushed through her system. Cosmic nebulae spiralling toward each other, tree roots pushing through soil, blood pulsing in veins, branching mycelium recycling organic matter. Spiralling patterns of energy repeated every second, everywhere, throughout time and space. "I understand," she whispered. "Thank you." With a soft sigh, the darkness began receding, like waves on the shore, wrenching Robyn back into herself, her hand still resting on the mosaics.

She blinked. Her arms ached from pressing against the temple wall. Robyn looked around and saw that a beautiful sunset illuminated the horizon. Terror seized her chest and she spun around. Lenti sat in the middle of the temple floor, exactly where she'd left him. "How long?"

"All day," Lenti said, his voice quiet. "The white light only just faded away."

Shaking, Robyn sat beside him.

"What did you see?"

Robyn remained silent until the sun had dipped below the horizon. "Everything is connected. *Everything*. Plants, animals, fungi – we didn't evolve away from each other. We evolved *together*. All life is connected through *energy*. Light, dark; life, death. Balance. The kindred ties that bind every living organism? It's the energy swirling through us, through the universe."

Lenti bowed his head and chanted something beneath his breath.

"What are you saying?"

Lenti took his time answering, his brow knotted in thought. "Energy within, energy without," he finally said. "That's the closest I can get in English. You saw the truth that surpasses all attempts at illusion."

The lab tent was empty, lit by a string of fluorescent tubes. Robyn worked through the night, running samples, mapping compounds. Lenti insisted on sitting at her feet, but the monk fell asleep in the early hours of the morning. Robyn carried him to her tent and tucked him in, hurrying back to her work. She filled a notebook with drawings in a vain attempt to capture the beauty of her vision. Swirling spirals of energy in different forms, repeated from the micro to the macro. Energy, matter – all of it the same. Einstein glimpsed the truth, but never followed it to its fullest conclusion.

As the sun rose, the fluorescent tubes flicked off and scientists began filing in. Robyn sat at her bench, buried in a mess of vials, scribbles and stacks of chromatograms. Hunger flared in her stomach. Later, she'd eat later. She returned to the work laid out on her bench. All life is part of the same ancient network of energy. Chemistry, physics, biology – it didn't matter. It all came down to the same thing. She just had to step back and examine it from a distance. All life was connected – plants, animals and fungi. All bound by the same kindred ties. A collective energy field that unified the universe.

Brock entered the tent and examined the whiteboard propped against the lab fridge. What yesterday had been a pristine printout of the three walkers' samples was now covered in scrawl. "Robyn?"

She laughed and hugged Brock, spinning him around the lab in her euphoria, ignoring the shocked look on his face.

"Robyn? Are you quite all right?" Brock asked.

She swayed as the lab started to spin around her; Brock tightened his grip on her arms as she fell against him.

I am nothing, yet I am everything, she thought.

Brock disentangled himself and propped his arm over Robyn's shoulder. "I think you need to eat something."

Robyn sat on Miranda's bed and ploughed through the breakfast tray Brock had brought her. Lenti burst through the tent, his hair mussed from sleep. "I failed in my duty to you." He dropped to his knees. "Forgive me, I did not mean to fall asleep and leave you without assistance."

"She's okay, kid, it's just low blood sugar," Brock said.

"I'm fine, Lenti," Robyn said through her mouthful. "It's not your fault. I shouldn't have worked all night, but I just got in the zone." She lifted the tray. "Want to help me finish this?"

Lenti's shoulders relaxed and he grinned. "Did you already eat the pastry?"

"Obviously." Robyn patted the bed next to her. "Come sit."

Brock and Miranda stood in front of the whiteboard they'd brought from Robyn's lab. Silent, they just stared at the hand-drawn amino acid sequences and organic compounds Robyn had annotated around the two strange peaks.

"She did this in one night?" Miranda whispered, glancing over her shoulder.

"I told you. She's the one," Brock said, his voice laced with pride.

Robyn passed Lenti the tray and stood, brushing

crumbs from her shirt. "Each peak isn't a discrete compound, it's a combination of compounds." She strode across the tent and pointed at the first peak. "Plant origin. A packet of plant DNA embedded in the convergence sequence." She tapped the second peak. "Fungal origin. Ancient fungi DNA also located in the convergence sequence. I confirmed the matches last night."

Miranda rubbed the bridge of her nose. "I'm still trying to understand exactly what this means."

"It means that separateness is an illusion. We're all the same. Humans, plants, animals, fungi. We're part of an energy field greater than ourselves. An energy field we lost access to when Nyx separated the spirit and physical worlds. Everyone except the walkers."

"And you," Brock said softly.

Robyn stared at the whiteboard, feeling her cheeks warm as everyone turned to look at her. "And me," she echoed.

5

Shield

Harvest implant chip, version 2.0

Patent number: 700657

Number of active chips: 2500

Description: 5mm x 5mm x 10mm silicon dioxide chip inserted into cerebellum. Base hardware for further applications. Monitoring and updates over encrypted network only. Neural binary code links to cellular energy metabolism derived from convergence gene sequence for external amplification; see Model A.2. Potential for remote activation and neural control when used in conjunction with retinal scanning software; see Report

34, section C for clinical trials and relevant updates.

Internal MRI memo, quoted in The Last Bastion of the Anthropocene, *Ester Akintola, the final UN Secretary General.*

Fang hunched into her coat as the harsh Alaskan wind nipped at her neck. Behind them loomed the High Frequency Active Auroral Research Program (HAARP) compound. Vulcan leaned on his cane and inched across the parade ground, his prosthetic clicking against the bitumen. Fang matched his speed, hands clasped behind her back, trying to look very much the capable scientist at ease despite the troop of soldiers accompanying them. Rifles glinted in the weak sunlight. The sound of drilling and hammering drifted over from the enormous radio array – an interwoven series of telegraph poles strung with electrical wires that covered nearly one third of the compound. Each pole bore four pylons that projected outwards at a ninety-degree angle. Fluorescent shapes clambered over the geometric spiderweb. A woman in coveralls and a yellow hardhat shimmied down one of the poles to meet them. "Final touches, sir. Would you like to do the honours?"

Vulcan smiled. "I would."

The woman reached for the bell at her hip and struck it three times. It seemed quaint until you remembered that traditional electromagnetic communications like walkie-talkies were useless without the radio array active, even over short distances. Tools fell silent as the workers returned to the ground. Fang heard the mountain breeze rustling through the deep wilderness that hemmed them in. Part of her longed to run into the shadows of the ancient forest and disappear.

"We've doubled the capacity of the array to stimulate the ionosphere in all conditions, as per your orders, sir," the woman said, handing Vulcan a thick receiver.

Vulcan lifted the receiver in the air and the radio array fizzled to life. The air crackled with energy, the telegraph poles hummed with it. Electricity arced between the pylons, drowning out the sound of the breeze, the forest, everything. It thrummed in Fang's chest, her feet, her hands. Vulcan leaned on his cane, a rapturous smile spreading across his face. *A dangerous spiderweb,* Fang thought. *Presided over by the deadliest spider of them all.* She glanced up at the sky. Nothing had visibly changed, but she knew that a bubble of high-energy electromagnetic radiation now protected them from the ravages of solar flares.

Her tablet dinged. It was Derek grinning, thumbs up. "The lab and command centre are back online," she told Vulcan.

It had been a long, uneasy week without consistent communications. Her progress in the lab had been stymied as machines cut out and data was scrambled. The uncertainty had made the convergers restless. Without tech and communications support, they'd been grounded. Half a dozen fights had erupted during training – a broken arm, a shattered femur, six lost teeth. In response, Vulcan had cut rations and increased the training load. The scuffles had stopped.

"Excellent news. We'll pick up right where we left off," Vulcan said and turned back toward the base.

Across the bitumen, helicopters powered up. A team of convergers clad in bodysuits and their animals ran toward them in formation. The chips implanted at the base of their skulls glinted in the weak sunlight.

Fang matched Vulcan's stilted shuffle, controlling

the urge to peel away from him. Vulcan stopped as they reached the base, dry-swallowed two red pills then turned his bloodshot gaze on her. "Now the lab and command centre are back online, you will personally oversee the training of the operators. You and Derek must be proficient in monitoring the implants. Alternate shifts. We cannot afford to lose any assets in the field."

"Yes, sir," Fang said as Vulcan and his troop of soldiers entered the base ahead of her and disappeared down the hallway. Taking a deep breath of crisp mountain air, she turned back to the radio array, the perpetual storm of crackling transmitters quieter here. Fang took in the arcing bolts of electricity and thought about how much energy was in the air. She shivered. The radio array kept them safe and allowed them to continue their research, while around them, the world crumbled. A safe haven that didn't feel safe.

She strode past the guards at the entry and pulled up comms on her tablet. "Derek?"

His face filled the screen. "You rang?" Behind him scientists bustled around the lab.

"Did we lose any data? Everything operational?" She tried to keep the tension out of her voice. Vulcan abhorred delays. These days, the Director was more on edge than ever; easily irritated and prone to rages. Fang guessed his convalescence was not going particularly well.

Derek ran a hand across his face and sighed. "We lost last week's sequencing data, but I'm replicating it now. It should only put us a few days behind schedule."

A particularly powerful solar flare had brought down the HAARP grid. It could have decimated months of data, but they'd still been offline for nearly a week, the longest outage so far. Fang rolled her shoulders, easing the tension. "I'll be in as soon as I've checked on progress down the hall. Vulcan's orders."

Derek nodded. "You running later?"

"Yeah. Meet you in the gym at 5pm?" God, she could use the oblivion of endorphins and dopamine. The diesel generators only maintained essential systems like auxiliary power, the barracks and kitchen. Leaving the compound wasn't an option – Vulcan had soldiers stationed at every entrance, ostensibly for their protection. The idea of running on tarmac around drilling soldiers, vulnerable under their judging gaze, held zero appeal.

"It's a date."

Fang swiped her tablet off. A date? Who was he kidding? At the reinforced door of the command centre, she pressed her palm to the scanner and the door slid open. Inside, cables dripped from the vaulted ceilings like veins, branching along the concrete walls to feed rows of monitors four-deep. In front of screens, technicians murmured into their headsets, their fingers dancing across the keyboards. On the front wall, an enormous screen flickered with a disorienting mass of video footage. Fang checked each of the sixteen segments. The sight made her dizzy. Paws, hooves, claws. Huffed exhalations, snarls and roars spat through the speakers. Focusing on one segment, Fang watched a bear tear through a training dummy, a soldier running beside it, issuing commands.

The technician closest to her paused his video feed and yanked off his headset. "Dr Fisher?"

At the sound of her name, the other technicians stopped work and the row of screens flashed to standby mode. Three months ago, this display of deference would have thrilled her. Not now. She dismissed them with a wave. "Don't stop on my account. I'm here to observe your progress with the training drills." The technicians glanced at one another then pulled their headsets back on.

Fang climbed the stairs to the central hub where a sleek, semi-circular desk housed an enormous monitor and the primary data banks. She palmed on the monitor, adjusted the headset, then settled into a chair to watch. It had taken months to synthesise sufficient quantities of her modified convergence activation doses. Long hours overseeing scientists in the lab, Vulcan breathing down her neck as she tweaked the genetic sequences. Derek had worked tirelessly by her side. They'd found a rhythm that somehow made the work easier. Still, she didn't trust Derek, or more to the point, *couldn't afford to* trust him.

The results were onscreen. Platoons of bears and humans drilled on a dusty field. Lions encircled and slashed a fake contingent of enemy soldiers. MRI soldiers rushed in to confirm the 'kills'. The sleek dance of orcas in the training pool sent a spike of fear through her system. Such raw power, the pinnacle of evolution, and all of it in Vulcan's hands. Fang gritted her teeth and issued commands to the technicians, coaching them through each new drill, her headset vibrating against her skull. The teams worked well, their training on simulations evident. But Fang knew one thing they didn't: no amount of training would ever match real-life battle.

Vulcan wanted them ready for whatever warped plan he'd concocted now. Rumours circulated about retinal scanning software under development. Apparently, the software would send strings of binary neural code deep into the converger soldiers' brains. The thought made Fang shudder. The prototype blasters were one thing. Months of experimentation and wizardry by Vulcan's tech team had resulted in weaponry that released dazzling arcs of bioelectricity. The sickening realisation the first time she witnessed the convergers training with them. No doubt the retinal scanning software would deliver equally compelling results.

Yet here the technicians sat at their monitors, their workstations littered with crumpled snack packets and stained coffee mugs, oblivious to the power soon to be at their fingertips. The ability to exercise global control over the divisions of soldiers and their formidable animals. Fang glanced up at the main screen. She did not need a chip implanted in her neck to be just as trapped as those convergers. Forced to keep up the façade and convince Vulcan of her dedication to the cause. It ate away at her like acid. She had no choice. No-one could survive the Arctic cold alone. And without the compound's protection from the solar flares, she had no way to contact the outside world. Anyway, who would she contact? Fang adjusted the headset and let the technicians' chatter drown out her doubts and fears.

6

Control

Terrorists. Mutants. Dangerous, non-human freaks. These are a sample of the inflammatory terms bandied about in what remains of the global media. The revelation of the convergers among us has resulted in terrible losses. Dispersing an experimental genetic activator, with a 30% mortality rate, is an unforgiveable atrocity. We cannot change what happened. All we can do is shape the future … and that future is bleak. Crop failures, food shortages, and extreme weather events that have baffled the world's meteorological survey teams and devastated the planet. Every continent flooded with refugees. How does one deal with a crisis on such an epic scale?

Like many before me, I am in exile. It was the beginning of the end for Greek dominance when they banished their greats: Aristotle, Plato, Seneca. Our one hope is the voice of Hypatia. May it reach more hearts, help us join together and forge a new future, while we still can. A future based on trust, acceptance and communion with Earth. If we don't, humans may survive, but humanity shall not.

Extract from **The Last Bastion of the Anthropocene,** Ester Akintola, *the final UN Secretary General.*

The gym was empty, thank goodness. Fang wasn't in the mood for small talk. She jabbed the remote and the blind against a side window eased open to reveal the snowy forest beyond the crackling radio array. She dumped her drink bottle and towel on a weight bench and warmed up, feeling the tension start to dissipate.

Being alone might be her safest option, but Fang regretted this missed opportunity to be more open with her brother, Bohai, about her work when she had the chance. She had no idea where he was and what dangers he might also be facing. The last time she'd seen Bohai was when he was still working for their father's tech firm. Although, he spent most of his time volunteering at a local orphanage, turning over a new leaf. Fang cringed. Who was she to judge? She had searched for his name in the lists of the dead and missing in the limited news reports. Not seeing his name did nothing to relieve her anxiety. If anything, it made it worse. Did her achievements, her sacrifices, count for anything if they didn't benefit the ones she loved?

No. Fang increased the settings on the treadmill and hoped the punishing pace would help her outrun her growing sense of foreboding. She felt trapped by her ego and ambition. When Miranda died, Fang had tried to wrest control of the MRI, but she'd miscalculated, and now she was Vulcan's pawn. The moment they'd touched down at HAARP, Weaving, Deckker and Vulcan held their own counsel, only parcelling out information to Fang on a need-to-know basis. The technicians deferred to her, but all Fang did was repeat Vulcan's instructions and observe the military train with its new weapons. Weapons made possible by Vulcan's genetically engineered convergence bond; a technology she had designed. Fang pushed herself harder, the treadmill whirring beneath her feet.

"Whoa, are you trying to break that thing?" Derek said, dumping his towel beside hers and jumping onto the neighbouring treadmill.

Fang slowed the machine and jogged. "Just a lot on my mind."

She watched Derek push buttons then settle into an easy lope. The last few months had been hard on him too. Since they'd been at HAARP, he'd become leaner, his face thinner. They'd spent long hours in each other's company. Early morning runs in the gym, shared breakfast in the staff cafeteria, then a run at night to ease the pressure of long days in the lab. An endless loop, on repeat. Fang didn't trust him, but if proximity counted for anything, Derek was the closest thing to a friend she had in here. If she were being honest, she probably wouldn't have lasted this long without Derek's stoic presence. And Fang hated this dependence on him, especially after what she did to him in Bulgaria. What sort of person doses a friend with propofol and knocks him out in her bid to seize control of the MRI? Derek would never forgive her if he knew; thankfully, he'd never shown any sign he remembered. Now Derek was her only ally. She couldn't afford to lose him. Fang grabbed her drink bottle and swigged, swallowing her fears.

Derek lifted a remote and the blind descended again, cutting off the pristine view of the snow-blanketed forest. A projector screen lowered from the ceiling and flickered to life. Curious, Fang bit back her protest and watched Derek navigate through a grid of video feeds. When he came to the feed from the convergers' gym, he expanded the video to full screen view.

Hewn into the bedrock, the convergers' gym was an enormous cavern strung with harsh lighting and industrial fans. At the press of another button, a cacophony erupted from the surround-sound speakers. Fang recognised some of the convergers from Bulgaria. Mikey and his lion, Daniel and the new bear he'd partnered with thanks to their induced convergence dose. The boys lifted weights, grunting with the effort, as their animals thudded their paws against the floor, keeping count of their repetitions.

"One hundred and fifty convergers, by last count," Derek said. "Whatever Vulcan is planning, they're ready." He glanced at her.

Fang shook her head. "Don't look at me." She thought back to the command centre. "It's military, but

I have no idea what scheme he's cooked up."

Derek increased the volume. Grunts, yells and thuds echoed around them. He nodded at the security camera in the corner.

Fang kept facing forward, head lowered as if she was intent on her run rather than making sure no-one watching the feed from the gym could read her lips. "There are groups of induced animal-human pairs in training but where, I don't know. Even the technicians in the command centre don't know. They may as well be playing video games. They record the biomonitoring statistics, make reports ... and now they've started practising simulated takeovers."

"Takeovers? You mean using the harvest implant chip? But I thought the retinal scanning software was nowhere near ready."

"Vulcan clearly thinks it is. With the software, real-time control will be possible."

Derek swore under his breath. "That changes everything. Now the convergers and their animals have the implant chips, the MRI will be in complete control. Not just electroshocks, but total neural control. This ... this is a nightmare."

Fang slowed her treadmill to warm-down mode. She's back looking through the glass of the experimental chamber. Ariana's spasming body, the electrical burns on her arms and legs, and the naked hatred in her eyes when she looked straight at Fang. "Ariana was only a test run. This is a whole new level of control."

Derek stopped his machine and mopped his face with his towel. "There were military buyers in Bulgaria – government representatives, dictators, private militia. Do you remember? Before everything went to hell. The day that ..." Derek trailed off with a frown.

Fang jumped off her treadmill, grabbing the bars to steady herself. "The day of the accident," she finished for him. "Yes, I remember."

Derek looked up at the screen. "Yeah. The accident."

"The MRI needs funds to keep this place going, but Vulcan would never cede control to warlords and dictators." Fang leaned against the bars of the treadmill and stretched her hamstrings, counting thirty seconds, switching legs. Then it hit her. "Shit!"

"The simulated takeovers," Derek said, slinging the towel around his neck. "Vulcan's sold the convergence technology to buyers around the world. They think they have bought an army, but those convergers are nothing more than Vulcan's sleeper forces. One flick of the switch and Vulcan controls a global army." Derek buried his face in his towel to stifle a scream. "Fuck. No wonder he's pushed so hard for the retinal software."

Fang slumped onto the weight bench, crushed by the enormity of what she, they, had done. "Vulcan sold our technology to the highest bidder, happy to let the world crumble as the solar storm approaches."

Derek clenched and unclenched his fists, staring up at the screen filled with battling convergers. "It wasn't enough to have his own private army, Vulcan wants to control the whole damn world."

Fang hugged her knees to her chest. She opened her mouth but no words came out. A tremor rose through her core; she couldn't stop shaking.

Derek knelt beside her and drew her to him. "Hey, Fang, we weren't to know. Vulcan is to blame, not us."

Fang leaned into his warmth, wishing she could bury herself in it and forget the cold truths and what she had done. "You and I are only alive as long as Vulcan considers us useful. Remember what he did to those convergers in the battle games."

Derek's eyes grew wide. Fang sat up. "He euthanised them." Derek pointed the remote at the screen. The volume died and the screen disappeared with a mechanical squeal, plunging the gym into stillness. The blind lifted to reveal vision of the snowy forest outside once more. The view calmed her and helped tamp down her exhaustion and fear.

Derek grabbed his drink bottle and turned his back on the security camera. "Let's talk in my room."

When they reached his door, he palmed it open and the floor lights flickered on. They stepped inside and the door hissed shut behind them. His room was identical to hers: single bed, desk, closet, tiny bathroom. Derek grabbed his chair and motioned to the bed. Fang sank onto it, acutely aware she was invading Derek's private space. This is where he slept, thought, dreamed. The only place he had any freedom. *And he let me in here*, she thought. Fang sensed Derek watching her. Blushing, she looked away and noticed a bottle of pills on the night stand.

"I don't sleep well," Derek said in a soft voice. "My brother needs constant care, medicine, and I'm not there for him."

"I miss my brother too." Fang kneaded her palm with her fist, anything to stop the frustration threatening to overwhelm her. "And my father. I'm scared for them. Everything I've done ... I just wanted to find a way to help people. To make my father proud. Not this."

They sat in silence, the absence of their loved ones filling the tiny room. Derek looked up first, his eyes finding Fang's. Something raw and vulnerable passed unspoken between them.

"Trust me, there's no point dwelling on the past." With a sigh, Derek stood and ran his hands through his hair.

Fang watched him pacing the confines of the room like a caged tiger. How many regrets did Derek have? He'd betrayed Robyn after helping her with the induced convergence doses. Had done Vulcan's bidding, blinded by the desire to get his PhD. Which made him what? Foolish? Selfish? But not unique. "It's painful, isn't it? I understand."

Derek couldn't look at her. Fang would never understand the shame he lived with every single day. Vulcan had finally approved his thesis. Derek was now *Dr Smith*. But the price of getting his heart's desire was so much higher than he'd ever imagined. Terence dead, Catherine held prisoner in a cell, and Robyn? "I've hurt anyone I've ever cared about."

Fang closed her eyes. The words could have been her own.

"You're my only friend," Derek murmured.

Don't say that! she wanted to shout. She'd been alone for so long. Trapped by Vulcan, throwing herself into her work to survive. Trusting no-one because who would she trust? Tears pricked her eyes. She lifted her gaze to Derek. "Me too."

Derek reached for her, enveloping her in a hug. She leaned into his shoulder as they held each other, an island of calm amidst so much uncertainty.

7

Iceland

We depend on vast swathes of agricultural land for nourishment. We require networks of satellites and wires for communication and electricity. How quickly civilisation crumbles when both these systems fail. We believed we were the apex of the evolutionary pyramid and we were wrong. Humanity has never faced a crisis like this. Perhaps if we had stood strong, like the brothers and sisters we are supposed to be, we could have borne it. But no — we turned on each other. Calamity renders us back to our basest instincts. Squabbling over remaining resources extends its reach to every continent; every city, every household. Country borders are as fluid as water. In a matter of months, nowhere on Earth will be safe. The sun doesn't recognise lines *on a map or fictional borders. It speaks the ancient language of energy and matter.*

Extract from **The Last Bastion of the Anthropocene,** *Ester Akintola, the final UN Secretary General.*

Fletcher screwed his eyes shut as he felt the jarring wrench of the transition to the spirit world. Head pounding, he pushed back against the nausea rising in his stomach, until it receded and left him feeling weightless. When he opened his eyes, he was standing on a rocky outcrop above a snowy plain, surrounded by a heavy white mist. Wind lashed him with sleet and Fletcher shivered.

Ana, the last earth walker, stepped out of the mist, grinning beneath her heavy furs.

Fletcher peered out into the grey, desolate sky. "What are we doing here, Ana?"

She pointed to a figure just visible on the snowy plain below. Fletcher watched the horse and rider approach. As they came closer, he made out the figure of a young girl riding a fine black horse bareback, her fur coat billowing in the wind. Several hundred metres behind followed a trio of riders, their mounts kicking up sludgy snow drifts. For a while, Fletcher watched their progress, then he turned to Ana. "They're headed straight for us."

She shrugged. "I guess they are."

The girl was clearer now. Fletcher could hear the dark horse's ragged breath as it pushed through the snow, see the spittle fly from its mouth. "How did she cover such a distance so quickly?"

"It's a memory. Our memory," Ana explained.

The young rider urged her horse onward, glancing over her shoulder at the men who pursued her. In a moment, she was almost on top of Fletcher and Ana and he stumbled backwards.

Ana stepped into the path of the oncoming steed. Oblivious to the earth walker's presence, the rider pressed forward, then simply burst straight through her. The air around Ana rippled.

The girl whirled her horse around. It heaved for breath as it danced, ducking its head, its flanks foamed with sweat. The men in pursuit quickly made up ground.

The girl leapt from her horse and prepared to face them. Beneath her fur cloak, her chest rose rapidly.

Though her hair was matted and unkempt, and her face smeared with grime, Fletcher knew this was Ana. Much younger, but the girl's eyes burned with the same determination as the earth walker. He waved a tentative hand in front of her face, but she didn't react.

The three riders halted on the outcrop. Their horses snorted and steam rose from their shiny, damp bodies. "Return the grain or prepare to die," shouted an enormous man. Not fat, but broad, his face half covered by a thick, wiry beard. "The vista bard is law. Hand me the barley, girl. I will not ask again."

The young Ana stood firm, her gaze defiant. "It is not yours to take."

Hairy jerked his head and, with a heavy thud, the other riders dismounted. The thickset men walked toward the young Ana, their movements slow and unconcerned. The girl held her ground.

Fletcher gripped his knife, ready to defend the girl. He glanced at the earth walker, but all she did was press a finger to her lips. "This is the good bit."

Good? This tiny girl might be brave but she was not strong enough to fight off two fully grown men.

Before he could protest, an ominous rumbling filled

the air. Thunder, Fletcher first thought, but then the earth beneath his feet shook. The rumbling grew into a heavy roar and the ground cracked open, zigzagging between the girl and her attackers. The split widened into a chasm that stretched deep into the ground. The man closest to the rift scrabbled desperately to maintain his balance at the edge of the growing chasm. Eyes wide with fear, he tumbled into the abyss, rocks cascading after him. The terrified horses whinnied and all but the leader's mount turned and bolted.

From deep within the chasm, a fiery glow sent plumes of steam and ash high into the air. The second attacker staggered backwards, desperate to escape the wall of heat. "Holy shit," Fletcher muttered. He'd just witnessed the birth of a volcano.

Ana turned and smiled. "Incredible, isn't it? The earth spirit found me."

By Fletcher's reckoning, the rift ran for at least twenty metres. There was no way Ana's surviving pursuers could double back. Through the smoke, Fletcher saw the young girl kneel with her head in her hands. Her black pony calmly approached and she reached out in wonder to the horse, her skin crawling with the familiar green glow.

"I still remember the feeling," Ana whispered. "As if I'd been broken into a million fragments and rebuilt. Everything made sense – why Inga and I could do more than the other children and their ponies."

The young Ana and her horse pulsated with green light. Fletcher's skin also flared green.

Following its instincts, Hairy's horse bucked savagely and dislodged the leader. The animal galloped back down the rocky mountain just as the chasm spewed an enormous burp of liquid fire. The two men didn't stand a chance. The rock beneath their feet melted and oozed around them. The air filled with their tortured screams. The pulsating green sphere protecting the young Ana and her horse, Inga, flickered under the onslaught of molten rock then blazed heavenward as the eruption ceased.

"The earth spirit moves the continents like toys, blesses the soil with fertility, carves mountains and valleys," said Ana, transfixed by her younger self and the green light dancing in the sky. "But much has changed since Nyx slowly wormed out of her prison. She has taken advantage of the air, sea and earth spirits' weakness in the years without a walker. She tricked me."

Sorrow washed over Ana's face. She turned to Fletcher. "You have to make it right."

Then whiteness blanketed him and Fletcher's ears filled with a sound like roaring water. "No, Ana, wait!" he yelled into the void.

Fletcher woke up in the semi-darkness of the cave, still wrapped in his sleeping bag. He rolled over and saw Bry kneeling by the butane burner, trying to coax a whisper of flame. Beyond the maw of their womb-like sanctuary, snow fell in infinite sheets.

Bry took the pot to the opening of the cave and filled it. He set the pot above the flame to boil and turned to Fletcher. "You saw her again."

Fletcher crawled out of his sleeping bag and shrugged on his parka. "We're getting closer." It had taken five anxious days smuggled aboard a fishing boat to get past the border patrols, followed by weeks of hiking through the Icelandic wilderness. His whole body ached, although his muscles were slowly hardening as his strength returned. Bry passed him a mug of tea and Fletcher relished the warmth through his gloves.

Meeting Ana on the solstice had changed everything.

She'd explained how Nyx had infected the earth spirit Gaia. How he was the only one who could free Gaia. Ever since, Ana kept dipping in and out of his mind when he slept, sharing snippets of her life. It was after one such dream that he'd stumbled into the farmhouse kitchen before dawn to find Bry sitting calmly at the dining table, reading by candle light.

Bry had understood. "You're walkers. Able to bridge the divide between humans and animals. Nature constantly searches for ways to connect with us. It's as if somewhere along the line, we lost the old ways of wholeness."

They were still talking when everyone else staggered into the kitchen for breakfast. After that, they fell into an easy pattern – long nights spent at the kitchen table poring over maps and charts. Bry translated Fletcher's visits with Ana into geographical and geological sense. Until one day Bry had pushed a heavily annotated map of Iceland across the table. "This is our route. We leave whenever you're ready."

And here they were, holed up in a tiny cave in the middle of the Icelandic wilderness, Fletcher's initial certainty replaced by growing doubts.

Bry pressed a bowl of porridge into his hands. "Eat up. What else did you learn?"

Fletcher ran through a collection of memories. "She stole barley, talked about something called the vista bard?"

"That fits with our estimated timeline. The northern hemisphere went through an extended cold period we now call the Little Ice Age – the seasons merged almost into one, creating a long winter. Greenland and Iceland were the worst hit. The glaciation caused extensive failure of cereal crops. Many died. Icelanders began moving away from a grain-based diet toward a marine diet. Lots of salted fish. And the vista bard came into effect – effectively serfdom under another name."

"Slavery?"

Bry scraped the last skerricks of porridge from his bowl. "Yes and no. The terms of the vista bard did entitle a labourer to move on to a new farm after a year. But the work was hard, the days long whichever farm you worked on. It would have been a bitter time to exist."

The wind angled inside the cave. Fletcher pulled his beanie lower over his ears.

"What happens if you find this earth spirit, Gaia?" Bry asked, pulling on his jacket and scarf.

Focusing on his breakfast, Fletcher hoped Bry wouldn't see the fear in his eyes. "I need to free Gaia from Nyx's grasp, I'm just not sure how exactly. I'm hoping Ana will show me once we get closer." The sense of failure blanketed him.

"Since you can't go into the spirit world, is your bond with the earth spirit enough?"

Fletcher gripped his bowl tighter. "I don't know. I couldn't save Ariana when she needed me. Or Eva. Ariana and Eli are real walkers – they're jetting around the world on rescue missions, saving people." It was a knife in his gut, twisted anew with each passing day. The solstice had shown him what he'd always feared: he was not as strong as the others.

Bry didn't answer immediately. Instead, he focused on meticulously repacking the cooking equipment, wiping each bowl and spoon clean with snow. Once he was done, he turned to Fletcher. "Did you know that I'm sixty-two? I still second guess my decisions, wish I'd done more to help. It never gets any easier."

"I know I could have done more." Fletcher wrapped

his arms around his knees. "It's like there's a wild thing inside of me, desperate to get out. A greedy, hate-filled, fearful beast fighting with the part of me that is kind, brave and loving."

The fear he strived so hard to keep in check rose up and threatened to paralyse Fletcher. His voice caught in his throat. "I don't want the beast to win."

Bry stared down at Fletcher huddled on the cold ground. "I believe in you, in what you're doing."

Fletcher stood and reached for his rucksack to hide the tears, but he wasn't fast enough. The older man drew him into a hug. Fletcher squeezed the mountain goat of a man back, whispering, "Thank you."

"Now come on," Bry said, releasing Fletcher and hoiking his rucksack onto his back. He pushed through the snowdrift covering the cave entrance and Fletcher followed close behind. The spine of the mountain range was aglow in the early morning light, the sky achingly bright now the snow clouds had moved on. Bry pointed to the goat track weaving sinuously into deeper mist. "Early days yet, boyo."

8

Vessel

We experience events of high-energy confluence regularly, yet we fail to see their utility unless directly affected. The aquatic superhighway – currents that funnel energy around the planet and drive our weather. Electrical storms, cyclones, tornados. Volcanic eruptions that dramatically expand the landscape. Things of beauty, and power.

Miranda Collins, Working Notes.

The ground under his feet swayed. Fletcher flailed to steady himself as the darkness resolved into blinding whiteness.

"You look like you're wrestling an octopus."

Fletcher blinked rapidly until his vision cleared. Ana stood there, wrapped in a fur cloak, her face tilted in amusement. He looked around. They were on top of a mountain, clouds buoying them upwards. A jet of steam forcefully displaced the cool air eddying around Fletcher's body. The clouds parted and revealed that they were on the edge of a gaping crater. Deep below him, magma churned, slow and viscous.

"This is how you can talk with the earth spirit."

Fletcher's foot slipped on ice-slick rock. He screamed, scrambling to keep his balance. Ana gripped his arm.

"It must be active," she carried on, indicating the clouds of oppressive smoke. "I hope you are luckier than me." A sad smile crossed her face and she flickered and began to fade. Fletcher reached for her, but he was already falling back into the blackness.

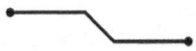

"Wake up. You're daydreaming again."

Startled, Fletcher dropped his protein bar into the snow. "I fell asleep? I didn't mean to." Fletcher retrieved the protein bar, trying to hold onto the threads of the dream-vision.

Bry zipped his rubbish inside his rucksack. "Time to get moving. We've got a lot of ground to cover today." A burst of static punctuated his words. Frowning, Bry fished a bulky radio receiver from his pocket and studied the screen. "Another damn solar flare."

Fletcher devoured the protein bar in two bites, shoving the wrapper in his coat pocket. "Ana showed me a volcano about to erupt."

Bry looked up from the receiver. "If my calculations are correct, we've been retracing Ana's journey almost exactly, but we need to hurry. We're still two days' hard hike from the next volcano, and it's due any day now. If we miss this one, it might be months until you get another shot."

"You knew?"

Bry stared out into the mist. He reminded Fletcher of an ancient Norse god surveying his dominion. "You, my daughter, young Eli. It's astounding how the three of you can harness energy. I figured you would need a dramatic energy input to reach the earth spirit. And since Iceland is one of the most volcanically active places on the planet, here we are." Bry threw Fletcher his pack. "So let's stop wasting time, ay?"

It had taken a day and a half of hard walking through thick snow to bring them this far. The volcano remained in sight but the monolith never got any closer. Fletcher pulled down his scarf and flinched as the snow whipped his face. "How much longer?"

Bry's voice floated back like a snatched whisper. "Another couple of hours."

Fletcher groaned and pulled his scarf back up over his nose. He fell back into step behind the older man. As they trudged along the ridge, Fletcher's thoughts returned to Ariana. What was she doing right now? Maybe more defence training or biology homework. He hoped she understood why he'd gone. Fletcher glanced up at the volcano and caught a glimmer of red. Ana had given him hope. Maybe he could still be useful. Maybe he'd find answers here.

Bry stopped abruptly and held up a hand. "Can you feel that?"

Fletcher closed his eyes and concentrated on the rock beneath his feet. There *was* something. A slight tremor then a rumble rippled through the ground.

"We have to hurry." Bry tightened his rucksack and broke into a jog.

Fletcher followed, struggling to cut through the snow. The tremors increased in frequency, jolting his legs. Reaching the top of the mountain seemed an impossible task.

They crisscrossed the face of the volcano. Fletcher gasped in the thin air, his heart pounding loudly in his ears as they clambered up the steep slope. A plume of smoke erupted turning the sky blood-red. Fletcher could just make out the rim, spewing dark smoke. It seemed like madness that they were running *toward* the deadly explosions when every instinct told him to turn tail.

Bry stopped, hands on his knees as he caught his breath. Then he straightened. "Come on. We're nearly there."

At last they reached the top of the mountain. It was shrouded in a thick ash cloud. Bry wrapped his scarf tightly around his head, leaving only a slit for his eyes. Fletcher copied him. Intense heat emanated from the depths, getting hotter and hotter as they neared the rim.

Fletcher coughed. Acrid smoke filled his lungs, the

hot air searing his skin. How the hell was he supposed to reach the earth spirit without killing himself?

Bry turned and indicated to Fletcher to hand him his rucksack. "When you're done, we'll need to hustle out." He gave Fletcher's shoulder a squeeze then walked away from the rim, away from Fletcher.

Fletcher felt like an idiot. Who stood on the rim of an erupting volcano and expected to live? But he hadn't come all this way to fail.

He chose a spot a metre or so from the rim and sat down. Fletcher crossed his legs, like he'd done with Eli and Ariana countless times before, and closed his eyes. He focused on slowing his breath and shutting out the wracking tremors, the clouds of choking ash, and the fear. Eventually his mind entered a space devoid of sound, the chaos left behind. His stomach lurched and his arms prickled with energy. Opening his eyes, Fletcher saw green light encasing his arms and grinned. His aura thrummed, enclosing him in a sphere as he lifted off the ground and hovered over the gaping mouth of the volcano. Fletcher's heart leapt. *Maybe I can really do this.*

Ana appeared through the billowing curtain of ash,

shimmering in the heat haze, like a mirage. She grinned and took his hand in hers. "Ready?"

A jet of steam whooshed upwards. Sweat beaded on Fletcher's forehead. "For what, exactly?"

"For this," she said and dived into the fiery abyss.

They plunged into the heart of the volcano, Fletcher too terrified to even scream. Bubbling, roiling magma surrounded them, but his green aura deflected the intense heat. When he closed his eyes, the heat disappeared and when he opened them again, they were standing in a dense forest.

Ana smiled. "You made it."

Fletcher stared at the greenery around them; the cool stream, the moss-covered rocks. "What happened to the molten cavern of lava?"

"The volcano simply provides the raw energy you need to cross over." She indicated the lush greenery. "This is the in-between. The walker state."

Hope filled Fletcher's chest. Eli and Ariana moved in and out of the walker state at will, but he'd never been able to enter it. Until now. "How long do I have here?"

"Long enough."

The trees parted and revealed a pair of dark-green

eyes. Entranced, Fletcher watched an enormous stag step into the clearing. Its long antlers were covered in moss, trailing vines and brightly coloured brackets of fungi. It was as if the creature was part of the forest itself.

Fletcher bowed to the magnificent beast. Waves of energy emanated from the stag, pulsating against Fletcher's ribcage. Its jade eyes examined him from head to toe. *It is dangerous for you to be here. You are of the chosen three.*

"I had to try," he said, his voice catching.

Fletcher felt the ancient voice probe his mind. It crept through the recesses of his grief and despair. An image of Eva rose in his mind and tears sprang to his eyes.

You have lost much.

"I couldn't save her." His voice broke across the words, but he was beyond caring. There were no barriers, nothing separating him from the earth spirit. He felt the burden lift from his shoulders and the sweetness of relief.

The stag knelt before Fletcher and touched its antlers to his temples. Fletcher jolted as a kaleidoscope of images flashed before his eyes.

Three to save the world, to restore the long-forgotten balance.

Fletcher saw forests filled with humans and animals walking together. "I've seen this before," he whispered. "When I first paired with Eva, I saw glimpses of the past, of how things used to be."

When war began and the land was ravaged, I saw what would come, the stag told him.

More images flooded Fletcher's mind. Converger against converger, bodies everywhere. The stag brought him back to the battle that had taken Eva. Mikey's snarl as his lion pounced at Eva's exposed throat. The blood, so much blood. Why?

I had not anticipated how humankind would separate from their partner animals. Nor what would happen when they did. Our two realms diverged and the other spirits and I closed the portal. We hoped that one day humankind would be able to bridge the two worlds and restore the natural balance. I still cling to that hope.

"Except things are worse than ever," Fletcher said, the familiar hopelessness settling on his shoulders.

Yet the walkers persisted.

Fletcher met Ana's teary eyes. She nodded, a thin smile on her lips.

Alone, they could only effect limited change. But I knew

a time would come when the walkers would rise together and repair the rift between the worlds.

"How? How did you know?"

The stag tilted its head, its green eyes appraising him. Its antlers still rested against Fletcher's temples, its breath a warm mist on his cheek. All of a sudden, it pulled away and stumbled backwards over the grass. The green light flickering along its flanks turned black. The stag pawed the ground, grunting and shaking its antlers, sending moss drifting to the ground like snow.

It is not safe. I cannot fight her for long. You must —

The stag stilled, its bare antlers glinting with menace. The spirit's voice sliced through Fletcher's mind. *It was foolish of you to journey here, young one. I have slumbered beneath the earth for many millennia, waiting for the ones who would come to restore peace, with naught but a temporary jaunt above the surface in all that wretched time.*

The temperature around Fletcher skyrocketed and with it his fear of the searing embrace of molten lava. The green light on his skin wavered as energy pooled behind his ribcage, immobilising him. Fletcher took a shuddery breath trying to fight Nyx's grasp, his unease turning to sheer terror.

I have waited too long. Now you will help me open the portal between the worlds. The stag turned around, eyes dark as obsidian. With a resounding boom, the forest faded.

Fletcher stared down from the edge of the volcano. Magma ricocheted off its walls, sending blistering heat spiralling upwards. The deafening roar made his ears ring. He spun around, looking for Ana, for Bry, for anyone to save him. Fletcher screamed as a surge of energy burst through his skull. It rippled through his limbs, coaxing momentary flashes of darkness across his skin. A string of images skittered through his mind: a dark void slowly filling with green, blue and red light; an ocean of bright stars; thousands of faces. He pressed his nails into his palms to stop crying out in pain.

You are mine now. When you open the portal between this world and the spirit world, I will be with you.

"Nyx," Fletcher grunted, straining against the force that kept him frozen, helpless.

I've festered on this planet for too long. No more.

Pain tore through his synapses, every nerve cell vibrating in rebellion against his own will. "I. Won't. Let. You. Do. This."

Yes, you will. When you enter the walker state, you will bring me to the air and sea spirits. Once I destroy them, I will be free of this meagre world.

Fletcher's body jerked sideways and he hit the snow hard. Energy crawled through his system, sinking into every cell and clutching tight.

Blood spilled from his mouth. "Eva is gone and I can't enter the spirit world, or the walker state." For the first time ever, this fact made him glad. Maybe this was how he could fight Nyx, stop the spirit destroying Earth.

Energy, life, is all the same. Through me, you will enter the spirit world once more. I will be your Eva.

A dark mist rose from the volcano and sent ash billowing into the sky. Grit swirled around him. Fletcher watched in horror as the ash cloud coalesced into a sphere of rippling dark energy. The sphere blazed, illuminating a bulky figure within. Stabbing pains seared his brain as Nyx greedily ravaged memories of Eva. Her soft brown fur, her galaxy-green eyes, the way she nuzzled his side in greeting. "No," he pleaded. "Those memories are mine."

No. You *are mine.*

"I'll never help you. Never!" Fletcher screamed.

Out of the vortex of ash, stepped Ana. Darkness rippled around her like a cloak, a cruel smile on her face. Nyx's voice overlaid her own. "It's too late. Luring you here was simple."

The green light on Fletcher's skin receded. Nyx's crushing grip blurred his vision. The spirit squeezed out every memory, every thought. Ariana running through a field of wildflowers, smiling at him. Eli grinning at him during a training run. Tears streaked through the ash on Fletcher's face. His world constricted, darkness rushing in from all sides.

Walkers, Nyx spat.

Fletcher wished for death, for oblivion, for an end to the torment.

No, walker. I need you a while longer.

Darkness surrounded him. No sight, no sound, nothing but pain.

Through the ash cloud, Bry saw the figure of a boy sprawled by the rim of the volcano. He ran to Fletcher and dropped to his knees. The boy's cheek felt warm beneath Bry's fingers. "Fletcher, wake up!" Bry said, pulling him upright.

With a gasp, Fletcher opened his eyes. He looked around. A fresh plume of smoke billowed around them. Ash-stained snow drifted from his jacket. He shook off Bry.

"The volcano is about to blow," Bry said, grabbing Fletcher's pack. Then he froze. Eyes wide, he stared past Fletcher. Out of the smoke and ash materialised a dark shape. "By all that's holy, what is that?"

An enormous brown bear lumbered toward them. Eva sniffed Bry's jacket and huffed in greeting before taking her place beside Fletcher. The boy placed a hand on her neck.

Bry stared at the bear in shock. "I guess you found what you were looking for."

Bry thought he saw a shadow as dark as midnight pass over Fletcher. He blinked and the light was gone but he felt sluggish, as if he'd woken from a long slumber. Bry shook his head. The important thing was that Fletcher was all right. Their journey had been a success.

Taking his pack from Bry, Fletcher started down the mountain with a confident step. "Come on. We need to get back to the others. There's no time to waste."

9

Trust

Electromagnetic blaster, modified version 2

Patent number: 700659

First production run: 2000 units

Description: 400mm x 50mm. Plasteel with vacuum arc chamber for bioelectricity harvest. Requires harvest implant chip hardware. Palm operated by user. Amplifies cellular energy metabolism derived from convergence gene sequence using neural binary code links.

Fatigue rating: High. Not to be used for extended

periods without medical observation. See Report 34, section E for clinical trials and relevant schematics.

Internal MRI memo, quoted in The Last Bastion of the Anthropocene, *Ester Akintola, the final UN Secretary General.*

Ariana sat beside Eli in the field behind the farmhouse. Her salamander Jericho perched on her head, warming himself in the sun. "It's reckless and just … completely idiotic," she exploded.

Eli refused to open his eyes. Instead, he took a deep, pointed breath. "I thought we were meditating."

Ariana picked a wildflower and twirled it in her palm. "We are. It's just that I can't believe Fletcher would leave without telling us where he was going. And how did he convince Dad to go with him?"

With a small sigh, Eli opened his eyes and gave Ariana his full attention.

"Don't they realise how much danger they're in? We need to be working together, not splitting up." Ariana passed the flower to Jericho, who snapped it up, creating a flurry of petals.

Eli rolled his shoulders and gazed across the field. "We've been over this a dozen times – ruminating on what has been is a waste of energy. We must assume Fletcher knows what he's doing."

"But he thinks there's something wrong with him; that he's somehow failing us … and now he's put himself in danger, and because of these damn solar flares we have no idea where the hell he is!" Ariana thumped the ground with her fist, her arms trembling. Jericho shimmied to the safety of Ariana's shoulder.

Eli gently squeezed her arm. "It royally sucks. Waiting around, running training drills with convergers. We're driving each other crazy. I can't wait for this solar activity to settle down so we can head out on more extraction missions."

He's right, and you know it, Jericho projected. *You all find this inaction crippling.*

And not knowing where my Dad and Fletcher are, or if they're safe, Ariana added.

It was as if Eli could read her thoughts. "We're doing everything we can to find Fletcher, but at least we know he's in good hands."

Ariana smiled at Eli. "You're right. I do feel a bit useless."

"Come on. Since we're the ones who can enter the spirit world, at least there's something we can do." Eli settled back into position and clasped his hands together.

Ariana closed her eyes and copied his posture, trying to push thoughts of Fletcher from her mind. But it was impossible not to remember him sitting beside her in this very field, heartbroken over losing Eva. Jericho nipped her ear, reminding her to focus, and eventually Ariana began slipping into the spirit world. But at the last second, Ariana stopped herself and hovered on the brink of both worlds.

What are you doing? Jericho projected. *Eli is waiting for us.*

Perhaps the sea spirit knows where Fletcher is. I have to ask. Around her flared an orb of blue light. She hung in the darkness as Jericho shifted into his spirit form, spiralling around her body.

Through the infinite blackness came the sea spirit's deep voice. *Sea walker. You are troubled.*

Ariana's skin prickled with goosebumps as all around her stars twinkled into existence.

I fear for the earth walker, Atlantis. I think he's doing something stupid and I'm not there to stop him.

Blue light flickered on Ariana's limbs as she floated in the in-between, the space between the physical and spirit worlds.

I cannot help you. The spirits split from each other long ago. You are now my only link to the physical realm.

Ariana's heart sank. Meeting with Atlantis had been her last hope of saving Fletcher from Nyx's control.

Once, the boundary between the spirit and physical world was fluid and humans moved between the two with ease. But humankind wanted more – they fought for resources, for imagined wealth and honour. The connection between the two worlds began to crumble and the number of convergers dwindled.

Sadness washed over Ariana. Imagine if she lost the synchronicity with Jericho? Humanity did not know what it was missing; what it had forgotten. *And Nyx?*

Nyx descended to Earth and fed off the growing chaos. Human hatred and fear made her strong. Together, we three, the air, earth and sea spirits, fought against her.

Ariana's blue aura flared at Atlantis' words.

Eventually, we managed to entomb her but at a price. We had to close the portal between the physical and spirit worlds, and so humans lost the ability to understand their animal partners. The only way we could maintain any connection was for us to weave our beings into the fabric of humanity. In so doing, we created the walker lineages; one for each of our realms. I live on through you, and pull energy from the swirling oceans and steady lakes; the air spirit from your rich and turbulent atmosphere; and the earth spirit from your young core. This is how we have kept the world from harm.

Now everything made sense. It all came down to energy. Nyx planned to harness the energy created by the solar storm to break these ancient bonds. And somehow, the walkers had to stop her. Her head throbbed. *But how? We can't stop the sun, can we?* There *must* be a way to stop Nyx. She directed a question to Atlantis. *How can we reunite the physical and spirit worlds without freeing Nyx? There must be a way of restoring balance that doesn't release a dangerous intergalactic spirit hell-bent on wiping us all out.*

Atlantis remained silent for so long Ariana feared the sea spirit had no answers. *It is my greatest wish to re-establish the connection between nature and humankind and see convergers walk the earth again. True balance can only be restored if the boundary between the worlds is torn down. Nyx's tomb in the physical world is weakening as the sun sings louder, and the solstice will give her the power she needs to break free, to once more roam the spirit world with impunity. Catastrophic destruction will follow. Only the walkers are capable of directing the energy required to vanquish her from both worlds. Only together will you succeed in your stand against Nyx.*

Ariana's hold on the walker state began to dissipate. She closed her eyes, saw lights flashing beneath her eyelids: red, green, blue. She slipped into the spirit world and joined Eli.

"Where have you been?"

"Sorry," she said. Jericho, in dragon form, landed lightly beside her. The sea spirit's words echoed in her mind. *Together.* "It took me a while to stop thinking about Fletcher."

Eli crossed the glade, greeting Jericho with a scratch behind his ear. The salamander-turned-dragon leaned into his touch with a throaty purr.

Una, wreathed in red light in her spirit form, landed beside them with a *whump* of air. Eli turned to her with a soft smile and she ruffled her feathers. Tilting his head toward Ariana, he said, "Still no sign of Fletcher or Robyn."

Ariana leaned against Jericho, letting the tranquil glade calm her worries. All of a sudden, the salamander's whiskers twitched. *Something is not right*, he projected. Ariana straightened, scanning the forest around them for the source of the disturbance. Una let out a cry, taking to the air as the trees in the clearing began shaking violently. They seemed to groan, lights sparking from their falling leaves. Darkness cloaked the bright sky, and the clearing turned from day to night. The wrongness of it penetrated Ariana's very bones. An icy wind pierced her skin, her muscles, and anchored itself in her skeleton. "Eli?" she shouted.

Through the darkness, Eli's fingers found hers and a dome of blue and red energy blossomed around them. Then the earth stilled and the sky brightened. The trees rustled their branches like a sigh of relief.

Eli released her hand. "I've never felt cold like that."

Ariana nestled close against Jericho. "It was more than cold. It seemed to choke out every emotion except fear."

Eli sat and brought his fists together. Ariana joined him. "Do you think it has something to do with Fletcher?" she said.

"I don't know. But I suspect we'll find out soon enough." Eli closed his eyes. "Let's get out of here."

Her father's study felt different with the twins in it. Less musty, more lively. Ariana and Eli looked over Kara's shoulder as she pulled up data on her laptop. "Another solar flare. The biggest one yet, which is weird. We're not due for another one until tomorrow, and we've been able to predict every flare so far." Kara chewed on her bottom lip as she looked over the numbers.

"You didn't notice anything strange?" Ariana pressed.

Kara shrugged. "I guess there's always an outlier. But otherwise, it's been business as usual. Aster's working on the satellite array, convergers are training in the south field, and the dinner crew is getting organised."

Eli steered Ariana toward the door of Bry's study. "Thanks, Kara. Speaking of training, we'd better get going. We're late as it is."

"Roger," Kara said, already back on her laptop and immersed in her work.

"What?" Ariana hissed once they were out of hearing distance.

"You heard her – nothing unusual happened here.

Maybe it was just because it's the first time we'd been in the spirit world during a strong solar flare."

Ariana paused. She hadn't thought about that possibility. "Maybe," she allowed. "But what about the darkness and the cold?" She thought of Atlantis' words. "Could the energy of a solar flare really penetrate both the physical and spirit worlds?"

Eli opened the farmhouse door. The day was crisp and cool. Across the field, convergers were stretching and warming up. He began jogging toward the south field.

Ariana ran to catch up, tugging on Eli's sleeve. "Or maybe Fletcher's in trouble."

"He's on his own journey right now. And he has your father." Eli turned around, jogging backwards. "He's not an idiot, Ariana. We have to trust him."

"But that's my point. We have no idea where they are, so we can't help them and we risk losing them both." Ariana stopped, choking back tears as she finally vocalised her greatest fear.

Eli skidded to a halt, his face pained. "Oh, Ariana, I'm so sorry. I didn't mean ..."

Ariana shook her head, willing the tears away.

Eli pulled her close. "I care about them too. Fletcher is like a brother to me, and Bry? He's basically a second father. I've never felt so lucky, but their welfare just isn't in our control right now."

Ariana pressed her face into Eli's shoulder. "Thank you, I needed to hear that." She straightened and wiped her eyes. "I wish we could do something, but you're right, worrying won't change anything. Their fate is in their own hands. I just hope they're being careful."

"Oi! You're late!" Jacob shouted, running over. He pushed his sweaty fringe out of his eyes. "We've finished running drills and now we're just mucking around. Want to join in?"

"Hurry up!" Sara yelled, her leopard, Ming, darting between her legs and almost knocking her over. Eli loped over to join Sara and a group of new convergers.

Ariana threaded her arm through Jacob's and forced a grin. "Guess that means you're stuck with me." They headed over to another team of convergers. "How's Poppy?"

Jacob's face brightened and he raised a hand to his ear. A bee flitted onto his palm and danced with excitement. "She's loving the wildflowers, though she's travelling further and further each day." Having said hello, Poppy buzzed upwards and disappeared into Jacob's messy hair.

Lucy broke away from her team of convergers and came toward them, her vampire bat hopping around her feet, matching the converger's fidgety energy. "Okay, how are we going to play this?"

Ariana studied the set-up. Eli stood with Sara and Basil on the other side of the field. A group of other new convergers whooped from the fence line. This had fast become one of their favourite games – basically touch football meets tag, except with four-legged team members.

"Hard and fast. You know the drill," Jacob said, jogging on the spot.

Lucy grinned. "Rightio. Alright, everyone, are you ready? On my whistle." She put two fingers in her mouth and issued a piercing note. "Go!"

They pounded toward Eli's team. Lucy flipped effortlessly over Basil, her vampire bat lifting her the extra metre she needed to clear him. "Got you!" Lucy shouted, slapping Basil's arm and landing in a roll.

Ariana and Jacob ran in tandem zigzags as Sara and

her leopard raced toward them. Sara lunged at Jacob and tapped his arm. "Sorry, buddy, you're out."

"Oh man," Jacob groaned. "Just one time I'd like to get through. Just once."

Lucy reached the fence line with a whoop of delight. "One point!" she yelled, joining the onlookers. She cupped her hands around her mouth and hollered, "Come on, Ariana!"

Sara and Eli circled Ariana. Heart pounding, she waited until the last second and sidestepped the pair. Pivoting, she dropped to the ground in a roll and nudged into the walker state. A surge of energy washed over her as she straddled the physical and spirit worlds. As Jericho spiralled upwards into his spirit form, Ariana grabbed his scales and pulled herself astride his back. They hovered over the field for a moment then dived toward the fence. Taking a deep breath, Ariana left the walker state and Jericho rocketed back to being a little salamander once more. She grabbed the fence with both hands, exhilaration coursing through her.

"Nice try," Eli called from the opposite side of the field, where he sat on the fence with Sara. "But it's a tie."

"Rematch!" Sara hollered.

Ariana grinned. Eli was right. She had to focus on the here and now, not spend every waking moment worrying about Fletcher and her father.

10

Puppets

Retinal scanning software, version 4.3.1

Patent number: 700658

<bugs detected?>

<error>

<error>

<none>

<update complete>

Description: Neural binary insertion code for real-time retinal imaging. Requires functional harvest implant chip as power source to perform binary inversion; see Report 34, section A for potential side effects.

Internal MRI memo, quoted in **The Last Bastion of the Anthropocene,** *Ester Akintola, the final UN Secretary General.*

Derek fumbled for his alarm, the floor lights brightening as the jarring noise abated. Rubbing the sleep from his eyes, he padded into the bathroom. A gaunt face greeted him in the mirror. Every day the same. Work, eat, sleep, repeat. Except now something had shifted. For starters, his room smelled different; Fang's presence lingered from the night before. He felt the dynamic between them had changed but would she have her mask back on today as if yesterday had never happened? He hoped not. He needed a friend here. Someone to talk to. He'd seen his own tiredness and fear mirrored on Fang's face as she sat rigid on the edge of his bed. Out of her element but willing to try and forge a new alliance. Perhaps it was time to trust her.

Derek splashed water on his face and reached for his toothbrush. Somewhere deep in the military complex, Catherine was being held prisoner, but were circumstances really any different for him and Fang? Neither of them were allowed to leave the compound or have any contact with the outside world. Vulcan insisted it was for their own safety, given the solstice was only months away and global order was crumbling. According to the Chief Director, HAARP was the safest place on the planet, except it didn't feel safe.

A wave of nausea threatened to overtake him. Derek clutched the sink. *Look what I have done to the people I called friends.* He hated himself, hated his weakness. Vulcan was ruthless, but he was right – outside of HAARP, there was no guarantee of survival. Not with the power Vulcan now wielded. Derek turned away from his reflection. *I can't change the past. I have to make the best of the current situation, starting with Fang. She's the only one I can trust; my only way out.*

Derek pushed open the command centre door. The room buzzed like NASA mission control on steroids. Technicians sat at their stations, intent on their monitors. Snack detritus and stained coffee mugs delineated the night shift about to clock off from the fresh-faced newcomers. Derek climbed the stairs to the central hub, his heart hammering in his chest. Pausing halfway, Derek looked at the enormous central screen that flicked from feed to feed, Fang's words echoing in his mind. *Real-time control.* Onscreen, soldiers drilled against dummies and sprinted around obstacle courses with their partner animals.

Derek palmed on the monitor and scanned the latest updates. No word on Robyn. The knot of tension in his chest loosened. So she was still safe, somewhere. *Or dead*, a little voice suggested. *Maybe even long dead.* It had been over three months since Robyn attacked the MRI compound in Bulgaria. He had to believe she was alive.

Derek pushed the thoughts away and skimmed the drills and active missions data. Most of the technicians monitored the training drills, but Alpha team oversaw a converger mission in progress. Vulcan's hand-picked favourites formed an elite crack squad for dangerous missions. Derek clicked on a smirking image of Mikey and pulled up the live retinal feed from his lion. The footage bounced as Mikey ran. Derek caught a glimpse of Daniel and his bear to the right. The pre-dawn darkness swallowed the convergers in their dark bodysuits but the lion's natural night vision showed everything as if it were full daylight.

"Who's on Alpha team?" Derek said into his headset.

"That'd be us." A group of technicians raised their hands. "They're en route but have not yet made contact. We're on it."

"Roger that," Derek replied. He pulled up the mission information and his stomach churned in dismay.

Mikey held up a fist and his team stopped. The two-storey weatherboard house looked neglected, the lawn too high, but a small vegetable garden down the side held new seedlings. A shiny pink bike was leaning against the fence. His lion prowled forward, head up, and sniffed the air. Mikey detected the scent of grass, linen and flesh. His lion huffed, impatient. Mikey ignored him and scanned the street. No lights penetrated the darkness. Power rationing had been in force for weeks now. Good.

He turned to the girl behind him and gave the

command. She knelt on the path and released a tiny scorpion, which skittered under the solid door. Moments later, the door clicked open, and the scorpion scuttled back to the girl's outstretched hands. She tucked it into the lining of her jacket and grinned.

Inside, the hallway was neat. Men's dress shoes and tiny gumboots lined up by the door. A vase of fresh-picked flowers stood on a narrow table. Mikey unholstered his blaster and signalled to Daniel. Together, they crept upstairs, pausing on the landing. Mikey nudged open the door. The dull yellow light of his blaster illuminated the sleeping figures on a bed. Mikey didn't hesitate. He raised the weapon and fired two electroshock bursts in quick succession. Daniel stepped inside and checked the bodies for signs of life. Satisfied, he gave Mikey the thumbs-up. In less than a minute, they were back on the street, the door closing behind them with a soft click.

"Mission complete," echoed in Derek's headset. The bluntness of Mikey's words sent chills down his spine. He re-read the briefing notes and pulled up the footage logs, skimming through the statistics, revolted by the *normality* of it all. Around the globe, Vulcan had systematically executed those who refused to comply with his vision – dozens of government leaders and military leaders assassinated. They were not innocent people – tinpot despots, corrupt government officials and terrorists among them. With the major league of nations destroyed, resistance had crumbled. Even the few commentators who had joined Hypatia online reached consensus: the shadowy leader of the MRI was on a trajectory to become the supreme commander on Earth. And Derek had sat back and watched it all unfold. Surely this had never been the MRI's intention or mandate. The previous Chief Director, Miranda, cannot have planned or foreseen this outcome.

His mind snagged on a hazy memory. Derek looked up from his screen: Fang's office, the day of the attack on the Bulgaria compound. There had been something in a folder, something important. Derek listened to the tech chatter through his headset and scanned the command centre. Images of deep jungle, desert dunes and deserted buildings. He tried to recall the memory but it eluded him. Derek shook his head and returned his attention to his monitor where gigabytes of biomonitoring statistics waited for him. Data to crunch, reports to file. He pulled up the statistics program and buried himself in work, soon absorbed in a world view from the perspective of bears and killer whales. A glimpse of what it must be like to be bonded with those majestic animals. It made him sick to his stomach. Vulcan had imposed slavery on innocent children and animals. Corrupting the convergent bond was an aberration of nature. And the end result? Murder.

Derek rested his forehead on the desk. When the time came, he would be responsible for manipulating the lives of more children and animals. At Vulcan's command, Derek would simply push a button; no less guilty than those who did the actual killing.

Gunfire erupted on the main screen and Derek's head snapped up. Actual gunfire. With growing horror, he watched a line of soldiers collapse under a combined bear-human attack. Real people, not training dummies. Bloody claws flashed and chilling grunts echoed around the command centre. Above the staccato of gunfire, terrified screams pierced the speakers. Derek turned away from the limp mangled bodies splattered across the screen.

Around him, fingers danced on keyboards, and the technicians' chatter swelled. "We got a hot one; damping down the signal."

"Geez, how did you not *see* that guy?"

"Bloody idiots …"

Bile hit the back of Derek's throat. Frightened people were dying, struck down by monstrous beasts. Derek sank into his chair. Biomonitoring statistics flashed onscreen; hundreds of individual heartbeats. Real heartbeats, real death.

An alarm sounded. The technicians fell silent and listened to the new instructions being relayed over their headsets. Derek grappled for his own, only catching the end of Vulcan's announcement: "… gone rogue, interfering with operations. Incapacitate their soldiers and terminate the assets."

He looked up at the main screen. The video feeds went dark then rebooted.

"Omega team, have you got a lock on that contingent coming up the rear?"

"GPS is kicking in now. I got it."

"Beta, can you take the flank?"

"Roger that."

"Get ready. On my mark."

Onscreen, a group of bears and their soldier partners froze, eyes wide. As one, the soldiers clapped their hands to the base of their skulls, their faces contorting in pain. An image of Ariana spasming under a powerful electrical current flashed through Derek's mind. Just as quickly, the soldiers straightened, their faces deadpan.

"Bring them around, now! The rest of the contingent won't be expecting an attack from their own soldiers."

Derek's headset crackled as the technician teams responded. The realisation dawned. *They're controlling them through the harvest implant chips.* Derek could not bear to watch the bloody destruction. *Everything Fang feared is happening.* Finally, when everything fell quiet, he dared to look at the screen. Confused and bewildered, the chipped soldier-animal pairs wandered among their fallen comrades.

"Is the final current charge ready?"

"Ready."

"Three, two, one."

Dozens of heartbeats flatlined on Derek's monitor. Soldiers and bears keeled over in a wave of death.

"And that is how you bankrupt an alliance of

nations," came Vulcan over the headset. The technicians whooped for joy and high-fived one another. They didn't understand the terrible truth. But Derek knew. This was no hyper-realistic video game.

Derek propelled himself out of his chair and strode into the corridor. He needed to find Fang.

She was in the lab, surrounded by racks of crimson vials. One glance at his numb expression and she peeled off her gloves with a snap. "Cafeteria," she said. "I'm desperate for coffee."

They said nothing on their way to the canteen. Fang steered Derek to an empty table then poured them each a coffee from the percolator. She put a mug in front of Derek. "What is it?"

Derek stared at the black coffee, the nausea rising in his gut. "Vulcan's moved on from training drills. I've just watched him take control of human-animal pairs he *sold* to other armies. He obliterated everyone."

Fang rubbed her temples. "Shit."

His anger surged. "That's all you've got? Shit?"

"What do you want me to do? Stroll in there and countermand Vulcan's orders?" Fang hissed, eyes flashing. "We're stuck in a compound in the middle of the wilderness. Our options are limited." Fang scrunched her eyes shut, her worst fear realised. Her work had given Vulcan this power to kill. She slumped over her coffee. "I hoped we'd have more time to find a solution."

A group of scientists from the lab entered the cafeteria and milled by the percolator. Two waved in their direction.

Derek waved back with a fake smile. "What are we going to do?"

"Survive," Fang said, throwing a forced smile at the scientists as they sat down.

Derek drank his coffee, ignoring the annoying buzz of conversation around him. He had to get back. Someone would report his absence. Vulcan would not be happy to find him absent from his command post at such a crucial time. Vulcan the puppet master forcing Derek to dance at the end of his strings.

11

Strike

When did we sink to such levels of barbarity? Using animals as weapons; nature red in tooth and claw. Our collective fear of monsters, of beasts with unimaginable strength, has now been realised in the flesh. How can you run from an animal faster and more agile than you? Fight back against superior strength? Hide from senses twenty-fold more attuned than our own?

Not much is known about the institute responsible for this atrocious molecular devilry. The Mitochondrial Research Institute (MRI) has issued no press release, no statement about their aims. Yet, from their actions, it is inevitable for one to conclude that they seek power. Their military now ranks on par with once-powerful *nations and is recognisable on every battlefield. Nowhere is safe – these unnatural soldier-animal pairs are found in regiments across the globe, their only function war and destruction.*

International Affiliated Press Syndicate, quoted in The Last Bastion of the Anthropocene, *Ester Akintola, the final UN Secretary General.*

Too many bodies and not enough air filled the hold. The dim fluorescent lights did little to brighten the gloom, casting shadows over rippling fur. Soldiers stood to attention, tiny compared to the fearsome beasts by their side. The bears huffed, big wracking breaths like the waves hitting the ship's hull. Vulcan shouldered past them. When he reached the stairwell, he turned and smiled. One hand resting on the cool metal railing, he regarded the ranks of telepathically linked human-animal soldiers. These warriors – his legacy – would become legendary. He shuffled up the stairs, his prosthetic clacking against the steel. Sunshine beckoned him onto the deck and, without breaking stride, he slipped on his sunglasses.

"We'll land in under twenty minutes, sir," said an officer. The man saluted then disappeared along the towering mass of shipping containers that lined the deck; fake cargo concealed the most important shipment hidden below.

Vulcan edged over to the rail and peered through the fog. The first glimpse of the mainland would be all his. He glanced at the two cargo ships flanking his and adjusted his earbud. "It's time."

"Yes, sir. Deploying first wave now. Delta team, report."

"Ready."

"Omega team, report."

"Ready to rummmmble."

Ripples spread out across the water and a gleaming pod of orcas broke the surface. They slid through the water, unencumbered by the soldiers riding on their backs. Then dived deep. Vulcan watched the water until it stilled. Ahead, the fog began to lift, revealing the Chinese mainland and dozens of ships in the harbour.

The Shanghai Cooperation Organisation (SCO), the alliance of Eurasian nations, had managed to wrestle a semblance of order from the chaos, signing nonaggression pacts with their largest neighbours, Russia and India. Vulcan moved into the shadow of the shipping containers and checked the time. The UN had already fallen under his hand. Now it was time for the SCO to be extinguished. From this chaos he would rise as polemarch. How fitting, when he ordered beings as powerful as gods, to restore the ancient Greek title for the supreme military commander.

In a matter of hours, the world would be his.

Staccato bursts of traffic noise punctuated the quiet. Smog and sunshine mingled in a glaring haze over the sea. A normal morning about to change forever. "Now," Vulcan ordered.

Every ship in the harbour imploded in a mess of screaming, ripping metal. Angry, oil-fuelled fires spiralled skywards, sending black smoke billowing over the water. The orca strike teams returned to the innocuous-looking cargo ships and Vulcan smiled when he heard the words, "Mission successful." Satisfied, Vulcan strode toward the waiting chopper, the pilot already yanking off the tarpaulin. He had a planet to rule.

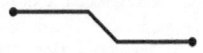

Smoke and screams filled the main screen in the central hub. Fang watched three cargo ships ram through the debris littering the harbour, clearing a path to the main jetty. Wave upon wave of soldiers and their animal partners disembarked and Vulcan's human-animal army descended on the city. Guns raised, claws out. Fang's headset thrummed with voices.

"Sector A, clear."

"Sector B, clear."

"Sector C – hang on – "

Gunfire filled one video feed and Fang flinched as bodies hit the bitumen.

"Sector C, clear."

"Proceeding."

Across the globe, Vulcan's human-animal armies descended on resistant countries. Each day brought a fresh battle. Here in the command centre, technicians sat at their terminals, hyped on energy drinks and adrenaline, monitoring biostatistics and live video footage from Vulcan's retinal conversion software. Fang forced herself to remain at the hub and witness Vulcan's army establish control of the city. Three long hours of carnage; all of it possible thanks to her research.

Finally, the technicians erupted into applause. "The city is ours."

Heart thudding against her chest, Fang nodded at them then left. Without really intending to, she found herself walking toward the cell block. The guards stood huddled together, watching the battle on a tablet, shaking their heads in disbelief and excitement, leaving Catherine's door unguarded. Fang rested her head against its cool metal. *What am I doing? Catherine isn't my friend. I can't come to her for counsel.* Yet something had driven her here. For God's sake, Catherine was one of them. She didn't deserve to be locked up like a criminal. *This is all my fault. I wanted to change the world and look what I've done.* It should be her in this cell, all alone. If she didn't keep producing results, keep Vulcan happy, it might be. Fang wished she could scrub her mind clean of all the death and destruction she'd just seen. If only she had made friends with Catherine and Robyn, if only Derek truly trusted her, things might have turned out differently.

Her tablet pinged. Vulcan. Fang ran her fingers through her hair and left the cell block. Outside, the shock of cold air needled her cheeks. On the parade ground, soldiers and convergers stood at attention. Behind them, the radio array arced with electricity. Vulcan's helicopter landed, sending dust spiralling through the snow. Fang held her anger tight, letting it warm her as she watched Vulcan greet the waiting entourage. Arrogance made him believe he was untouchable, god-like, but he was just one man. The MRI was just one organisation. The convergence gene just one ancient mutation. Fang joined Derek on the bitumen. *Every problem has its solution.*

12

Poppy

Every organism from the three main branches of life relies on mitochondria to create its cellular energy. Tiny remnants from the dawn of time. It cannot be a coincidence.

The temple walker lineages are ancient, stemming back to the haze of the emergence of sapiens. Is it not such a great leap to envisage a world in which existence was fundamentally different? A world in which beings of pure energy coexisted with living creatures and imbued them with powers beyond our modern comprehension. Power to communicate with each other and to use the cosmic energy of the universe that flows through each and every one of us. We have lost touch with this power, but not the mechanism to deliver it: our mitochondria. This potential slumbers in us all, waiting to be reawakened.

Brock Williams, Working Notes.

Poppy rode the spiralling air currents down toward the mountain top. The ancient song hummed through her antennae as she followed the powerful trail to the sacred place. This was the furthest foray she'd made. She had to skip across the fabric of the spirit world to search the physical, drawn ever closer to the energy signature of the guide. Weeks of traversing deserts, smoking remains of cities, and deep forests. Poppy revelled in the intoxicating lure of the guide, sweeter than the pull of a field of pollen-heavy flowers. She landed on Robyn's shoulder as the guide moved in the ways of the old ones, coaxing energy from the quartz penetrating deep into the mountain. White light thrummed on Robyn's skin as she paused, raising her hand to stroke the tiny bee.

Poppy flickered and disappeared, hurtling between worlds, emerging into a field filled with wildflowers where a boy sat, eyes closed, a hive swarming around him in a kaleidoscope of light. Poppy drew closer, pulled into the vortex of russet fur. With a flash, the hive transformed into a single bee, which alighted on the boy's shoulder.

Jacob opened his eyes and smiled. "Thank you, Poppy."

Kara drummed her fingers on Bry's desk, impatient for the fluctuating signal to resolve into something stable. "Weeks now," she groaned. Entire weeks of grounded operations as a surge of solar flares decimated communications everywhere.

Kate leaned back in her chair. "Yup. Without the internet, we're blind, deaf and mute."

"Useless, you mean." Kara stood and thudded into the kitchen, empty but for the lingering scent of toast. The microwave read 7am. The walkers and convergers would be training. Opening the door, Kara watched

Ariana and Eli move through a series of tai chi movements. Blue light shifted readily across Ariana's skin, Eli swathed in red by her side. They were strong, and getting stronger.

Kara thought of Fletcher trying to access his own aura and a wave of guilt washed over her. She slumped on the doorstep. "If I'd been more attentive, I might have realised he was planning to leave. I could have helped him."

"Hey, that's not fair," Kate said, passing over a mug of coffee. "It's been crazy: establishing an operations base here in Wales, co-ordinating the new medical and military personnel, keeping everyone safe. We've been pretty freaking busy, sis."

Kara couldn't absolve herself quite so readily. "Robyn would have noticed."

Kate stretched out in the gentle sunlight and pulled her sister close. "I miss her too."

They watched Ariana and Eli raise their arms and bring them down to their navels, energy pulsing around them in a sphere.

"None of us would be here if it weren't for Robyn," Kate said. "Ariana and Eli, the convergers we've rescued from the MRI compound in Bulgaria – none of them would be safe. They'd be tortured as experimental subjects or dead. What we're doing – it's important. We're carrying on Robyn's legacy."

Kara gripped her mug tight. "I know. I just wish she was here." She still couldn't bring herself to think of Robyn as truly gone.

Someone shouted their names. Kara turned to see Jacob sprinting across the field. He stopped at the steps and rested his hands on his knees to catch his breath.

"I'm guessing you have news,' Kate began, just as Jacob blurted, "Robyn's alive."

"Robyn's alive?" Kara dropped her mug as she scrambled to her feet, ceramic shards skittering down the steps.

Grinning, Jacob straightened. "She's in Laos."

Kate cupped her hands around her mouth. "Ariana! Eli! Get over here, and bring the others!" She grabbed Kara's arm and dragged her into the kitchen, steering her stunned sister into a chair at the dining table. "Food, she needs food. Bit of a shock."

"I'm on it." Jacob crammed bread into the toaster as Ariana, Eli and Sara raced inside.

"Robyn's okay." Kara straightened with a huge grin, the weight of months of uncertainty finally dissipating. "She's alive!"

"What do you mean? How … I mean where … did you find her?" Ariana exclaimed.

"Poppy," Jacob declared, pushing a plate stacked with jammy toast into Kara's hands.

"What? You're kidding?" Eli exclaimed, snatching a piece of toast and jumping up on the counter.

"Okay, okay, everybody calm down." Kara banged the kitchen table with her fist. "Let's hear what the man has to say."

Jacob paced the kitchen, too excited and bursting with pride that Poppy, his tiny little bee, had been the one to crack this open. "I didn't want to tell anyone in case we failed, but Poppy and I have been trying to locate Robyn for months. It's been hopeless. There was no trace of her. Then, all of a sudden, there she is."

"Where is there, exactly?" Ariana looked from Jacob to the twins and back again. "More information?"

Kate chewed on a piece of toast. After she swallowed, she said, "It's possible she's been in the spirit world this entire time."

"Exactly." Jacob grinned and popped more bread in the toaster.

Sara saw Eli about to nab the last piece of toast and snatched it away. At his scowl, she broke it in half and shared. "Is that even possible?" she asked.

Ariana pulled Jacob into a hug. "Of course it is. Lenti said he'd been in the spirit world for nearly a thousand years." She let go of Jacob as her excitement gave way to confusion. "But then if Robyn has been in the spirit world all this time, why didn't Eli and I find her? We looked everywhere."

Kate ducked into Bry's study and returned with a map. Wiping her fingers clean on her shirt, she rolled it out on the table. "Laos," she said, jabbing at a small country in northern Asia.

Sara leaned over the map, toast crumbling across continents. "Shit, that's a long way from Wales."

"Why Laos?" Ariana pressed.

"Sara's right," Eli said, leaning back against the wall. "There's no way she just decided to travel to Laos. For one, it's near impossible with all the current conflict. Plus she wouldn't just leave us like that."

Poppy buzzed in Jacob's ear. He nodded. "Poppy

found Robyn on a mountain, near the ruins of a building built on a rocky outcrop."

Ariana turned to Eli, blue light humming on her skin. "You don't think maybe …"

Eli's red aura flickered in response. "It's not a coincidence she disappeared on the mid-year solstice. Somehow Robyn used the power of the solstice to travel through the spirit world to the walker temple in the physical world. Even I have never managed to do that."

"Holy shit," Sara and Kate said in unison.

Kate traced a path between Wales and Laos. "Wow."

"Let's fire up a chopper and go and get her," Sara said, heading for the door.

"Not so fast." Kara glanced at her twin sister. "There's the small problem of the solar flares."

"Yeah, while there's so much electromagnetic radiation in the atmosphere, we're grounded, guys." Kate wiped off the toast crumbs and carefully folded up the map. "It's a no go."

Sara slumped against the door frame.

"There'll be a window soon, won't there?" Jacob pressed. "We have to try."

Kara shook her head. "The flares have become

increasingly unpredictable. It's getting harder and harder to estimate when the next clear period will be or how long it will last."

"So we will have to reach Robyn through the spirit world." Ariana turned to face Eli. Before he could remind her how many times they'd already tried, she added, "If she meditates in the spirit world again, we can find her. I know we can."

"With communications down and the MRI taking over, it's our only shot." Kara stood with renewed determination. "But please be careful. I know the solar activity makes the transition jumpy."

Kate clutched the map to her chest. "And we can't afford to lose you too."

Robyn picked her way through the loose quartz up to the temple ruins, Lenti following on her heels. The ancient wooden beams seemed to stretch up to the heavens, urging her to look upwards and embrace the vastness of the universe. She felt light, as if she might float away on the wind. As she stepped inside the once resplendent temple, she felt a sharp tug on her sternum and gasped.

Lenti stopped beside her. "What is it?"

Robyn concentrated on the energy eddying in her system. "I think the walkers are trying to reach me." She pressed her hands to her ribcage. "I can feel them."

She slowed her breathing. Last time she'd crossed over to the spirit world, she'd lost three months in the physical world. She couldn't afford for that to happen again. In the time she'd been here with Miranda and Brock, she'd poured all her efforts into the lab work. But to contact the walkers, she'd have to risk returning to the spirit world.

The cool breeze ruffled Lenti's robes as he took a respectful step back. "I will watch over you from here. If you do not return within the hour, I will come."

Robyn placed her hand over the boy monk's. "Thank you." Then she sat down and closed her eyes. She focused on the out breath, exhaling the fear and summoning the familiar feeling of passing into the spirit world. When she opened her eyes, she was relieved to see she was sitting in the true temple with its pristine tiles and golden ceiling. Robyn stood up and traced the walker lineages with her fingers. A shaft of light illuminated the figures and made them dance across the walls. Red, green and blue travelling in parallel until they reached the orb surrounding the mosaic versions of Ariana, Eli and Fletcher and merged into one. Lenti had told Eli they might be the last walkers ever. But what if he was wrong?

Robyn sat in front of the final section of the ancient relief. The physical and spirit worlds had been separated long ago when Nyx was imprisoned deep within the earth. As the sun strengthened, so too did Nyx. But logically, it must also increase the walkers' powers.

And mine. Robyn clasped her hands in her lap. If Nyx could escape, that must mean there was a way to reverse the separation, to reunite the physical and spirit worlds. Robyn studied the mosaic versions of Ariana, Eli and Fletcher, surrounded by the tiny white tiles, the same as her energy aura. Combining red, green and blue light gave rise to pure white light. Was that why all three walkers had been called at the same time? Certainty flooded her mind. Of course, the sun song, Nyx. The walkers were finally strong enough to open the boundary between the physical and spiritual worlds. Together, they could restore the energy currents to all living things and bring the world back into balance. This is what they were here to do.

You are the true guide, Robyn. Liro's words finally made sense. It was her job to protect the walkers and to make sure they accomplished their task.

Robyn pushed herself to her feet and bowed. *Thank you, Liro.* As she turned, the temple walls faded until she stood alone on the mountain top, bare except for the ancient tree reaching skyward, roots like knuckles clutching the cliff face.

The push and pull sensation of the walkers' energy tethers guided her down the stone steps and back into the forest. The soil beneath her bare feet pulsed with life. Light trickled up through the dark earth, branching out ahead of her, leading her through the trees, the pull in her sternum growing stronger with every step. Eventually, she reached the edge of the glade and the guiding light disappeared. Robyn stepped into the clearing and smiled at the two familiar faces.

Ariana screamed and ran across the grass, throwing herself at Robyn. As they hugged, Jericho twisted downward in his spirit form, his blue scales glinting with light as he orbited around them. Eli joined the pile-up, Una hopping lightly across the grass and tugging Robyn's jeans with throaty cries of delight.

"I've missed you. All of you," Robyn said, reaching out to include Jericho and Una. "I'm sorry I've been gone so long." Extricating herself from the group hug, Robyn wiped her eyes on her sleeve. "I can't believe how much you've all grown!" She laughed, realising she sounded exactly like her mother.

"I'm so glad you're back," Ariana murmured into Robyn's shoulder. "It's been so hard without you."

Robyn pulled Eli and Ariana closer, feeling their energy tethers thrum against her ribcage. "I'm here now, and even better, I think I've figured out how to stop Nyx. But we need Fletcher too."

Ariana's smile evaporated and she stepped out of Robyn's embrace. "We don't know where he is."

Eli stroked Una's glimmering feathers, his smile fading into sadness.

The combined force of both walkers' hurt and fear hit Robyn and she winced at the pain. As much as she didn't want to add to the walkers' distress, Robyn had to tell them the truth. "My old supervisor, Brock, and the former Chief Director of the MRI, Miranda, are studying the temple and your convergence genetic sequences." A wall of shock and outrage slammed into her. Doubling over, Robyn gasped at the pain.

"What?" Ariana and Eli yelled in unison, staring at her in disbelief.

Robyn held up her hands, desperate to make them understand. "It's a long story, but the short version is that Miranda and Brock faked their own deaths in order to set up a rogue unit to pursue the MRI's original intended objectives. They have nothing to do with Vulcan."

For a long moment, neither of the walkers said anything; even Jericho looked startled and Una snapped her beak in agitation.

Eli laid a comforting hand on the osprey. "Seriously?"

Ariana paced the glade, Jericho winding his way around her torso, his scales glittering with blue light. "If you trust them, then we should too," Ariana finally said. "Although for the record, I hate it."

Robyn took Ariana and Eli by the hand. "Come with me – I want to show you something."

As they linked hands, energy welled in Robyn's abdomen and their energy tethers strengthened her own. Closing her eyes, she focused on their destination, and with a flash of white light the glade disappeared.

The temple shone on the mountain top, doors flung

open, inviting them in. Una and Jericho took to the air and circled above the temple, sending shimmering trails of red and blue energy spiralling in their wake.

"I've never seen it like this," Eli said, letting go of Robyn. He stared at the temple's golden ceiling, his face reflecting the warm light. "Every time I've been here, it's been a ruin. But with you, the guide, I can see what it once was."

"It's beautiful." Ariana stepped over the threshold, twirling to take in the detailed mosaics. "The energy is so much stronger here. Sharper somehow."

"Your history is recorded on these walls," Robyn said, leading them to the tiles depicting the three walkers. "And a roadmap for us to stop Nyx."

Ariana studied the mosaics. "How?" she whispered. It seemed impossible to defeat an otherworldly spirit of such great power, especially when Nyx had nearly destroyed the walker lineages.

"This is why we need Fletcher. The last earth walker accidentally freed Nyx from her earthly prison. In the process, Nyx infected the earth spirit. Fletcher is the missing link," Robyn explained.

"You mean Nyx infected Fletcher." Ariana turned

away from the wall, her voice cracking as she swiped at her tears. Robyn absorbed her sorrow through the walker's energy tether. "He kept saying he was diseased, that this was all his fault, and I tried to tell him it was all in his head." She stamped her foot and blue light expanded around her, rattling the temple walls. "Except he was right, wasn't he?"

Eli wrapped his arms around Ariana and held her there until her aura started to fade. "That explains why he could never reach the walker state or summon his energy aura," he said.

"That's why he's trying to be a freaking hero?" Ariana muttered. "He's trying to put things right – on his own."

White light skittered across Robyn's limbs as she thought of Fletcher training by her parents' earthship, desperately trying to reach the walker state, and failing every time. The anger he'd directed at himself as he tried to match Eli and Ariana's skills. It felt like a lifetime ago now. "I wasn't there for him when he needed me."

Eli let go of Ariana. "Hang on a minute. Without Eva, Fletcher can't cross into the spirit world or reach the walker state. So the only way he can try to find the earth spirit is in the physical world."

"But Fletcher has no protection against Nyx," Robyn shouted, releasing a mass of white light.

The temple hummed beneath their feet, sound resonating through their chests. Robyn brought her energy under control, felt it renew her and strengthen her connection to the walkers. "We have to find Fletcher before Nyx does. If we don't she will destroy him."

13

Quantum

There is much I still do not understand about the energy source represented in the temple. It is clear that the mosaic-work depicts the bond between human and animal and this is a source of significant energy. The question is, where does this energy come from? The mosaics suggest there is another world parallel to this one, from which this energy stems. This has significant implications for the future of technology, of energy, for humanity. It has the potential to be the healing salve for the terrible wounds we have inflicted on this planet and to our brethren: the living beings with which we share an ancient kinship.

Brock Williams, Working Notes.

Derek sat on the floor of his quarters, his back against the bed. He flipped through the pages of a worn folder. The photographs and notes seemed familiar. He studied a photo of temple ruins, another of a dirt-smeared woman with an archaeological trowel. "What is this?"

Fang handed Derek a cup of tea and leaned over his shoulder. "That's Miranda. She was my PhD supervisor, and the Chief Director of the MRI before Vulcan. These are her notes."

Despite the late hour, Derek was instantly alert. He cradled the mug in his hands as Fang sat down next to him. She pulled a woolen blanket down from the bed to cover their legs, tucking them into a cosy cocoon. Derek tried not to notice the pleasant warmth of her leg against his. He spread the photos across the floor and flicked through the notebooks. "How'd you get this?"

Fang looked at the splayed photos. "Brock gave them to me, before he died."

Derek tried to sort the contents into some kind of chronological order. His fingers froze on one photo. He stared at a mosaic of three teenagers and their animals. He swore it was Eli, Ariana and Fletcher, but there was no way their existence could have been predicted thousands of years ago.

"When Miranda first showed me that photo, I didn't really listen to her. I thought her talk about spirits and energy was all nonsense. But then I met Eli and Ariana." Fang blew on her tea before taking a small sip to test the heat.

"And Fletcher," Derek added, examining the photographs. He tapped on the image of an ancient ruin. "What's the significance of this place?"

"According to Miranda's notes, there is a temple that is home to an order of monks dedicated to preserving the walker lineages." She picked up the photo. "Miranda spent years studying the ruins and reconstructing the mosaics. I never understood why."

"You've had these for months," Derek said, flicking through the notebook. *What else was Fang hiding?*

Fang returned the photo to its spot on the floor. She turned to face Derek. "Honestly? I didn't know if I could trust you." She smoothed the blanket over her feet and raised her mug as if giving a toast. "Forgive me?"

Derek faltered at the hopeful look in her eyes, seeing his own fear and pain mirrored in their hazel depths. "It's been a while since I could trust anybody," he said softly, raising his own mug to clink hers. He turned back to the photos to hide the faint blush blooming on his cheeks. "What conclusions have you reached?"

"Science has not helped us explain the walkers' abilities. We got nowhere trying to understand Ariana's aura. Vulcan's electromagnetic weapons barely scrape the surface of the energy source the walkers and convergers represent. It is well beyond our understanding of what is scientifically possible."

A memory flashed: Ariana chained and convulsing in the shock chamber. Derek shuddered. Weeks of data had led nowhere; they'd tortured the sea walker for *nothing*. Derek hated it, hated himself.

Vulcan now had more than a dozen functional convergence activation sequences. His army was growing more powerful by the day. Images flared to life in Derek's mind. Claws cleaving flesh, the terrified screams of the dying, the staccato of gunfire. "I don't believe in spirits, Fang."

"Neither do I, but think about this: the walkers' existence was predicted thousands of years ago. Their emergence now can't be a coincidence." Fang ran her fingers across the photographs, trying to divine their meaning. "In Bulgaria, you mentioned a parallel world. What did you mean?"

The first time Ariana and Fletcher had crossed over to what they called the spirit world, Derek had been shocked when he and Robyn found them sitting frozen by the stream, like they were unconscious or dead. "It's not a physical place – their bodies remain physically here. And, to be honest, I never asked them about what it was like in the spirit world. I think a part of me never believed them. I don't know." He shrugged.

Fang pulled her knees up to her chest with a sigh. "And I didn't listen when you first told me."

Derek looped a tentative arm around Fang's shoulders, was astonished when she didn't pull away. "I don't blame you. The whole idea is crazy. But don't you think that if your supervisor was studying this temple, there must be more to it?"

Fang leaned against Derek's shoulder, drawing the blanket tighter around them. "I think the answer lies somewhere in Miranda's notes. Two places at once," she murmured. "Funny."

Derek picked up one photo after the other and studied them. There was Miranda standing next to a young man wearing a bamboo hat, his face cast in shadows. Yet, something about him was familiar. Hazy thoughts pricked at Derek's mind but refused to come into sharper focus.

"Oh my God," Fang exclaimed, untangling herself from the blanket and jumping to her feet. She raced over to Derek's desk and grabbed a pen and paper. "This problem is beyond biology, beyond chemistry. This is about physics."

"Physics? Not my specialty," Derek said. He cringed as Fang pushed aside his stack of books. "Those were organised alphabetically!"

Fang frowned at him and shook her head. "Heisenberg's Uncertainty Principle means we cannot simultaneously measure the position and momentum of a particle. But the principle can also be applied to energy and time. If time is more constrained, then energy is less constrained, and vice versa."

Fang dumped her cup on Derek's desk and drew

two overlapping circles. "Here's us, here in the physical world," she said, writing the words in the left-hand circle. "And this is the spirit world," she went on, annotating the right-hand circle.

Derek tried to remember his second-year physics classes. He was desperate to keep up with Fang's brilliant mind.

"Quantum theory predicts that we can know where a particle, or energy, or in this case, a person is, but we can't accurately know *when* they are there, or *how fast* they're travelling." Fang's eyes shone as she glanced up at Derek. "That would explain why you could see their bodies in the physical world whilst they were actually visiting the spirit world." Fang traced the two circles again with her pen. "Can you imagine the incredible amount of energy that gives them access to?"

"But then what the hell is this?" Derek said, pointing to the tiny overlap between the two circles. "An in-between state?"

Fang beamed at him. "Exactly! Quantum theory also predicts a state in which it is possible to know both location and momentum, energy and time. This could be the source of the walkers' power."

Derek couldn't tear his eyes away from Fang's drawing. With two simple circles, she'd been able to conceptualise the physical and spirit worlds. *And she's on my side.* Hope surged through his system.

"In which case, if the in-between state has even more power than the spirit world then the walkers are human nuclear reactors!"

"Correct." Fang drummed her fingers on the desk, frowning in thought. "Humanity has never dreamed of such power." Then all the joy left her face. She turned back to her diagram and scrunched it into a ball, hiding it in her pocket. "We cannot tell Vulcan about this. Imagine if he had access to such a vast amount of energy."

"There's no way in hell I'd ever tell him," Derek assured her. It suddenly felt imperative to pack away the photos and notebooks. He glanced at his watch. *3.10 am.* They'd been here for hours.

By the time he stashed the folder in a drawer and locked it, Fang had fallen asleep on his desk, her head pillowed on her arms. Derek pulled back his bedclothes and carried her to bed, then gently tucked her in. Wrinkling her nose, Fang rolled over with a sigh.

Derek folded a spare blanket in four to use as a pillow and lay down on the floor beside Fang. He shook out a second blanket and pulled it up to his shoulders. Wherever Eli, Ariana and Fletcher were right now, he hoped they were safe. He'd made so many mistakes but maybe now, thanks to Fang, he might finally be able to make amends.

Fang woke to the sound of running water. She sat up and rubbed her eyes. It came back in a rush: Derek, the folder, her quantum theory explanation for the walkers' abilities. A blanket lay in a tangled heap on the floor. *I slept in Derek's room.* Fang tore off the covers. Thank God she was fully dressed. She must have been so exhausted she'd passed out. The clock read 7.15 am. She'd missed her gym session and the cafeteria would already be bustling. Fang grabbed her jacket from the back of Derek's chair and slipped into her heels. Derek had seen her asleep, her blouse crumpled, and her makeup was probably smudged so she looked like a racoon. How humiliating. It made her skin itch. *Pull it together.* Confiding in Derek had made everything about being here at HAARP more bearable. Friends even. But she was still escaping before Derek finished his shower. As Fang punched in the code, the water stopped and Derek called her name.

Shit. A wave of guilt washed over her. "Yes?"

Derek stuck his head out the door, steam billowing behind him. "Sorry. I didn't want to wake you."

Damp curls framed Derek's face and even though his torso was wrapped in a towel she could still see his naked chest. *I don't know how to do this.* It had been so long since she'd had either a lover or a friend, she couldn't remember the rules. Fang forced a smile to hide her embarrassment. "I need a shower. I'll see you in the lab later?"

Derek stepped out of the bathroom, dripping water on the floor. "I'll work through Miranda's folder and see if I can find anything else." *God, was Fang blushing?* He moved closer as she fumbled by the door.

"Great," Fang squeaked. She punched in the rest of Derek's door code and mercifully, the door slid open.

"Hey. Last night – you were brilliant," Derek called out as the door closed behind her.

A passing soldier smirked. Fang's cheeks burned. Shower, she needed a shower.

14

Jump

Every generation forgets the sins of the past. It believes itself to be above petty foibles and character flaws. Until they are revealed in their own hearts and it is too late. Dictators thrive in difficult conditions. People willingly give up their sovereignty for the illusion of safety. We have learned nothing from two World Wars and the terror of the Cold War. Humankind's lust for power cannot be tamed. Again and again, our basest instincts rise up as soon as conditions get tough. Today, we face the greatest challenge to our survival as a species and a self-styled dictator has announced himself. Each and every one of us must make the hard decision to do what is right.

Extract from The Last Bastion of the Anthropocene, *Ester Akintola, the final UN Secretary General.*

It didn't get any easier. He just got more used to it. Eli scanned the faces in the cargo bay; Sara, Basil and Jason sat quietly, deep in their own thoughts. As mission leader, he knew they'd follow his orders, but if something went wrong, like what had happened to Chris on their last sortie, the guilt was his alone. Outside, trees flashed by beneath them. Eli checked his parachute straps for the fourth time. They were just as secure as they'd been a few minutes ago.

The pilot's voice crackled over Eli's earbud. "Approaching jump site." Eli stood and slid open the heavy door. Wind whipped at his hair, buffeting his face and straining against his body. Eli gave the signal. "Form up."

As always, Sara was the first to her feet but she looked pale. Eli squeezed her shoulder. Her leopard, Ming, bristled when Sara patted her head through the reinforced box. Basil's wolf whined and Jason's jaguar huffed. The sedatives were kicking in, but the animals knew what was coming, and Eli didn't need to be the earth walker to know they weren't thrilled about it.

"And … go," announced the pilot.

Eli jumped out into nothingness. He fell fast, faster than he'd thought possible. Air tugged at his lips, his eyelids, and rubbed his face raw. The force was incredible. Una dived beside him; her wings pinned to her sides. He counted the seconds then yanked hard on his release strap. Fabric billowed and Eli slowed with a jerk as the parachute filled with air. He grinned as the others mushroomed above him. "Everyone good?" he said into his earpiece.

"Yeah, Selene is loving this," Jason responded.

Eli craned his neck to see the jaguar clutching at Jason's arm in panic.

"Can't say Lupa is enjoying it much either," said Basil, his voice muffled by the fur of his writhing wolf.

The tail of Sara's leopard twitched violently like an overcharged grandfather clock.

As the ground came into view, Eli pulled on the joists and oriented the parachute to slow him down. "Okay, we're still coming in hot," he said to the others. "Spread out and get ready for a bumpy landing."

He hit the ground at a run, the momentum of the

parachute still behind him. He rapidly disengaged the straps, slowing as the parachute dropped off in a puddle of fabric.

"Arrrgh," cried Jason behind him.

Eli launched sideways to avoid a collision. Jason rolled over, his parachute tangling around him until the jaguar slashed open an escape hatch. The cat tumbled out, hissing at the indignity of it all. Around them, the rest of the team landed in a graceless set of bumps and yells.

"Get off me, Basil. Seriously." Sara pushed her way out from underneath the boy and his wolf. "Ow. You're heavy, you know that?"

Eli grinned at the sight of them. "What a crack unit."

"Hey, it wasn't my genius idea to throw ourselves out of an aircraft into the forest," Sara snapped back.

Eli faced the green-speckled mountains looming above them. In between solar flare bursts, the twins had managed to send word of a rendezvous point deep in the Serbian mountains. By Kara's estimate, at least a dozen convergers received the message. "This is our last extraction mission; we have to make it count."

"Let's hope they're up there," Sara said, pulling her

rucksack onto her shoulders as they waited for the others to ditch their parachutes. Their earbuds released a high-pitched whine and Sara grimaced. "Another flare," she said, yanking hers out and stowing it in her rucksack. "No comms, then."

They hiked in silence. Eli tried to lose himself in the rhythm of his footfalls and the sounds of the forest. For a while, it worked. The big cats prowled ahead and Una soared above the enormous trees providing intel from the skies. In the dappled shadows of the overgrown logging trail, she told Eli what he already knew. They were alone.

After an hour, Eli signalled to the team to break. Jason and Basil had fallen behind and it wasn't safe to separate. Sara yanked off her rucksack and rummaged for snacks, tossing Eli a water bottle and a muesli bar. "Where do you think Fletcher is?" she asked, unwrapping one for herself and flopping on the ground, using her rucksack as a backrest.

"Good question." Eli swigged water and removed his own rucksack, rolling his shoulders to loosen them.

"He never talked to you about leaving?"

Eli dumped his rucksack next to Sara's and sat down.

"I've replayed every conversation a hundred times, but after Eva died, he retreated into himself and I didn't want to push him. I figured that if he ever wanted to offload, he had Ariana."

"I doubt he'd have come back from the edge without her."

Eli thought about Ariana and Fletcher's hidden smiles, the way they gravitated toward each other, like distant planets making their own new solar system. He imagined Sara taking his hand, eyes bright, laughter on her lips. Eli shook off the thought. "Even before he lost Eva, he was frustrated." Fletcher had abandoned them all, but it was Ariana who he'd hurt the most. Proof it was unwise to open up your heart like that.

Jason and Basil's voices floated up the trail behind them. Eli jumped to his feet. "Come on, we must keep going." He busied himself with his rucksack to hide the butterflies tumbling in his stomach, then took off down the trail, ignoring Jason and Basil's complaints that they hadn't had a break.

Sara raced to catch up with him. "Because he couldn't reach the in-between?"

Eli slowed and reflected on her question. How

readily he slipped into the spirit world and the walker state that lay between the two worlds. As if he'd always known how. "He couldn't reach the earth spirit, like Ariana and I had found our sea and air spirits."

"Meaning he couldn't talk to his past lives, like you do with Clara. No wonder Fletcher had struggled," Sara said.

"Ariana and I can ask our past selves for guidance, but Fletcher is alone."

"Do you know why?"

Eli looked up at the sliver of sky visible through the tree canopy, focusing on his link with Una. He flitted into her consciousness, revelling in the cool breeze, the freedom of gliding above it all. The air spirit lived in him, in their bond. But now Nyx, the dark spirit, having once almost succeeding in destroying the walker lineages, wanted to return and obliterate life itself. "Robyn says Nyx infiltrated the earth spirit over a thousand years ago. It is her who limits Fletcher's connection to the walker state and his past lives. It must be awful to be cut off from the flow of cosmic energy."

"I only feel a minute portion of what you have access to, but I can't imagine living without it now. It's part of me." Ming loped past, flicking her tail at Sara before bounding ahead up the trail and disappearing around the bend.

Eli and Sara lapsed into silence, following Ming's pawprints, focusing their energy on climbing the steep incline Ming had made such light work of.

At the top of the ridge, they stopped to catch their breath. A pink twilight sky clutched the green haze of the forest in its embrace. Ming wound through Sara's legs, purring in greeting. The cat's eyes glinted as her natural night vision kicked in.

"Ever since Fletcher disappeared, I can't shake the feeling that I should never have given him so much space," Eli said. "I should have made him talk to me. Then we might not be in the current situation."

"We've all changed. Not just Fletcher. It doesn't mean we've lost him forever," Sara said, her heart brimming with compassion for the boy by her side, the walker who wanted to change the world for the better. The boy who didn't want to leave anyone behind.

Una dived through the final threads of pink in the sky then landed on Eli's shoulder. "I hope you're right," he said, eyes fixed on the sunset. The peace was broken by Jason and Basil groaning about the climb. Eli turned to the boys. "You guys need to be fitter. You can't afford to keep falling behind." He glanced at Sara. "I need to check in with Ariana."

"Camp will be set up by the time you get back, right guys?" Sara said, removing her pack and tossing it at the young convergers.

Jason caught it and shared a despairing glance with Basil. "Right," they grumbled in unison.

Eli opened his eyes. Stars splayed before him and a fire burned at his back. He turned round and saw the teens had been as good as their word; camp was set, dinner was on. Jason passed him a bowl of steaming rehydrated tagine. Eli hoped it tasted as good as it smelled. The big cats stretched out in front of the fire, purring contentedly. The bright eyes of Basil's wolf peered through the darkness as it patrolled the perimeter.

Sara raised her eyebrows and shrugged, by gesture rather than words asking Eli for information.

"Apart from seeing Ariana – no sign of Fletcher."

By the dancing firelight, Eli could see written on their faces the same despair he felt. All of them wanted the same thing: hope. Hope they would survive this. Hope that the MRI would be stopped and Nyx destroyed. It was more than he could give them. Eli pushed aside his meal. "I'm going to bed."

He'd no sooner curled up in his sleeping bag when someone unzipped the tent flap. Sara stood silhouetted in the doorway, her long hair loose around her shoulders. "Sorry to disturb you, but there's only two tents …"

Sara unrolled her sleeping bag and lay down beside him, so close Eli could smell the sweet apple scent of her shampoo. "Gosh I'm exhausted," she yawned, elbowing Eli through her sleeping bag as she got settled.

"Goodnight," he whispered. Energy skittered through his veins and sleep took an eternity to claim him.

15

Forest

Fungi constitute the third branch of life. Their hyphae ripple through the soil, linking the trees to each other, funnelling energy across the Earth's surface. Like animals and plants, they too rely on mitochondria. For reasons we do not fully understand, the three branches diverged millennia ago. Why? And what was the exact nature of the link between them that was severed? Whatever the answers, the fact remains; we all share the same basic biochemical machinery. The issue is, we have forgotten how to use it.

Eli woke to sounds of Ming's gentle snores outside the tent and Sara curled against his stomach, one arm flung across his chest. Despite everything they'd been through, she looked so peaceful; he wanted nothing more than to snuggle into her warmth. He wondered how he could slip out without disturbing her. He shuffled awkwardly to one side, gently lifting her arm out of the way. Sara stirred and rolled onto her side. Eli stepped carefully over her and escaped into the early morning freshness of the clearing. The embers from last night's fire glowed faintly. Ming yawned and stretched then padded over to say good morning. Eli added another log to the fire and patted the leopard while he waited for the wood to catch. From her perch on a tall branch high above the campsite, Una projected, *Sleep well?*

Heat flushed Eli's cheeks, and it wasn't from the fire. He busied himself making porridge; a meal guaranteed to stick to their bones and fuel a long day's hike. Once he'd added the finishing touches – a smattering of dates and walnuts – Eli yelled out "Breakfast's ready." On cue, Jason and Basil tumbled out of their tent.

Sara unzipped the tent flap and emerged, yawning and attempting to untangle her hair. Abandoning the effort, she grabbed a bowl. "Smells good."

Eli was smiling so much he dolloped porridge on the ground instead of in her bowl. Jason sniggered. Basil elbowed him in the side and mouthed shush. Mortified, Eli passed Sara the serving spoon and made a point of sitting on the opposite side of the fire where he faced the rising sun.

Today meant another long walk, but he was confident they'd reach the rendezvous point by nightfall where he hoped the new convergers would be waiting. He stood and passed the last oaty remnants to Una. "Time to pack up and get moving, guys."

Eli killed the fire with soil while Sara and the boys went to the stream and filled the water bottles. By the time they'd returned, Eli had spread out the map and was studying the landscape through Una's eyes, comparing the contours. He looked up and pointed to a faint path that led around the base of the hill. "If we go this way, we avoid a steep gully and can make quicker progress along the face of the ridge."

The jaguar and the wolf peeled off and were soon

camouflaged by the dense scrub. Una had spotted no-one yesterday, but Eli wasn't chancing it. He signalled to Jason and Basil to take the rear guard and returned the map to the side pocket of his rucksack. "Alright, let's go."

The sun was high in the sky by the time they stopped for lunch. Jason slumped to the ground, fanning himself as he lay back on his rucksack and the cats and wolf sprawled in the shade, panting. Basil slathered peanut butter on bread and passed the first sandwich to Sara. She ripped it in two and stuffed one half in her mouth, the other she tossed to Ming, who caught it mid-air.

"So the plan is that we make sure everyone has arrived safely, then call in the extraction chopper, right?"

"Right," Eli agreed, catching the next sandwich.

"In the wilderness in Serbia." Basil lobbed Jason a sandwich, his wolf's eyes following its arc all the way into the safety of the boy's hands.

"The middle of nowhere might be our best option. Less chance we'll be spotted," Eli said over a mouthful.

"And less chance we'll be killed," Sara added cheerfully.

Jason and Basil exchanged glances.

It wasn't a question. Sara looked around the weary circle, seeing the same resignation in the others' faces. "To the media, we are either freedom fighters or terrorists. Thanks to Vulcan's armies, millions of people fear convergers."

"We're not exactly popular, are we?" said Jason.

"Hey, neither were regular baths but they soon caught on," Basil joked, dusting off his hands and getting to his feet. His wolf appeared on the edge of the narrow clearing and snorted. "Come on, slowpokes. Her highness says it's time to hit the trail."

Eli must have stood up too quickly; Basil's voice faded to a dull thrum. He had to close his eyes to stop the forest spinning around him. His head felt like it had come loose from his shoulders. Then everything stopped. Eli smelled frying oil and cumin, heard the distant chatter of a bustling street. He opened his eyes. There, in the middle of a dusty alleyway, stood Clara.

"You just disappear? Then don't call for weeks? You're lucky I'm still here." She spun on her heel and stormed off, disappearing through a fluttering string of clothes and rags.

With a deep sigh, Eli followed. Right now, he was

probably slumped on the ground, scaring the crap out of everyone. He needed to return to the physical world, but after he'd found out from Clara if she could help in any way. After all, this whole extraction business was her idea – she had a tactical brain.

He emerged through the curtains of clothes to find Clara perched on an old gasoline tin, the raven on her shoulder. "I'm not avoiding you; it's just a bad time," Eli said, bowing lightly, hoping to appease the last walker. "It's an honour to see you again."

Clara spluttered and clapped a hand to her mouth. Laughter racked her shoulders. The raven squawked indignantly and hopped to the safety of a rafter. "Sorry," she managed between breaths. Clara waved at her surroundings. "I'm not exactly royalty."

She was younger than Eli remembered. Maybe only a few years older than him. Ariana had said Yves appeared to her as an old man. Shouldn't Clara be ancient too?

Clara slid off the gasoline tin and picked up the hem of her sari. "Come. Let me show you my life." With a click of her fingers, they were plunged into darkness. Roaring filled Eli's ears as they tumbled through the void. He prayed he wouldn't be sick. When they finally stopped, he gagged at the foul stench that greeted them. In the semi-darkness, Clara spoke.

"I started work in this tannery on my tenth birthday," she said. Eli made out a line of impossibly thin, grimy children scraping hides of flesh and fat. The arms of one young girl trembled with the strain as she held the red raw hide with one hand and slid the knife with the other.

Eli's stomach churned. The smell, the noise – how could these poor children stand working here?

"I had no-one. Except my raven."

Eli looked around and spotted a jet-black raven high in the timber beams, silently watching over the skinny little girl.

Clara clicked her fingers. They were in the midst of a throng of people moving between ramshackle slums. Eli spotted young Clara slipping through the crowd, the raven bobbing on her shoulder. They followed her in silence as she turned left then right, weaving her way between the slums until she reached a huge open drain running parallel to the shanty town. The little girl slid down the side, waded through the open sewer, then climbed up the other side. She wrenched open a tiny grate that concealed a small space. Only big enough to contain a foul blanket, a cracked cup and a tiny doll. The girl crawled inside and pulled the grate closed behind her, swallowed by the darkness. Eli shuddered in horror.

"When I was fifteen, I realised my relationship with my raven, Jagun, was special. I found my way into the spirit realm, to Lenti." Clara's face wore a blissful expression. "It became harder and harder to return to the physical world. Every time I woke up and looked through the grate of my little hole, I wondered how one person could make a difference."

The scene changed again. Birds soared around young Clara. Crows, ravens, scavengers of every sort. They dipped their beaks to scoop up the morsels she threw to them.

"It took a long time, but I found my tribe." Young Clara raised her arms to a sky that was filled with choking clouds of black smoke. "It was clear what the factories were doing to them. To us all. But try as I might, I couldn't stop them." Her outstretched arms fell to her sides.

"One day I didn't come back," Clara whispered. "I crossed over to the spirit world and left my body behind for good." She pointed to the centre of the enormous filthy drain. There lay the curled form of a girl hugging an emaciated raven surrounded by a silent circle of birds.

Angry tears pricked Eli's eyes. "This should never have happened to you."

Clara clasped Eli's hand in hers. "You can change it all, I can feel it. You're getting closer."

Everything started to fade. Eli's dizziness returned. "Closer to what?" he shouted, desperate for answers.

"Restoring balance will take the three of you, together. But it will require the ultimate sacrifice." Clara's voice was so loud it sounded like it was in his head. Then she hurtled away and darkness fell.

Sara shook Eli hard enough to make his teeth rattle. He swatted her hand away. "I'm here. Get off me."

"You've gotta tell us when you're going to the spirit world," she said, shaking him again for good measure. "You scared the crap out of Jason and Basil," she added, taking an unsteady step back.

Eli shielded his eyes from the blinding sun and immediately winced at the jarring pain in his elbow.

"Ow!"

"You fell pretty hard."

His visit with Clara flashed before his eyes. "Sorry, I didn't plan this one."

"What happened?" Sara grabbed her rucksack and pulled it onto her shoulders.

"I … I saw Clara again. The last air walker."

Jason's jaguar, Selene, appeared from further down the trail. He folded the map and shoved it back in Eli's pack. "If you're okay to travel, we better hoof it. Still a fair bit of ground to cover."

Eli struggled to his feet, stiff after lying in the same position for so long. "I'm fine. Sorry, guys."

"Okay then, good. I'll go scout ahead," said Basil. He nodded at Jason and the pair bounded away hot on the heels of their animals.

Sara waited until the two convergers had disappeared before pressing Eli for details. "What did you find out?"

Eli said nothing as he loaded his pack and started up the track after Jason and Basil. Clara's life had been so brutal … so painful. What happened to her should never happen to anyone, let alone a child. "She had a hard life. She had no family, or friendship," he said, glancing at Sara then back to the track. "She told me we'd fix things, but it would involve a sacrifice."

"What kind of sacrifice?"

Eli shrugged. "I don't know. I came back here before I could ask." The image of Clara's frail, undernourished body, her horrible death in the wide drain, filled his mind. What would he be willing to sacrifice to prevent such suffering? Everything.

Sara grabbed Eli by the arm and forced him to a halt. "You listen to me, Eli. You're not making any heroic gestures, okay?" She stood in front of him, blocking the path. "Whatever it takes to make things right, we'll figure it out together. You said we're family now. You're right. There's a reason we found each other." She gave him a quick hug then spun on her heel, hurrying to catch up to the others.

Eli's burden lifted a little. Clara was right; he wasn't alone.

16

Test

Energy is at the heart of every major advance in civilisation. The discovery of fire, natural oil and gas, and the power of electricity fundamentally changed the world; for better, and for worse. Wars have been waged over access to energy sources. Now is no different. This dictator controls energy derived from the connection between humans and animals. He has harvested that energy via modern circuits and utilised it with devastating consequences. The power this self-proclaimed polemarch wields means he controls the energy system of the future. It is no surprise then that countries are falling like dominoes under his hand.

Extract from The Last Bastion of the Anthropocene,
Ester Akintola, the final UN Secretary General.

Ancient trees surrounded the clearing, their branches reaching out to form a natural dome. The hut in the centre of the dappled grass was long abandoned; a leaning, decomposing ode to a distant era. Dozens of tents mushroomed around it. Eli dropped his pack and wiped the sweat from his forehead.

"We made it," Sara murmured by his side, taking a lug from her water bottle.

Basil and Jason approached the tents and dozens of wary kids and teenagers spilled out with their animals.

At the sudden crowd, Una fidgeted on Eli's shoulder, her unease rippling down his spine. He stroked her feathers to comfort her. He shared her fears. This was the largest extraction they'd ever attempted. A group this large was vulnerable and too many people knew where to find them. Across his mind flashed a vision of Mikey wielding his blaster, bodies splayed across a bloody courtyard.

Eli got that creepy feeling someone was watching him. He turned around and spotted a lean man in glasses. He smiled at Eli and stepped forward, hand outstretched in greeting.

Recognition flooded Eli. "Bohai." He ran to meet the man and gripped him by the shoulders. Without Bohai's help, he would never have escaped the MRI compound in Beijing, and never have met Ariana and Fletcher. "What the heck are you doing here?"

"The orphanage where I volunteer has been smuggling people out of China since the SCO fell. Last month, it was raided." He pointed to a little girl lying on the grass tickling a baby otter. "I escaped with Cho, but all the convergers we'd hidden were taken." Bohai's shoulders slumped. "It's just us now."

Eli pushed away the sense of unease. Newcomers circled Jason and Basil, some with hopeful expressions, some hanging back. Eli recognised himself as these kids must. A stranger clad in dark, carbon polymer armour, a powerful osprey on his shoulder. Jason and Basil towering over them, smiling, but still equally as intimidating. Sara crouched down next to a young boy, letting him reach out to play with Ming's tail.

Eli examined the surrounding mountains, glad for the deep cover the forest afforded. "Time to go. We need distance between us and this campsite."

Sara stood up and closed the gap between them. "Wait, isn't this the rendezvous point?"

Eli glanced at the expectant faces then back at Sara. "We can't take any chances."

"Do you know something I don't?" she murmured.

"It's not safe to stay in one place." His promise to Clara echoed in Eli's mind. "Dozens of people know the co-ordinates for the hut. We can't risk arranging the pick-up from here, not after last time." He didn't need to say more.

Half an hour later, the lone hut stood empty, all traces of the camp removed.

"Basil, scout ahead for a good place to stop," Eli said, "and Jason, take the rear guard."

The convergers nodded, and Basil disappeared down the trail, his wolf by his side. Bohai went to follow, but Eli asked him to walk with him. They had a long night ahead. May as well gather some intel on what had been happening while they were at it. Sara walked hand in hand with Cho. Jason had lifted one of the smaller children onto his shoulders, a marmoset monkey peeking out of the girl's jumper. Eli and Bohai traded stories in whispers.

The rising moon lit the path. It made walking easier but it also exposed them. They needed to get the convergers deep into the woods and safety.

A figure emerged from the shadows. Una ruffled her feathers. *Basil,* she projected.

The converger jogged toward them, his wolf beside him. "Found a decent spot for the pick-up. It's a clearing but surrounded by thick forest. There's a cave nearby where we can catch some sleep. We'll be well out of sight from anyone above. It's just us and the wilderness."

"Good work. Wait for us there and direct all the convergers to the cave. We can't afford for anyone to get lost," Eli said.

"On it," Basil said, then once more disappeared into the night.

Sara watched this exchange with growing pride. Eli had matured since she first met him. He was a fully formed walker now. "You're good at this being a leader thing," she murmured.

Embarrassed, Eli ran a hand through his hair. He'd never been a leader before. The title slid across his mind like a stone skipping across water. It had always been just him, his parents and the Mongolian wilderness, following the patterns of generations. Moving camp, herding, the warm sun on his back or the icy bite of winter. A world where his biggest worry was whether the foals would survive the first frosts.

Not anymore. Now every lost converger was a physical ache. He frequently woke up drenched in sweat. Nightmares in which his friends suffered and died because he wasn't strong enough to save them. He didn't feel like a leader.

She's right, young one. You look to the survival of the many, Una projected.

Eli trudged in silence as he thought about the many extractions he'd commanded, the way the others looked to him for guidance. "Thank you," Eli said. He reached up and stroked Una's neck. *And you, too.*

Cho yawned and Bohai picked the little girl up, cradling her in his arms. In a moment she was asleep. Looking over his shoulder, Eli nodded at Jason, who had drifted back to serve as rear guard. Illuminated in the moonlight, Jason's jaguar prowled in a wide arc behind the slower members of the group.

Ahead, Basil whistled and his wolf leapt into the undergrowth. "Here!"

Eli followed the whistle, picking his way down the slope to a jutting outcrop of rock. Below the ledge was a long cave lined with dry sand. "Good job. This will be perfect." He clambered halfway back up the slope to where Sara waited. "It's a good spot. Let's get everyone settled. Tell them to grab a few hours' sleep. We'll be heading out at dawn."

"Roger that," Sara said.

Dumping his rucksack, Eli checked their co-ordinates on the GPS. The convergers shuffled inside, Jason bringing up the rear. Bohai and Sara passed around rations, making sure the little kids didn't miss out. They'd walked all night, and the poor things were exhausted. And, although it was freezing, they couldn't risk lighting a fire. Eli kept watch as everyone found a space to sleep and crawled into their sleeping bags. Their eyes shut the moment they laid down.

Sara unrolled her sleeping bag and passed Eli a chocolate bar. "Saved you one."

"Thanks. I owe you." Eli devoured the chocolate and was licking his fingers when Una swooped inside the overhang and landed on his shoulder. Remembering how cranky Sara had been this morning when he disappeared without warning, he told her he was leaving to check in with Ariana.

"Tell her I said hi," Sara replied, wriggling into her sleeping bag and pulling the zipper up to her eyes.

Eli sat on the folds of his sleeping bag and slipped over into the spirit world, his aura blooming on his skin. He found Ariana waiting in the glade, Jericho floating above her.

Una, too, expanded into her spirit form, her feathers glimmering with red light. Eli hugged Ariana. "It's good to see you. How's everything back at base?"

"Everyone's feeling a bit stir crazy, me included." Eli opened his mouth to ask the obvious question. Ariana shook her head. "No news from Dad or Fletcher either."

Eli sighed. "Soon, I know it."

"I hope you're right." With a nod, she shimmered and disappeared.

By the time he returned to the cave, no-one was awake. Eli curled into his sleeping bag and gazed at the stars beyond the lip of the cave. Energy looped through his system, a calming push and pull that eventually lulled him to sleep.

A cacophony of sound ricocheted through Eli's head. Clutching his skull, he focused on the competing voices, the brush of startled wings, the sound of stomping boots.

Una stirred beside him. *Beware, air walker. They are coming.*

Eli opened his eyes. Outside, the barest hint of dawn edged above the horizon. Throughout the cave, convergers lay sprawled in their sleeping bags like fat caterpillars. Eli dipped into the stream of consciousness, flitting from the mind of an owl to a sparrow. They showed him a group of convergers in bodysuits emblazoned with the distinctive white stripe of the MRI, guns strapped across their shoulders. A Blackhawk on a rocky outcrop, blades still whirring. *The MRI.*

Eli scrambled out of his sleeping bag and shook Sara awake. She went to scream and he smothered it. Furious, she whipped his hand away.

"What is it?"

"The MRI have found us," Eli replied, keeping his voice low. "Wake Jason and Basil. Get everyone up and ready to move." Eli closed his eyes. *I should have split up the main group, made separate camps. It would have been harder to track us. Damn it.*

Sara unzipped her sleeping bag and felt around for her boots. "What are you going to do?"

Eli dipped back into the layered warnings echoing through his mind. "I'm going to stop them."

Una perched on the lip of the cave then launched into the air and disappeared into the brightening sky. Eli followed her progress as she rose above the trees, the wind rippling her feathers. *They're too close*, she projected. *There's no time to escape.*

Through Una's eyes, Eli saw a group of MRI convergers step onto the trail near the cave. A bear sniffed the ground and huffed. A boy, Daniel, rubbed her side.

"Spread out either side," Daniel said. "The idiots have trapped themselves against the cliff. We'll flank them, give them nowhere to go."

Like a storm, anger surged in Eli's chest. His mind expanded and reached out across the valley. Eli skimmed the minds of thousands of birds. *Help us.*

He waited, straining to hear the birds answer his plea. At first, nothing; then the faintest tremor shook the earth. The leaves in the trees around the cave rustled. Eli smiled.

The MRI squad paused, glancing uncertainly around them. "What the hell was that?" hissed a girl, drawing her weapon.

The thrum of a thousand wing beats filled the air. Eli's perspective tilted wildly as he skimmed the minds of the birds coalescing around Una; a murmuration of disparate species. Unlike the extraction at the school, when he'd sent out the call and felt the answering surge of birds descending, this time he was able to maintain the connection with the entire cluster.

"Holy shit," screamed the MRI convergers as a living, breathing super-organism stained the sky black.

It rippled through Eli's mind and red light blossomed on his skin. It grew within him, tendrils of energy shifting and slotting into place.

Now, he projected.

The flock dived; a storm of beaks and claws collided with the MRI convergers in a maelstrom of shrieks and screams.

Sara grabbed Eli's arm. It took all his effort to distance himself and open his eyes. "Head north," he managed to say. "The choppers will be here soon."

Then he closed his eyes and plunged back into the deadly storm. Claws raked flesh. Human screams looped through his mind. Eli pushed energy into the connection, jumping between minds in the space of nanoseconds, experiencing the melee from every angle, every elevation, all at once. He grimaced as fiery pain blistered his skin, the crack of rifle against bone, the searing pain of electroshock bursts. Black spots appeared in his vision as he lost members of the connection. Birds fell to the ground senseless. He saw it all.

The MRI stumbled backwards in disarray. Eli held on. Sara needed time to get the convergers clear. All he had to do was concentrate. A dazzling wave of pain sliced through Eli's neurons. He grunted in shared agony as another shock sizzled through his body. The torture layered upon itself, building, building. His eyes shot open. *No.*

Mikey snarled, striking at the birds harrying his lion, and raised his blaster to knock yet another from the sky, twisting his boot into the skull of one kill. Ignoring the birds swooping at his head, he slammed on his blaster and aimed at a powerful eagle diving low, its talons extended like switchblades. The luminescent yellow charge struck the eagle in the chest. Current arced through its body and the bird of prey flailed and dropped.

The chip in Mikey's neck responded, clawing at his skull as it repowered the blaster for his next shot. So what if each recharge left him a little drained? He could handle it. The air crackled with yellow spikes of electricity. The birds retreated from the assault. Mikey punched his fist at the sky.

The squad spread out behind Daniel and Mikey. At his signal, the soldiers snaked around the southern edge of the rock face. They had lost two of their own – a needless waste. Eli would pay for their deaths.

Eli swayed and steadied himself against the cave wall. His mind felt as if pieces of a neural jigsaw puzzle had suddenly been hurled through the air.

In his mind, Una's voice was strong and steady. *Get out, now.*

Eli straightened and raced to the cliff face. He jumped and hooked his arm over the roof of the cave, hauling himself to a low crouch on the rock. His synapses still thrummed with energy, making the hair on the back of his neck stand up. He sensed movement to his right and spun around. Sara pressed a finger to her lips. Beside her, Ming's tail twitched in readiness.

"Basil and Jason are leading them away," she whispered.

"You should have gone too," Eli said, stumbling as adrenaline surged and receded through his system, leaving him dizzy and drained. Sara grabbed his arm to steady him, her eyes blazing with determination. "I'm not going anywhere. We're here to protect the convergers from the MRI." She released him and turned to face the oncoming forces, a warrior framed in the sunlight. "We fight together."

Eli drew her close and, just for a moment, held her tight, Sara's heart beating in time with his own.

Una dived toward them. *They're coming*.

Eli and Sara stepped apart. Slowing his breathing, Eli moved through the sequence of ancient movements and energy cascaded through his system. Red light danced on his skin, mirroring the dawn behind them.

MRI convergers emerged from the forest, guns held

against their shoulders. Stars of yellow light crackled from the muzzles.

"Good morning, Eli," called Mikey, his lion snarling at his side.

Ming matched the lion's prowl, shielding Sara and Eli from direct attack.

"Bird boy. We have orders to take you alive and kill the others." Mikey rolled his shoulders and stepped forward, releasing a flash of electricity.

Eli deflected the current with his red energy aura and sent it rocketing into the air. Taking a deep breath, he expanded the energy field to fill the space between them and Mikey's squad. Eli pushed through into the walker state and Una expanded into her spirit form. She loomed over him, flapping her wings to hold position. Sara shielded her eyes from the brightness.

Mikey froze, his face pale as he stared at the enormous spirit-osprey. Then he shook his head and whistled. "Well, that's new."

Several MRI convergers stumbled backwards. Annoyed, Mikey yelled at them to form up and they rejoined the advance. At his command, dozens of arcs of electricity ricocheted against Eli's aura.

Fang watched Eli's energy shield deflect the electrical blasts. Amazing. It took her breath away. Below her, the technical teams argued, filling her headset with chatter. "Enough," she snapped. They fell silent. "Omega team – what's our status?"

"We have no defence against that energy shield … thing. Should we give the order to pull back, ma'am?"

Eli's energy field was the most beautiful sight. What else was he capable of? One thing for sure, Eli was no longer the quiet teenager she remembered from Beijing. He'd grown into a formidable fighter. A *walker*, Derek had called him. Given the astounding amount of energy he wielded, could Miranda's notebooks hold the truth? "Get me a reading from Mikey's implant chip. I want to know the energy level."

"Gamma range. Way too high. They need to disengage," came the immediate response.

"No. Hold the current pattern." Fang enlarged the image of Eli on the screen. She had to see if the walker could overcome Vulcan's blasters, the harvest implant chips. Because if that was possible, maybe she'd found the way to defeat Vulcan.

Eli gritted his teeth and strengthened his energy field, trying to hold Mikey's squad at bay, but he was exhausted. The red light began flickering and the sphere retracted. Una slowly shrank back to her regular size.

From further up the trail came agonising screams. Eli's heart sank. *No – not the others.*

"You piece of shit," Sara yelled, sprinting past the last vestiges of Eli's red energy. Yellow bolts of electricity flashed toward her. Ming leapt onto the lion's back while Sara grappled with Mikey, pushing aside his blaster. He stumbled, recovered, then jammed the butt of the blaster into Sara's stomach. Grunting, she doubled over and Mickey sneered, ready to take her out. It was all the time Sara needed. She pivoted and smashed her elbow into Mickey's mouth. Blood spurted from his cut lip.

"Ariana told me everything I need to know about you." Sara dropped to one knee, threw his weight over her hip, and slammed him into the ground. "That'll teach you to smirk at me, asshole."

Eli whirled through the tai chi forms, knocking over convergers with each new surge of movement. A thin sheen of red light flared on his skin, adding power to his attacks. He barely registered his opponents. His eyes were trained on Sara.

The lion roared under Ming's attack. The leopard tore her claws along its thick hide, exposing its underbelly. Mikey scrabbled for his blaster and shot a searing bolt of electricity thudding into Ming's side, sending the leopard sprawling. Sara froze, her face contorted in pain. She clutched her stomach and dropped to her knees.

From further up the trail, a single blaster shot echoed through the trees. Eli turned and saw Sara doubled over on the ground. He raced to her, slinging her arm over his shoulder and dragging her upright. At her feet, Ming let out a piteous meow. Sara winced. "Come on, girl, please," she murmured through her tears. The leopard stirred, paws twitching.

Mikey pushed himself upright, his face contorted in rage.

Hold on, they are coming, Una projected. Red light gleamed on her feathers, wreathing her in gold as she launched herself at Mikey, forcing him back and scattering the remaining convergers.

Above the noise of the battle, came the rhythmic

thwack of helicopter blades. Eli looked up and saw the choppers silhouetted against the bright sky.

"Fall back!" Mikey called, his voice thick and slow, like molasses.

Thwack, thwack, thwack.

Mikey walked toward Eli. He towered over the walker but Eli didn't flinch. "Next time," the converger snarled. "I'll finish you, orders be damned."

Rage coiled in Eli's stomach. How many convergers had Mikey and his unit killed? Innocent children who had been led into a trap. He sat Sara down next to Ming and, eyes locked on Mikey, drew a figure eight around his torso. Red light flared around his body. Eli pushed out his arms and red energy surged from his outstretched palms. Mikey somersaulted through the air, collided with a tree, then lay still. Eli's vision clouded. Darkness swooped in and claimed him.

"Omega team, co-ordinate retreat," Fang said into her headset.

"Roger that."

"Six losses – if we'd retreated earlier –"

"No," Vulcan countered, striding into the command centre, Deckker and Weaving at his heels. The technicians desisted.

Fang stood at the central hub. The other directors nodded briefly in her direction.

"We do not retreat. We can sustain the losses. The team leaders?" Vulcan said as he climbed the stairs, his cane thudding on each step.

"Mikey and Daniel are accounted for, sir."

"Excellent. Preventing the walker's rescue mission was never our main objective."

A female technician pulled off her headset. "Sir? But our orders …"

Vulcan stared the woman down. The other technicians focused on their screens. Vulcan snatched the energy readouts from Fang's hand. "I trust you have the data on the blasters test?"

She nodded and pulled up the statistics on the screen.

"And the boy's energy aura?"

She fought to maintain a neutral expression. "Able to withstand several blasters, but not for long."

Vulcan smiled. "Now the game begins in earnest."

17

Prodigal

Geological surveys revealed that the
temple is built on a bedrock of quartz.
While quartz is common in sedimentary
rock, the purity of the crystal at the
temple site is unprecedented. Quartz
is an unusual mineral because of its
inherent piezoelectric properties – the
ability to generate electricity when
mechanical or heat stress is applied to
the crystal structure. Today we exploit
this property using a range of synthetic
materials in industrial and manufacturing
applications: our smartphones, the
development of robotics and the world's

electricity grid all rely on piezoelectricity. But the purity of the outcrop in Laos raises questions. Did the monks accidentally stumble across the quartz after they had chosen the temple site, or did they choose the site because of the crystal? And if the latter, did they harness its piezoelectricity? Like everything observed here, it seems unlikely that the monks happened upon this site, that it was mere coincidence. The inevitable conclusion must be: this site was chosen for a reason.

Brock Williams, Working Notes.

It was so very dark, and so very cold. Fletcher sat with his arms wrapped around his legs, darkness hemming him in from all sides. He had lost track of time, of what it felt like to control his own body. The ancient voice penetrated the deepest recesses of his mind, trickling through his synapses like poison. *Let me in. You cannot hide forever.*

Fletcher said nothing. Perhaps he had to conserve his energy, fight to control even this small corner of his consciousness. A door materialised out of the dark recesses of his memory: the front door of his house in Durham; a fragment from his life before pain and loss. It thudded as a great weight collided against it.

Let me in, earth walker.

Never.

The spirit's frustration rippled through their shared neurons. The sweet lilt of Fletcher's mother came through the keyhole. "Fletcher, honey? Let me in, sweetheart. I promise everything will be all right. Just open the door."

Fletcher pressed his nails into his calves, fighting the urge to run to the door, fling it open and fall into his mother's embrace. *Nyx needs me to reach the spirit world. As long as I can fight her, Nyx is powerless to destroy the planet.* He rocked back and forth, clutching this small thread tight in his mind. *I can't give up. I have to save my friends.*

Silence, stillness. Fletcher choked back a sob as he closed his eyes, focusing on his memories of home. When he opened them, he found himself sitting on his bed, the darkness gone. His bedroom was exactly as he remembered it, right down to the faded quilt his mother had sewn for him. He pulled it around his shoulders, inhaling its faint cedar scent, and explored the rest of the empty house. His fortress. *If I can create this, I can hold out against Nyx.*

The house shook; dust fell from the strong beams Fletcher's father had built.

I will have you soon enough, walker. Then you shall know true despair. Nyx's voice reverberated in Fletcher's ears.

Fletcher flinched, pulling the quilt tighter around his shoulders as he struggled to hold out against Nyx's barrage. He repeated the words over and over. *I can't give up. I have to save them.* The pressure squeezing his brain eased. Sweet relief. Then terror.

Let's go visit your friends, shall we?

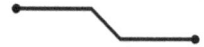

Kara frowned at her monitor. Solar flare activity continued to jam the comms link. It had been more than a day since they'd had any contact with Eli and his team. Kara hated flying blind.

A warning flashed in the bottom corner of her screen. Kara pulled up the video feed. "Holy shit!"

Two horses trotted down the driveway. Kara zoomed in on the image. A lean muscled figure rode toward the house. "Fletcher?" she said, flooded with relief which quickly morphed into concern. The earth walker looked haggard. There were dark circles under his eyes and his features were sharper than she remembered. Kara shut down the alarm and pushed back her chair. She found Ariana at the kitchen table, hunched over a huge map, her fingers pressed against the tiny nation of Laos.

"They're back."

Millisecond transitions of confusion, hope then anger washed over Ariana's face. She slowly stood, wiping her palms on her jeans. "Fletcher," she said, her voice breaking. "Dad."

Ariana raced out of the house. Kara followed her and stopped by the front door, watching Ariana stride across the gravel. The sea walker stopped halfway, staring at Fletcher, as if reassuring herself he was really here. When the earth walker dismounted, Ariana broke into a run, her eyes glittering with tears. They met in the middle of the driveway in a crushing hug.

"I'm sorry," Fletcher whispered into her hair.

Ariana pushed him away. "You're *sorry*? You've been gone for months. No word, nothing." She jabbed a finger in his chest in time with her words. "You. Could. Have. *Died.*"

Fletcher ducked his head in apology. Ariana turned to embrace her father. "I missed you too."

"Well, we're back. And very contrite," Bry said with a grin, his hand over his heart. "And I promise not to leave again." He glanced at Fletcher, then whispered, "I had to try, Ariana. For his sake."

Ariana pulled her father close again, inhaling his familiar outdoorsy scent. "Thank you." She turned to face Fletcher. "Did you find what you were looking for?"

Fletcher smiled and picked up Ariana, twirling her around, before gently placing her down. "I sure did, and then some."

Ariana's breath caught in her throat. How long had it been since she'd seen Fletcher smile? Maybe this journey had helped. Maybe she'd worried over nothing, and Robyn was wrong about the earth spirit and Nyx.

Fletcher whistled and an enormous brown bear emerged from the bushes lining the driveway. It stepped into the sunlight and cautiously sniffed the air.

Ariana gasped, shaking her head in disbelief. "It's not possible."

Fletcher ran a hand across Eva's flank. "I know, right? I didn't realise just how much I missed her until she came back."

But while the words sounded okay, Fletcher's intonation sent a shiver down Ariana's spine.

Ariana watched Fletcher climb the stairs, his legs corded with muscle. The way he moved made her uneasy. He looked different. He carried himself differently. Like the old Fletcher but not. What exactly happened while Fletcher had been away?

Fletcher paused on the landing. "I'm sorry I left without talking to you, but I wasn't sure you'd understand why I had to go to Iceland. You and Eli are so connected to the sea and air spirits, and I just … wasn't."

The familiar guilt washed over her. Despite the long hours of training he'd put in trying to access the walker state, Fletcher had never been able to connect with the earth spirit. Forced instead to witness how effortlessly she and Eli slipped between worlds. It must have been hell to watch them. "I do understand, but I still wish you'd trusted me."

Eva huffed and stretched, her flanks rippling with muscle. Ariana couldn't comprehend how the bear was really back. She'd seen Eva shot, watched her blood spread through the water of the MRI compound in Bulgaria. *Eva had died.* Yet here she stood at the bottom of the staircase, looking mournfully up at Fletcher. Something was off about this new Eva though; something Ariana couldn't put her finger on. The old Eva had always nuzzled against her looking for a pat, eyes wide and trusting. But there was an air of coldness about this Eva. She seemed closed off, distant.

Ariana climbed the stairs, leaving the bear behind. Her thoughts returned to Fletcher's mysterious journey. "Is it different now? Are you connected with the earth spirit?" At the landing, she took his hand and flinched at how cold it felt. Ariana studied his face, mapping every new furrow, the shadows under his eyes, the pronounced sharpness of his jaw. A haunted expression flashed across his features. For a second Ariana didn't recognise him, then he laughed and pulled her in close, kissing her forehead.

"Of course it's different now! For one thing, I have Eva back." Fletcher grinned.

But his flippancy made her uneasy. She stared up at Fletcher's hazel-flecked eyes, darker than she remembered. "Before you left, you told me that there was something wrong with you. That you were diseased, useless," Ariana paused, leaving him space to explain why he was behaving like this.

Fletcher frowned and shrugged. "Did I? I don't remember saying that."

There was definitely something wrong with his eyes. Somehow pretending not to be watching her, yet she kept catching him scrutinising her when he thought she wasn't looking. It was a bit creepy. Ariana met his gaze. "What happened when you met the earth spirit?"

Joy filled Fletcher's face like he was having a religious experience. "She made me whole again." He wrapped his arms around Ariana and pulled her into a tight hug. "The earth spirit told me how to stop Nyx. Don't you see, Ariana? I can finally access the spirit world! I've redeemed myself."

"Don't." Ariana broke his hold and stepped away. Fletcher flinched like she'd slapped him. Realising she'd hurt his feelings, Ariana backtracked. "I mean, don't push yourself so quickly. You've had a huge adventure," she said with a reassuring smile.

Fletcher turned away and pushed open the door to the room that had once been her bedroom. It had since been repurposed as a hang-out space where Eli, Sara and Jacob kept their stuff. Fletcher rummaged through garbage bags overflowing with clothes looking for something in his size. The last time Ariana and Fletcher had been alone in here, he'd kissed her so sweetly she thought she might combust. Did he still feel the same way about her? Or had the harrowing trip changed him? She had to know what he'd found in Iceland. "Did you … did you find any trace of Nyx?"

Fletcher spun around; his arms full of clothes. "I told you, I found the earth spirit." Frowning, he strode past her. "Where's Eli?"

Ariana rubbed her shoulder where he'd bumped into her. "He's on a mission."

Fletcher tensed and he stopped on the landing. "The moment he gets back, we need to agree on a plan." Then he bounded down the stairs, ignoring Eva, and headed for the bathroom.

The door slammed behind him. Ariana's eyes brimmed with tears. What had happened to the warm, vulnerable boy she cared so much about? Fletcher was hiding the truth.

Robyn's days passed in a blur. Up at dawn to train with Lenti, then into the lab to her notes and scribbled drawings, and the three vials of walker blood: earth, air, sea. Blood samples preserved from Eli, Ariana and Fletcher, courtesy of the MRI. Miranda had delivered a thick stack of photocopied field notes, and Brock had added his working notes to the pile on her lab bench. Robyn stayed up late into the night, absorbing everything the pair had gleaned from decades of studying the temple site. She had tacked photos to the whiteboard – the temple surrounded by workers; a young Miranda and Brock smiling as they strained against the sun in their eyes. And the temple itself, which gleamed like polished crystal, as if carved from the very rock beneath its foundations.

She stopped only whenever Lenti appeared with a tray from the mess tent. Each night, she collapsed into an exhausted sleep, dreaming of a world in chaos, Vulcan's enslaved convergers, and Catherine. Always Catherine. Far away, alone, vulnerable, scared, tortured. Her subconscious crafted increasingly terrifying scenarios where Robyn failed to save Catherine. She'd jerk awake, covered in sweat, and lie there until dawn. Paralysed by fear, she'd focus on her breathing until light leaked into the sky and she could summon the energy to do it all again.

The vials on her lab bench glittered like liquid rubies in the early sunlight. Robyn opened her notebook to a scrawled sketch of three overlapping circles. Inside each circle, she'd written *plants, animals, fungi*. Everything had felt so *clear* in her vision, but now that clarity had dissolved, leaving her grasping at threads. Vainly, she tried to weave them back into the stellar tapestry she was part of.

Lenti entered the tent, carrying a mug of tea and a plate of toast. He put Robyn's breakfast on the corner of the lab bench, bowed, then settled cross-legged on the floor and closed his eyes.

Robyn returned her attention to the circles. They kind of looked like *cells*. The noise in her head went still. In humans and animals, mitochondria carried the convergence sequence. Grabbing a fresh sheet of paper, she sketched a simple eukaryotic cell, circling the mitochondrial energy apparatus. Fungi also need mitochondria. Plants produced energy by chloroplasts, but their cells still needed mitochondria to produce ATP, the energy currency used by all living beings.

"That's it!"

Lenti started and looked up at her. "What is?"

"All three main branches of life depend on mitochondria. The walker convergence sequence includes both plant and fungal components because they're all connected. They all depend on this ancient symbiosis. The kindred ties that bind us to the planet and to all living things. See?"

Lenti stared at her picture, trying to divine the sense of her words and images. "At the temple, we made daily offerings of fresh fruit, mushrooms, whatever was in season."

"Yes, of course. The monks understood the importance of this symbiosis." Robyn held one of the glass vials up to the light. "The convergence mutation has lain dormant for thousands of years, ever since the physical and spirit worlds separated. Those who carried the mutation never realised their potential."

"When you created the activation dose you unlocked the convergence sequence." Lenti bowed his head, hands clasped in the prayer position. "For that I am eternally grateful."

Robyn smiled at Lenti, glad that at least one person didn't blame her for the destruction her discovery had caused. "To restore the balance, we have to open the boundary between the physical and spirit worlds, which requires all three walkers." Robyn tutted and sighed. "Fletcher."

"Is missing, and if he finds the earth spirit, we're – what do you call it – toast?" Lenti held up a slice of jammy toast and took a thoughtful bite.

"Somehow, we have to help Fletcher overcome Nyx's hold over him." If it wasn't already too late. Robyn slid the vial back into the rack and returned the samples to the fridge.

Lenti rose and stood at the lab bench, examining Robyn's diagrams. "Nyx has had centuries to infiltrate the earth spirit and centuries more adrift in the void between worlds. This ancient spirit had access to power we can never know."

Robyn studied the boy monk. His hair seemed to grow inches every day. He had tucked it behind his ears, which made him seem old and wise and daggy all at the same time. How had Liro managed to hold her off, and save Lenti and preserve the walker lineages in the process? Robyn rested her forehead against the cool metal of the fridge door. "You're right. We can't underestimate Nyx." She traced the birthmark that bisected her right eye, the mark she shared with Liro and every guide before her. "I'm the guide. I'm supposed to find the solution, but we're running out of time."

"You need a break." Lenti steered her away from her lab bench toward the fresh air and sunshine. "And something proper to eat."

At the tent entrance, Robyn noticed the screen in the corner of the lab flicker to life. A familiar face appeared. "Vulcan," Robyn said. Dread quickly gave way to anger as she remembered the gun he had pressed against Catherine's spine and her girlfriend's barely suppressed terror.

"Citizens of the world. I am Vulcan Manning." He

flashed a grin that failed to reach his eyes. "When I was young, I joined the military because I believed it to be honourable; a means of preserving life and defending those who could not fight for themselves."

Vulcan folded his hands in front of his chest, a posture designed to make him seem contrite. As the camera zoomed in, he raised his gaze. "I was wrong. I no longer recognise country borders or the sovereignty of nations. Today, I address you as global citizens."

Robyn stared at the screen. She despised yet feared this dictator. A man who sought to bend the convergence sequence to his will. She hated how helpless he made her feel.

"Over the past few weeks, my armies have systematically overhauled oppressive governments throughout the world. To date, your countries have been governed by fools who believe the impending solar storm is a disaster. It is not. This is the opportunity for a brighter future. Today, I give you your freedom."

Robyn sensed Brock and Miranda join them in the lab. No-one said a word.

"I will lead humanity into a new era. A world without boundaries, without conflict, hunger or fear."

"Arrogant bastard," Miranda spat, sitting on a nearby stool.

Brock nodded, brow furrowed. "I was afraid it would come to this."

"Within the fortnight, every government must deliver formal surrenders. Failure to recognise me as polemarch of this new world will not be without consequences." The camera panned across lines of convergers wearing bodysuits with the trademark MRI white stripe. By their heels sat their animals wearing plates of dark armour.

The screen dissolved into blackness. Fear curdled in Robyn's stomach. Lenti bowed his head, crestfallen. "There are so many under his sway," he murmured. Robyn steered the dazed monk to a lab stool and helped him sit down.

"Polemarch my ass." Miranda pinched the bridge of her nose. "I knew Vulcan was power hungry, but this is insane."

"The world is in chaos. Without other options, people simply surrender." Brock thumped the nearest lab bench and starting pacing the tent. "If Vulcan thinks the solar storm is his chance to seize power, he is a fool.

With Nyx freed, life on this planet will cease to exist."

Miranda rubbed the tension in the back of her neck. "Vulcan never believed in the existence of spirits. Remember? He hated the idea of beings with greater power than us. When I presented the MRI with my findings from the temple, Vulcan refused to believe any of it was possible. Except the ability to connect with – and control – animals."

Robyn's gaze moved between the two determined scientists. Miranda, Brock and Robyn were allies. Together, they must prevent Vulcan seizing total control and restore balance to the planet. It was time to put all her cards on the table, to truly trust them. "If we open the boundary between the physical and spirit worlds, I think we can stop Nyx."

Miranda sat up. Brock stopped pacing and joined them, his eyes wide. "Are you positive? Nyx is not to be trifled with."

Robyn nodded. "I know, that's why we need Fletcher."

"Apart from the fact that he has gone missing," Miranda said.

"The bigger issue is not where Fletcher is but that Nyx has infected the earth spirit that resides within him."

Miranda and Brock shared a look. Miranda gave a slight nod and Brock turned to Robyn. "Vulcan cannot be allowed to wrest power over the world."

"Go on then," Miranda said with a low chuckle. "I know you've been dying to tell her."

Brock smiled. "I think it's time we introduced you to our side project."

Robyn ran her hands through her hair, utterly dumbfounded. "What side project?"

Brock stood at the tent flap and, with a flourish, gestured for Robyn and Lenti to follow him. "C'mon. I think you'll like it."

Except for the hammock strung in one corner, Brock's tent was an extension of the lab. Glistening shards of crystal, carefully refined and faceted, sparkled like gemstones on the stainless-steel benches. On a hotplate, a magnetic stirrer churned a bubbling solution sending a herby aroma wafting through the tent.

Lenti picked up a crystal and closed his eyes. "Oh," he whispered. "You're right – I do like this side project."

Brock selected another crystal and weighed it in his palm. "This entire mountain top is a geological anomaly.

It's predominantly made of quartz crystal, the purest I've ever seen. The temple is built on a bedrock of it."

He placed the crystal in Robyn's hands. Instantly, the walkers' tethers clarified into a single note, pulsing against her chest. Energy swirled through her system and behind her eyelids flashed red, green and blue light. "Oh," she said, mirroring Lenti's quiet exclamation. She grasped at the faint thread of Fletcher's green energy tether. It was the first time she'd felt the earth walker since she'd returned to the physical world. "It does feel different here. Clearer, somehow."

Miranda walked the length of the bench, rainbow refractions glittering against her shirt and the canvas behind her. "Quartz is piezoelectric. This mountain acts as an enormous natural transmitter and receiver. I believe that's why the boundary between our world and the spirit world is weakest here and why the monks chose this location for their temple. It's a direct cosmic antennae channelling electromagnetic radiation."

Robyn remembered how she'd been drawn to the temple in her dreams, how being here on the mountain top brought her so much clarity. It all made sense now.

"This is how Liro could overcome Nyx," Lenti

whispered in awe, looking up at Robyn.

Surprised, Miranda regarded the boy monk. "Exactly. I think we can harness its potential to do so again."

Robyn closed her fist around the crystal and felt its energy thrum through her veins.

Brock chose a circular piece of quartz and raised it to the light, sending a cascade of rainbows spiralling around the tent. "The quartz acts as a powerful electromagnetic amplifier," he said, his expression thoughtful as he admired the rainbows dancing across the tent walls. "To think – we mine for gold and metals, yet we've never viewed quartz as valuable, even though it shares the same silicon oxide structure as the circuits that made the computer age possible." He passed the curved quartz band to Robyn. "The crystal heightens your receptivity and that of the walkers, but we believe it is devastating to Nyx."

Robyn studied the band and smiled at her old supervisor as understanding dawned. "A piezoelectric collar."

Brock nodded. "Precisely."

"If we jam Fletcher's frequencies, he can't be the conduit for Nyx to enter the spirit world or the walker state."

Lenti scrutinised the collar and frowned. "But how

will you put it on him?"

Ariana's blue energy tether tapped insistently against Robyn's ribcage. She gestured to Lenti to follow her before turning to Miranda and Brock to explain. "I have to talk to the walkers."

Robyn and Lenti sat on the cool stone floor of the ruined temple. She brought her fists together and closed her eyes, but her mind refused to calm down. Vulcan's ultimatum and Miranda and Brock's side project competed for neural space. They had a fortnight. Not nearly enough time to stop Vulcan *and* Nyx. She focused on her breathing, allowing the flow of thoughts to still, then crossed into the spirit world.

When she opened her eyes, Robyn blinked in confusion. She expected to be in the glade but she remained in the temple. Across from her sat Ariana. "How'd you get here?"

"Ugh, finally! I've been waiting for *ages*." Despite her attempt at levity, Ariana's face was drawn.

Robyn pulled the sea walker into her embrace. Fear and uncertainty surged through her system as Ariana sank into the hug. Her shoulders shook with suppressed sobs. "It's Fletcher," she managed, all pretence at levity gone. "He's back, but he's different. I don't know how but somehow Nyx has an even stronger hold on him."

Ariana took a deep breath and raised her gaze to meet Robyn's. "He found the earth spirit."

Robyn processed Ariana's words. She felt sick. She'd hoped she still had time to find Fletcher and prevent Nyx from fully parasitising the earth walker. Too late. Robyn stood and followed the line of mosaics. They glowed with the energy from her fingertips, calling to her, awakening something buried deep in her subconscious. "The solstice is only two weeks away." Robyn paused, focusing on the push and pull of energy in her system. She found what she was searching for; a feather-light tendril connecting her to the earth walker. "He's still in there. And while he is, there's still a chance Fletcher can help us defeat Nyx."

Robyn turned from the mosaics, remembering the weight of the cool crystal in her palm. "And I have a plan."

18

Threat

I cannot begin to imagine what it would be like to be bonded with an animal; to experience the world as they do. To feel a deep kinship with the Earth and to truly understand my place in the circle of life. Yet this ability exists and has been reawakened by force. I envisaged the social and cultural upheaval such a revelation would cause but not the devastating consequences of its power being used for death and destruction. My objective has always been to reinstate the order of monks who originally worshipped and served in this temple, to restore this sacred place as an energy centre. I believe this is the only way to guide those with this ability and to create a better tomorrow. My only hope is that I am not too late.

Miranda Collins, Working Notes.

The roar of the landing helicopters reverberated in Ariana's chest. There were six, each packed with rescued convergers. It was the largest and most brazen extraction they had ever completed. And by far the most dangerous. Eli jumped from a still hovering helicopter to greet the medics rushing from the barn. As the helicopters powered down, dozens of people followed him across the field toward the barn for processing and debrief. Heart pounding in her chest, Ariana waited.

Eli peeled away from the group and jogged toward her. His armour was pitted with scorch marks, a chunk of his hair was missing, and an ugly red burn seared his scalp. Una clutched the strap on his shoulder, swaying with the movement. Eli stopped in front of Ariana. "The MRI knew we were coming."

"But you still saved the convergers."

Eli glanced behind him. Despite the lingering after-effects of the blaster, Sara insisted she was fine. She and Ming guided the new convergers into the barn. "*We* saved them." Eli lowered his gaze. "Not all of us came back."

Ariana saw a stretcher covered with a blanket being trundled toward the barn. Her heart sank. Under the thin cotton lay one of her friends, lost to them forever.

"Jason didn't make it. Basil's pretty badly hurt." Eli blinked away tears. "It was a good plan, it was supposed to *work*, damn it. Instead we nearly died."

Ariana threw her arms around Eli's neck and drew him close. "You did everything you could."

The tightness across Eli's shoulders faded as he slumped against her. "They all had these blasters." He ran a grimy hand across his face, smearing dirt and blood across his cheeks. "Mikey had a similar one at the last extraction, but I didn't see it up close."

Ariana remembered the taser guns they'd been forced to use in the battle games when she was held captive by the MRI in Bulgaria. "Electroshock weapons?"

Eli nodded. "They never seemed to run out of charge." He kneaded the cords of tension in the muscles in his neck. "And every one of the MRI convergers have one of those chips."

Ariana's hand flew to the base of her skull where, not so long ago, a MRI neural hardware chip had been implanted. Beyond the invasion of her own body, she hated how it allowed the MRI to control her. With a shiver, Ariana pushed aside the thought. "You need food and rest. You all do." Ariana urged Eli toward the farmhouse. "And you need to debrief the twins and Aster."

They walked side by side across the field, each reliving their own nightmares.

"Nothing we do seems to make a difference," Eli whispered.

Ariana stopped walking. Tamping down her own fear, she looked Eli in the eye. "It makes a difference to the convergers you saved. Because of you, they're safe. All of you," she added quickly before Eli could remind her he hadn't acted alone.

Eli squeezed her arm. "I needed to hear that." He ran his fingers through the wildflowers that dotted the field as they kept walking. "There's still so much beauty, so much goodness in the world."

At the farmhouse, he stopped and cocked his head as if listening. "Something's different." He closed his eyes and red light flickered on his skin. "I can't put my finger on it, but something has changed."

Ariana slid into the gap between Eli and the door. Her fingers thrummed a nervous rhythm on her chest. "Fletcher's back. But he's not … not himself."

Eli swore softly under his breath. "Fletcher found Nyx."

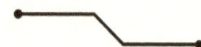

"I know how we can stop Nyx," Fletcher said, a triumphant look on his face.

Eli and Ariana glanced at each other then back down at the kitchen table. The twins noted the walkers' lack of enthusiasm and hid behind their laptops.

Undeterred, Fletcher continued. "We have to open the boundary between our world and the spirit world." Eva placed her head in his lap and huffed.

Kate felt a chill and pulled the blanket tighter around her shoulders.

The veins in Eli's neck flared as he fought to maintain his composure. "And how exactly do we do that?" he said, leaning back in his chair, away from Fletcher, accidentally dislodging Una in the process. She landed smoothly on the fridge and ruffled her feathers in silent protest.

Fletcher chuckled and scratched Eva under the chin. The bear grunted in pleasure. "Isn't it obvious? The earth spirit said the three walkers needed to be together in order to open the bridge between the worlds."

Ariana shivered. It was the middle of summer, yet since Fletcher's return, they'd all taken to slipping on a cardigan or wrapping themselves in blankets and scarves when they were in the house. It was like he sucked all the warmth from his surroundings, leaving behind a bleak cold that lodged under her skin, in her bones, like a disease.

"Clara told me the same thing," Eli said. "The spirits are the solution to everything."

"It's been hundreds of years since the three walkers were called together," Ariana whispered. "Hundreds of years since the sun emitted this much energy to Earth."

"She's right," Bry said, entering the kitchen. In his hand he had a bunch of electrodes that he passed to the twins. They started attaching them to a blipping console. Bry retrieved a knotted cable from his pocket and started teasing it apart. "As a result of the unique mutation on your convergence sequence, you walkers steer a tremendous amount of cosmic energy through your bodies." Seeing their shocked expressions, he added, "I did read Terence's reports, you know."

Her brother's face flashed before her, followed by darkness. Ariana pushed against it, the energy tumbling through her system and displacing the despair. She glanced at Fletcher. Constant vigilance.

Fletcher yawned and stretched. "Well, I'm ready when you are."

Eli nodded slowly, grinding his fist into his palm, the tension raising the veins in his forearm. "If we open the boundary, we will stop everything. Restore balance."

"Exactly," Fletcher said, slapping Eli on the shoulder. Cold danced around him, like a living, breathing entity.

The twins positioned the heavy console in the centre of the table, electrodes spilling out like limp noodles. Kate hooked up Eli and Fletcher while Kara pressed two electrodes to Ariana's temples and one on her ribcage.

Ariana squirmed. The circular plasters felt sickeningly familiar on her skin. For a second she was thrust back into the MRI's experimental chamber where excruciating bursts of current fried her synapses.

Jericho flicked his tongue against her cheek. *You are safe here. It is only a memory.*

Ariana watched the earth walker. He was so excited it was all he could do to stay seated. It felt wrong. Fletcher had never been able to access the walker state. Even the thought of trying used to fill him with dread. Now he was excited about it? Ariana shuddered. Pushing away the rising panic, Ariana nodded at Eli and Fletcher. "Let's do this."

Bry passed Kate the final cable. She fiddled with the baseline readings on the monitoring console then looked at the three walkers. Eli was calm, Ariana seemed anxious and Fletcher was obviously excited. She shivered at the icy chill in the air. "So, how does this work, exactly? Do you just cross over to the spirit world and *bam*, the boundary between the spirit world and the physical world is destroyed?"

Kara nudged her sister out of the way to double check the calculations. "It's not that simple, sis. All three of them have never crossed over into the spirit world together, so we don't know what to expect."

Eli rubbed where the electrode attached to his neck. It was super itchy and he couldn't wait to get this whole experiment over and done with. "In the walker state, the space between the two worlds, we can connect to all of our past lives and communicate with the spirit linked to our reincarnation cycle."

"With the increased solar activity, together we might have access to enough energy to finally break through the barrier holding the physical and spirit worlds apart," Ariana added.

"Might? Are you guys sure about this?" Eyebrows raised, Kate looked up from the console.

Ariana felt like vomiting. Robyn's plan echoed in her mind. *I just have to hold out long enough.*

You are strong enough. We are strong enough, echoed Jericho from his perch on her shoulder.

The room fell silent. "Be careful," Bry whispered in her ear. "Any sign of trouble and you get straight out of there, promise?"

Ariana nodded, folding her hand around the reassuring weight of the quartz in her pocket. Robyn had pressed the smooth crystal into her hands in the spirit world only days ago, and Kara had set the ridge of quartz into a metal collar. A failsafe.

"Ready?" Eli whispered.

"Ready," Fletcher and Ariana answered in unison.

Ariana closed her eyes. The room fell away, replaced by utter blackness.

Ariana hovered in the void. Tiny pinpoints of light blossomed in the darkness, like diamonds scattered across folds of velvet. Around her body, blue light flickered to life.

Fletcher and Eli appeared out of the nothingness. Ariana's skin prickled as her blue aura flared outwards in every direction. Red light surged around Eli. Their auras intersected and kept expanding. Ariana gasped as energy surged through her body and poured into the darkness. She felt power in her veins, her very bones. She'd never felt so alive.

This is definitely new, Eli projected.

Ariana looked over at Fletcher. He was staring at his arms, as if willing his green aura to appear. *No ... I shouldn't be here ... Please ...*

Fletcher sounded panicked and Ariana's heart leapt. This was the real Fletcher. She reached out for the earth walker. *It's okay, Fletcher. We're here. I'm here.*

You don't understand. Then he froze. Dark light enveloped his body. Fletcher rolled his neck and leered at her.

Horrified, Ariana recoiled as dark energy swept outwards from Fletcher toward her and Eli. When the darkness hit the blue and red streams of light, her energy sagged. Invisible fingers tightened around her throat and the blue light stopped pouring from her body and instead was sucked inwards. And it was cold, very cold.

Ariana glanced at Eli, wreathed in the dark light, his hands clutching his throat. *Fletcher, stop,* she pleaded. *This is Nyx, not you. You have to fight her.* A blade of pain lanced through Ariana's skull.

Fletcher's eyes were as dark as the void around them. His voice snaked into her mind. *Today I remove the last blemish. Today the walker lines will cease.*

He raised his arms and Ariana's chest constricted. Dark light raced up her arms, over her chest and around her head. All that was left was the faintest hint of blue.

The monitors screeched and all three sets of electrodes flatlined. The walkers' bodies slumped. "Holy shit," Kara yelled, jumping to her feet. "Get them out of there, now."

Bry dropped beside Ariana and started ripping off her electrodes.

"Don't!" Kate cried. "It'll overload the system."

"What the hell?" Bry shouted. "Why didn't you tell us this before?" He cradled Ariana to his chest. "Don't leave me, Ariana. Come back."

Kate grabbed Eli by the shoulders. "Can you hear me? You need to come back. Now."

Kara's fingers flew over the keyboard. This couldn't be happening. They couldn't lose them. Not now, after everything they'd been through. Jamming the emergency switch on the monitoring console, she hoped to hell the walkers would survive to forgive her for the pain she was about to inflict.

Ariana fought, concentrating on her breath and the energy swirling inside her body. Somewhere in the distance, a voice called her to come back. She heard Eli scream. His aura had shrunk to a faint red halo of light surrounding his head. Fletcher's words rang through her skull: *Today the walker lines will cease.* Certainty displaced fear. Fletcher planned to kill them both and, by virtue, destroy the walker lineages. Never again would a walker be reborn in the physical world. This incredible bond linking humans and animals would disappear.

No. Focusing on the sliver of blue light on her skin, Ariana pushed her aura outwards, trembling with the effort.

The voice in her mind kept building. *Ariana, come back. Come back.* With a silent scream, she pushed against the invisible fingers strengthening their grip around her throat. Blue light flickered, then flared, on her skin. A surge of red echoed her call.

Ariana, come back.

Kara hunched over the console, her eyes wild. "It's not working!" she yelled.

"I've increased the current. Try it now," urged Kate, head buried in her laptop.

Kara dialled up the power and the air around them sizzled. Sparks showered the walkers but still they didn't move. She banged her fist on the kitchen table. "C'mon, you guys."

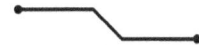

In the physical world, Robyn and Lenti sat in the ruins of the temple, meditating. Miranda stood to one side, where she had set up a Geiger counter to measure Robyn's energy response. Brock filmed them on his tablet while a group of lab technicians took notes. All of a sudden, Robyn doubled over and screamed. In horror, they all watched her claw at her throat, gasping for breath.

Robyn felt Ariana and Eli's energy tethers crackling with energy. She focused on drawing external energy into her system and funnelling it through the walkers' energy tethers. Darkness edged her vision. Sweat dripped down her spine. In the background, the steady whine of the Geiger counter increased in pitch.

"Stand back, everyone! Reaching critical levels!" Miranda shouted.

Straining with the effort, Robyn pushed energy through the tethers. The mosaics on the temple walls began to dance, glittering in the sunlight. Beneath her, the crystal bedrock hummed with power.

Brock passed his tablet to one of the technicians, then crouched beside Robyn and whispered encouragement. "I don't know if you can hear me, but I've always known it would be you, from the first day you entered my lab. Your intellect, your strength, even in the face of failure. You can do this, Robyn."

Darkness blurred her vision, paralysed her limbs. She was only a vessel for the energy churning through her and she was steadily emptying. Brock's voice faded. The sound of Robyn's heartbeat thudded in her chest like a distant star.

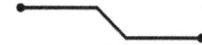

Ariana gasped. The vice-like grip around her throat disappeared and, with a rush, she tumbled back into her own body. She heaved for breath, like a swimmer hitting the surface. The room spun around her, slowing, then stopped on her father's face. "Dad?" she sobbed.

"Ariana." Bry enveloped her in a hug.

Eli's body shook. He spluttered and coughed, wild-eyed as he tried to get his bearings. Kate and Kara hunched over their laptops. Ariana held in Bry's embrace. Then he saw Fletcher.

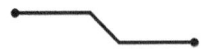

Robyn greedily sucked in air as the pressure around her throat loosened. Brock and Lenti grabbed her by the arms and helped her to her feet. Miranda stood over a laptop, scrolling through the results from the Geiger counter. "Impressive readout. Did it work?"

"It worked." Robyn shook with adrenaline as she remembered Nyx's dark energy, the power the spirit wielded through Fletcher's body.

With a gasp, Fletcher stirred, eyes wide and uncertain.

Ariana ripped the electrodes from her skull and stood up, her chair crashing to the ground as she scrambled to get as far away from Fletcher as possible.

"What the …" Kate began.

"Ariana? What's wrong?" Bry followed her across the kitchen to where his daughter pressed up against the pantry door. Eli joined them.

Fletcher's eyes darted between Ariana and Eli. "I remember the void, the stars. Your auras kicked in. Then …" He stood, kicking his chair so hard it shattered against the wall. "It should have worked, damn it!"

"Whoa there," Kara said, hands raised as if trying to calm a skittish horse. Eva stepped between her and Fletcher and growled, the throaty sound reverberating around the kitchen. The temperature plummeted.

Ariana reached into her pocket, toying with the piezoelectric quartz collar. *Now. I have to do it now.* Summoning her courage, she stepped around Eva and faced Fletcher. "What happened in there? Are you okay, Fletcher?"

The tension in his shoulders disappeared. He ran a hand through his hair and Ariana recognised the boy she cared about. As much as she hated what she was about to do, she had no choice. In one smooth motion, she took the collar from her pocket and clinked it shut around Fletcher's neck.

Fletcher yelped and yanked at the collar. Confused, he stumbled backwards against the kitchen table. "What have you done to me?" he screamed, his eyes feral. Eva snarled and pressed herself against the earth walker.

The collar began beeping, a steady, insistent sound. The temperature in the room began to warm.

Ariana edged away, finding her father's hand. "It's

for the best," she said. "It kills me to have to do this to you, believe me."

Fletcher's eyes went black and he snarled.

Kara held up a slim receiver, her thumb hovering over the button. She caught Fletcher's eyes and smiled. "Doesn't kill me, though." Uncertainty crept across him and he turned to Ariana.

"This is to protect you," she said, fighting the tears that threatened to fall.

"And incapacitate you. Let's not forget that part," Kara said.

She pressed the button and Fletcher fell to the ground. Eva howled. Fletcher screamed, convulsing under the barrage of current. Then he lay still, his bear collapsed by his side.

Robyn stood in the ruins of the temple, staring at the mosaics, as the walkers' energy tethers stabilised against her ribcage. A glimmer of white light played over her skin.

Lenti eyed the tiles as if seeing them for the first time. "The mosaics are made of the same crystal as the bedrock?"

Robyn nodded and smiled.

Brock ran though the readouts from the Geiger counter while Miranda fussed over the laptop. "The readings confirm your hypothesis, Miranda. The quartz collar has jammed Fletcher's frequencies and contained the energy spike." Brock grinned at Robyn. "You did it."

"Now it's impossible for him to enter the spirit world or the walker state," Robyn said, getting to her feet. Overcome by dizziness, she leaned against Lenti until it passed. Seeing Fletcher like that – no, Nyx – had been terrifying. Her heart ached for the earth walker.

"With any luck, Nyx will remain trapped within Fletcher's body until we can figure out how to be rid of her for good," concluded Brock.

Miranda packed up her laptop and passed Brock the Geiger counter. "Yes, it's a temporary reprieve at best."

Brock slung the machine over his shoulder. "And there's still the pressing matter of Vulcan."

Robyn straightened, the push and pull of energy from the temple filling her with renewed strength and determination. "Yeah, he's next."

19

Inhibitor

We've communed with animals since the dawn of time. All over the planet, there are ancient cave paintings depicting humans living, working and sleeping alongside animal kind. We've examined everything about them, yet no-one ever thought to examine the paint. Until now. And what an interesting concoction it is; plant dyes, bacteria, fungal spores, and oil from the human hands that mixed it. Proof that life is not separate: we are more powerful together. Ancient humans knew this. Maybe now, thousands of years later, we're beginning to remember.

Brock Williams, Working Notes.

Robyn pipetted solution into the vial of blood on her bench, agitating it to mix the protein matrix with the blood cells. Heart in mouth, she watched for the tell-tale colour change that would indicate disruption of the convergence sequence, but the vial remained red. *Damn it.*

Sighing, she scrawled a line through her latest attempt at a deactivation sequence. Similar failures filled her notebook. Brock and Miranda were right – in order to stop Vulcan, they had to incapacitate his induced convergence army. And they were agreed, Fang's environmental virus activators held the key. Thank God Brock had managed to smuggle out samples of Fang's work when he'd fled the base in Bulgaria. Samples Robyn was busy putting to good use. She had to admit, Fang knew her shit – these activators were top shelf.

"Dr Greene?"

It took Robyn a moment to register who the person was talking to. She still wasn't used to her new title, but Brock and Miranda had insisted she'd more than earned it. Robyn turned to see that a scientist had brought a fresh rack of vials.

"Anything yet?" Robyn asked her.

The woman shook her head and placed the rack on Robyn's bench. "We're working our way through the combinations you suggested, but none have bonded with the convergence sequence."

Robyn cursed. She'd stayed up all night reading scientific papers and writing out a list of inhibitor combinations. For days, it had been all hands on deck testing each one, trying to unlock the key. To no avail. *It has to work, it just has to.* Robyn remembered Vulcan's ultimatum: surrender or die. She smiled at the scientist. "Thanks for the update. Keep working through the list – I'm going to get some air."

Yanking off her gloves, Robyn stepped out into the sunshine. Lenti emerged from his tent and followed her, her discreet shadow. She pretended not to notice but in truth, his devotion, his belief in her, kept her motivated. They had to find the key – for her friends, for the walkers, for every converger on the planet. Especially now Fletcher was back. *Fletcher.* The way he'd channelled tendrils of dark energy toward Eli and Ariana. The sensations she'd experienced through their energy tethers. It was awful. The memories pierced her consciousness when she slept. Ever since, Robyn woke up covered in sweat and gripped with pain.

Robyn and Lenti passed the temple ruins and stopped at the base of the ancient tree. She sat in the embrace of its tangled roots. Lenti chose to perch on top of a thick root that grew precariously close to the mountain edge. Warmed by the golden light of the setting sun, Robyn watched the clouds scuttle through the valley below. She ran her fingers along the gnarled surfaces of the surrounding roots. There was moss, clusters of cup-shaped orange mushrooms, and tiny seedlings that reached for the sunlight through cracks in the rock. Life – always striving, colonising new places, adapting, evolving. Never in stasis.

Lenti plucked a dandelion and scraped a cluster of the cup-shaped mushrooms. "Every morning, we made an offering of life at the temple, like this." He tipped the flower and mushrooms into Robyn's open palms. "I think the key you seek is right in front of us, not in the lab."

Robyn studied his gift. What an idiot she had been. Lenti hadn't just been following her around – he'd been listening, thinking, trying to help her. Not her shadow but her cipher. She looked up into the canopy of branches intertwined above their heads. The tree of life. Humans, plants, animals, fungi. All part of a greater whole. The walkers' chromatograms had two peaks. Plant and fungal compounds. She stared at the delicate flower and mushrooms cupped in her hands, her mind flooding with certainty. "You're right," she said, scrambling to her feet so fast the young monk fell backwards, landing on the ground with a thump.

"Bloody hell, Lenti, you've cracked it!" She pulled him to his feet. "Come on! I need your help."

Three hours later, Robyn held aloft an Erlenmeyer flask filled with a viscous green liquid as if she were a magician who had just pulled a rabbit out of a hat. Brock and Miranda looked at it, then at the thin layer of soil, leaves and mushroom stems that littered the bench. Miranda shrugged. "You did what, exactly?"

Lenti, standing tall in his very own lab coat, pushed his safety glasses on top of his head. "We've made an inhibitor."

"Right," Brock said, looking to Robyn for confirmation.

Robyn brushed the debris aside with the sleeve of her lab coat. "Think about the walkers' protein signatures in their chromatograms – their convergence sequence creates both plant and fungal compounds. Thanks to Lenti, I realised that's exactly what we need to disrupt Fang's viral activation sequences: plant and fungal DNA."

"Go on," Miranda said, pulling up a lab stool. "I'm intrigued."

Robyn swirled the flask, exhilaration coursing through her system. "This is a highly concentrated extract of plant and fungal cells."

"That explains why the smell in here is so *intense*." Brock covered his cough as he moved closer to the bench.

Robyn sniffed the air. All she could smell was a distinct note of earthiness. She raised an eyebrow at Lenti and he wrinkled his nose. "It does smell pretty bad."

Robyn scanned the lab. The desks closest to hers were conspicuously empty. The scientists working through her list of traditional inhibitors had moved to a cluster of benches that caught the breeze through the open tent flap. "Okay then. It smells bad."

Lenti grinned and took the flask from Robyn. He placed it carefully on the bench then passed her a vial of pale-white liquid.

Robyn showed the vial to Brock and Miranda. "This is the inhibitor. I've spliced plant and fungal mitochondrial genes into the human convergence sequence."

Lenti brought over a rack of vials, each containing a tiny amount of blood. "These are some of Fang's viral convergence activation sequences," Robyn explained as she loaded a pipette full of the white liquid. "Let's hope my hypothesis is right."

Miranda leaned in closer. "What are we looking for?"

"Colour change. I've added an indicator dye to the inhibitor. If the blood solution turns purple, it means the inhibitor has bound to the convergence sequence." Robyn took a deep breath to steady her nerves. If her hands weren't full, she'd cross her fingers. "Truth time."

She depressed the trigger on the pipette and dispensed three drops into the first vial. The individual droplets splashed the surface of the sample, penetrating deep into the vial, then slowly dispersed.

Miranda slumped on her stool. "Nothing."

"Wait," Brock said, touching her arm. He picked up the vial and gently agitated it to mix the two liquids.

The solution turned a violent purple.

No-one said a word. Robyn carefully repeated the procedure with the remaining two vials. Brock agitated each one and again: an explosion of purple.

Robyn stood frozen, still holding the pipette. She couldn't believe it – it had *worked*. Brock and Miranda stared at the bright purple vials. Lenti started dancing around the lab.

"You've done it," Brock said, breaking the shocked silence. "You've found a way to stop Vulcan."

Robyn shook her head, still struggling to believe she'd actually done it. Her mind raced. "Unfortunately, the inhibitor is only temporary. Once it's introduced to the bloodstream, the foreign DNA will only remain stable for a few hours."

Brock laughed. "But the MRI won't know that, will they?"

Of course, Brock was right. Why hadn't she thought of that? Robyn held up the rack of vials, admiring the row of purple. It finally hit her – after all this time, she'd found a way to fix the damage she'd unwittingly caused by creating the original activation dose. The MRI had twisted her work, leading to the deaths of millions of people. Now she could start making amends. Some of the guilt lifted from her shoulders. Robyn felt lighter than she had in a long time.

Miranda checked the time and reached for her laptop. "We only have a few days until Vulcan's ultimatum expires. We have to start synthesising the inhibitor right away."

"And we need a distribution vector," Brock added. "Perhaps a projectile weapon of some kind? Miranda, do you remember those designs the institute commissioned? Some of the old supplies are in storage here. I could take a look and see if they could be adapted."

"Great idea," Miranda said, eyes glued to her screen. "I'll start manufacturing the inhibitor – we'll need all hands on deck."

Lenti joined the ex-MRI chief. "I'll help."

Brock paused in the doorway to the tent. "In all the excitement, I forgot," he said, pulling out his tablet. "Thanks to a temporary lull in solar activity, your friends managed to get an encrypted data package through."

Robyn snatched the tablet from Brock. "What? Why didn't you tell me?"

Robyn sat alone in her tent, Brock's juiced-up tablet on her lap, and watched the week-old recording. Onscreen, Catherine stood staring into the mirror, hands braced against the sink. She looked gaunt, unsteady on her feet, bruises snaking around her arms and collarbone, her shoulders shaking. Even though the recording didn't include sound, Robyn could tell she was crying. Robyn touched the screen, crushing guilt and despair flooding through her. *I'm sorry, Catherine. Sorry I wasn't there for you when you needed me.* Nearly four whole months. Robyn bit her fist to stop the tears. *I wasn't there for you, or for Fletcher. This is all wrong, and I'm not sure how to make it right.* How must Catherine feel? Abandoned, worthless, alone. *I'm going to get you out of there. I'm going to rescue you. I swear it.*

"Knock knock." Brock stepped through the tent opening with two steaming mugs. Robyn swiped her eyes and took a steadying breath. "Thank you," she murmured as she accepted the tea.

Her ex-supervisor sat beside her. "Are you all right?"

When Robyn didn't reply, he took the tablet and shut off the video feed. "She's your friend."

Robyn pulled the blanket from the bed and wrapped it tight around her like a cocoon. "Catherine is my girlfriend."

Mug halfway to his mouth, Brock paused. "Oh." His ears turned a delicate shade of pink. "I'm so sorry, Robyn."

She rubbed her eyes with the heels of her hands. "Four whole freaking months."

Brock studied the footage of Catherine. "Do you know where she's being held?"

Robyn knew what he meant, the video gave away no details. "Kara and Kate said she's being held in an ex-military compound in Alaska. It was an experimental radio array that Vulcan brought back into commission."

Robyn tapped the tablet and brought up an encrypted file. "The twins have managed to get a basic map of the MRI's operations base. It's well fortified, remote, and packed with soldiers and convergers. From what they've been able to gather, it seems the MRI uses the radio array to protect their own communications integrity. It's the reason why they've been able to send their convergers and army into the field with such ... success."

Brock skimmed through the file, eyes bright with excitement. "This is exactly what we need. Now we know where they are, we can bring your inhibitor to them. Together we can stop Vulcan, restore a sense of balance to the world."

Brock's zeal was contagious. He was right – they now had everything they needed to stop the would-be polemarch in his tracks. "I need to rescue my girlfriend," Robyn said, pushing her blanket cocoon aside with renewed determination. "And I'm going to make that bastard Vulcan pay for what he's done to her." Her birthmark flared and white light shimmered on her skin. She turned to Brock. "Let's go. We've got work to do."

20

Offer

Hermits, recluses, spiritual gurus — many have left civilisation in search of enlightenment by communing with nature. Leaving behind the constructs of society, they find their true place among the tree of life: just one living part of the many, all channels of pure cosmic energy. But the rest of us, we're too busy getting to work, watching TV or thinking about what we'll have for dinner to wonder about the energy eddying around us, calling us home.

Brock Williams, Working Notes.

"It comes down to energy," Vulcan said, rapping his cane against the floor. Catherine jumped in her chair, her wrist cuffs rattling with the movement. Today's outing was an anomaly; she only ever left her cell to visit the shock chamber. Compared to the stark white chamber and her cell, she found Vulcan's office overwhelming. Catherine breathed in the scent of the leather furniture and the cool fresh air that trickled through the window. For a moment she didn't care what Vulcan wanted; she just wanted to feel the wind on her face, to press her toes into the snow.

"I'm not a spiritual man," Vulcan continued, moving to look out the window at the convergers running drills. "Miranda believed in beings beyond our comprehension; gods, almost. I think she went a little loopy before her unfortunate death."

Catherine focused on the notes of pine in the air, sensing Vulcan didn't want to be interrupted. What could she say, anyway? She'd never known the previous Chief Director. Since she'd been held prisoner, her old supervisor, Deckker, had visited her once and only then to deliver a spiel about complying with Vulcan's wishes. It still amazed her to think she had been part of the

MRI's web for years without ever realising it. Deckker hadn't really been her supervisor; he was an MRI agent assigned to monitor her and her work. It made her skin crawl, but months in solitary had dulled every urge except the instinct to survive.

"The ones you call *walkers* are different, yes, but the principle is the same in the convergers. The bond generates a significant amount of energy. Power that can be harnessed." Vulcan turned away from the window and faced Catherine. "We've improved the blaster design but Dr Fisher assures me there is room for more progress. I want you to work on the project."

The memory of Mikey aiming his blaster, the unbelievable pain as the electroshock zinged through her neurons, came back to her. It made her sick to her stomach. *Rot in hell.*

Someone rapped on the door and Vulcan replied by jabbing his cane against the floor. "Dr Fisher will give you a tour of the facility," he said, waving his cane at Fang, who now stood in the open doorway. She nodded at Catherine. "Shall we?"

It felt like a trap. Why would Vulcan want her to work on the project? He must realise she'd do everything she could to sabotage his efforts. Vulcan rapped his cane again in irritation. Catherine stood, her cuffed hands in front of her and, swallowing a retort, followed Fang into the hallway. Two soldiers detached themselves from the wall to follow at a discreet distance. *Why now? Why not leave me in my cell?* The soldiers' boots clicked against the concrete. *Because the stick didn't work. Now they're trying the carrot.*

They entered another wing with one wall made entirely of glass. Catherine stopped in her tracks. Snowy mountains beckoned over an emerald-green forest dusted with white. She edged forward and pressed her hands against the glass, the restraints biting into her wrists. She wanted to drink it all in. The gentle cascades of snowfall as the trees swayed, the glittering motes of light. Condensation formed on her palms and she pulled them away, relishing the icy cold, dreaming of the wind dancing around her, ruffling her hair, carrying her far away from here.

Fang stood by Catherine's side and pretended to admire the view. "I apologise for your treatment thus far, Catherine. Vulcan can be … harsh," she murmured.

Catherine flinched, wary of these overtures of

friendship. She opted for a neutral response. "I'm not sure harsh covers it."

Fang clicked her fingers at the soldiers. "Please remove her restraints – she's not going anywhere."

A soldier ran a metal wand over Catherine's wrists and the cuffs clicked open. Catherine rubbed her wrists and flexed her fingers, relishing the sudden taste of freedom. *What the hell was Fang playing at?* She'd basically handed Catherine to Vulcan. Because of Fang, she was being held prisoner, tortured, isolated. Another voice niggled at the back of her mind: *Then why did Fang save me when Vulcan had a gun pressed to my head?* Catherine risked looking at Fang. Her face was a calm mask but the dark circles under her eyes made Catherine wonder what kind of pressure to succeed Vulcan placed on Fang.

Fang kept her gaze locked on the view. "I'm sorry for my part in all this. These last few months ..." Fang turned, just enough to meet Catherine's eyes. Self-conscious, Catherine pulled the collar of her crumpled fatigues up over the scars and bruises, but not before Fang had a chance to see the damage. Fang looked momentarily stunned then recovered and went on. "We should be working together. We're running out of time."

"For what? For the MRI to take over the world?" Catherine spat. She didn't want Fang's pity, but she was right. Time was one thing they didn't have.

Fang pressed a hand to the window with a frown. "Dr Smith and I convinced Vulcan that you would be an asset to our research team." Fang broke off and glanced at the soldiers. But she needn't have worried, the men were distracted by a passing colleague and the three were staring at a screen. Fang lowered her voice. "The Chief Director underestimates the power of the solar storm, and doesn't believe in Nyx. But I do. The solstice will magnify the intense power of the solar storm allowing Nyx to break free. We can't let that happen, but we only have a limited window of opportunity."

Catherine stared at Fang in disbelief. "To do what? For you to have another attempt at overthrowing Vulcan and wresting control of the MRI?"

Fang abruptly turned on her heel and started off down the hall. "Come on," she called over her shoulder. "Lots to see."

The soldiers stopped gossiping and glanced between the two women. Catherine had no idea what game Fang was playing, but if the choice was between following her or being stuck with the soldiers, it was no choice at all. She hurried to catch up.

"The cafeteria," Fang announced, opening a door to reveal a huge room filled with long tables and a servery. Scientists sat nursing coffee and biscuits. The smell of hot toast, eggs and bacon wafted over from the bains-marie. It made Catherine's mouth water. Fang beckoned her closer. "Keep your voice down. Vulcan's lackeys may not be the brightest, but they tend to remember anything yelled in their general direction."

"What did you mean about the potential of the solar storm?" Catherine hissed.

Fang glanced at the soldiers. "The convergers' gym and quarters are directly below us," she said, then set off again. She reminded Catherine of a guide on one of those cheap holiday tours. They went down another corridor and almost bumped into a group of convergers. The teenagers gave Fang a quick salute then disappeared into the heavy-duty lift, their animals placid by their sides. Catherine stared at them in shock. They didn't look like teenagers – they looked like hardened soldiers. Is this where her research had led? It felt like a kick in the guts.

Fang lowered her voice. "Dr Smith and I have reconstructed some of Miranda's and Brock's research. It seems Brock has left us some breadcrumbs to follow."

"Dr Smith? You mean … *Derek*." Catherine stopped in the middle of the corridor, stunned. "Derek never believed in any of it."

"The breadcrumbs have proven rather convincing," Fang continued, ignoring Catherine's comment. They turned into another hallway. "This is the scientific staff wing. Your room – contingent on accepting Vulcan's offer – is here." She motioned to the scanner inset into the wall, saying, "It's already coded to your DNA signature."

Catherine pressed her palm against the silicon screen and the panel lit up. The door retracted, sliding into the wall cavity with a hiss of air. Inside reminded her of a hotel room; a comfortable bed, soft light, a desk, with one major exception. An enormous window framed that incredible view of snow and conifers. Catherine broke into a smile.

"You'll find civilian clothing in the wardrobe. There is a tablet in the desk drawer, access code to the internal network, everything you need." Fang returned her smile.

If it weren't for the white lab coat, she looked every inch the hotel concierge.

Catherine sank onto the bed. It was so soft she could lie down right now and sleep for a million years. In truth, there was only so long she could survive alone in her cell. And what good was she to anyone rotting away down there? Catherine looked at Fang, all poised and confident to the point of arrogance. Saying yes to Vulcan's poisonous offer might mean she could figure out what Fang and Derek were up to. More to the point, she might find a way to either stop them or help Robyn and the walkers.

Fang moved to leave then hesitated, lingering on the threshold. She turned to face Catherine. "You know, it was pure chance that I ended up on this side of the war and you on the other." She went to step forward, corrected herself, all poise momentarily lost. "Maybe in another life, we might have been friends ..."

Catherine leapt to her feet. In two strides she was across the room and standing toe to toe with Fang. "Friends don't hold guns to each other's backs," she said, and pushed past Fang out into the hallway.

Fang followed, the door hissing shut behind her.

Maybe she'd never be able to bridge the abyss of anger and fear that separated her and Catherine. "I guess not," she said quietly. With a small shake, her poise returned. She gestured down the hall. "This way."

The gym, the library, the recreation room; Catherine took it all in. Finally, Fang paused by a reinforced steel door. "This is where you'll be working with either Derek or myself." She palmed the scanner and the door slid open.

Catherine was speechless. The laboratory seemed to go on forever, filled with a legion of scientists. Catherine scanned the room until she found the one person she was looking for. He stood by the sequencer talking to a group of scientists who seemed to be writing down every word he said like devout followers. As if he felt her gaze searing his skin, Derek looked over his shoulder. Catherine swallowed. She'd dreamed of the day she'd make him pay for what he did; for abandoning them, stealing their research, and torturing Ariana.

Derek left the group, their pens hovering over their tablets, and strode toward her. He stopped several paces short. "Catherine. It's ... good to see you."

You could have seen me any time; you knew where I

was. Trapped in a cell while above me, you lived in comfort working as Vulcan's protégée. Steeling herself, Catherine managed a curt, "Derek."

"Have you considered Vulcan's offer?" Derek asked.

Catherine hated the eagerness on Derek's face, but she hated herself more. If she went back to that cell, she'd go insane. She was about to make the same choice Derek had all those months ago. She turned to Fang. "Are we allowed outside?"

"We're allowed anywhere within the compound boundaries."

Catherine imagined the cool mountain air on her face, the wide open landscape; a place she could breathe. "Then I accept."

Catherine woke in a tangle of warm blankets. Sensor lights flicked on and the room gradually brightened. She sat up in a rush. This was definitely not her cell. The events of yesterday flashed through her memory. She'd accepted Vulcan's offer to join the research team. This was now her room. Catherine fumbled for the remote and, at the touch of a button, the blinds rose to reveal the snow-covered forest. Tugging a blanket around her shoulders, she stumbled over to the window. Outside was an unblemished world, bathed in the rosy glow of dawn. A momentary sense of peace washed over her.

Catherine shook herself free of the blanket. She might not have had much choice, but she had every intention of turning this situation to her advantage. Opening the wardrobe, she examined the rack of clothes. After months in dark fatigues, they looked garish. Had Fang picked them? Catherine pushed aside the thought. It was best not to trust Fang. This charade was simply an attempt to gain her co-operation. Catherine pulled out a pair of jeans and a white t-shirt. She added sturdy boots, thick wool socks and a long, warm cardigan.

She paused in the doorway of the bathroom, fearful of what the round vanity mirror might reflect back. Her cell hadn't run to such luxuries; only bright white walls and the abyss of her mind. Tentatively, she stepped toward the mirror and raised her eyes. She barely recognised the woman staring back. Her hair was now a mess of blonde waves. It softened the hardness of her hollow cheeks and sunken eyes. Catherine examined her bare arms, the way the scar tissue along her wrists and forearms glistened under the light when she moved her arms. The sight tugged at her, remembered pain snaking through the scars. With a gasp, she gripped the edges of the sink. *I'm going to make them pay for this.*

Once showered and dressed, Catherine palmed opened the door. She peered up and down the hallway. It was empty. No soldiers lurked outside her door, waiting to trail her around the compound. It made her feel nervous.

Her heart thudding in her ears, she forced herself to step out into the corridor. Catherine drew herself tall and walked with a confidence she did not feel – out of the staff dorm wing and past the gym and cafeteria. Freedom fluttered in her chest like a bird eager to leave its cage. She relaxed into her stride, but when a heavyset door in the next hallway hissed open, she squeaked in alarm. Out stepped Derek, and with head bowed over his screen, he ran straight into her.

"Shit! Sorry," he said, stumbling backwards in surprise. The door slid closed behind him, but not before Catherine glimpsed a bank of computers and an enormous screen filled with video feeds.

"You're up early," Derek said, swiping his tablet off and shoving it in his pocket. "Breakfast?"

His affable manner did nothing to conceal the dark circles under his eyes, his crumpled shirt. Had he been working all night? Catherine's gaze flitted to the enormous door. What did it hide?

"The food's not as bad as you'd expect," Derek said, starting off down the hallway. He paused and stared at Catherine until she gave in and followed him.

The clock on the cafeteria wall read 5.30 am. The place was empty except for the man at the servery who yawned continuously as he filled their trays with scrambled eggs, sautéed greens and thick slabs of sourdough.

Catherine's stomach rumbled.

Derek chose a table with a view over the forest. As she sat down, Catherine realised this was also the furthest possible point from anyone wishing to overhear their conversation.

Derek started apologising as soon as they sat down. "I'm sorry. I never wanted any of this to happen."

Catherine ignored him and instead concentrated on savouring her first forkful of proper nourishment in months. Derek watched her, his meal untouched. "They fed Ariana well … but I guess they needed to keep her strong."

Catherine swallowed, registering the truth of his words. She was only useful if she co-operated and supplied the MRI with information or research. Neither of which required her to be healthy or strong. To date she'd been fed enough to keep her alive, nothing more.

"I don't know how you resisted so long. I don't think I could have," Derek said, rubbing his chin.

Catherine studied the thin ridge of stubble across his chin. Whatever Derek had been doing in that sealed room, he'd pulled an all-nighter.

After she'd mopped her plate clean, Derek pushed his untouched tray across the table. She mumbled her thanks and made short work of his breakfast too. Only then was she prepared to talk. "How long do we have until the solstice?"

Derek stacked their plates on the tray and pushed it aside. "A few weeks."

Alarm rippled through her mind. *I've missed so much. Trapped, useless, no good to anyone.* "So soon?"

Her shock must have shown because Derek grimaced. "I'm sorry."

She lifted a hand to stop him. "Don't apologise again."

Was Derek telling the truth? If so, time was a luxury they didn't have. Somehow, she had to figure out a way to stop Vulcan and to help Robyn, and fast. She looked at Derek, sitting there with that earnest look on his face. Assuming it was true that between them Fang and Derek had orchestrated her release, then maybe they'd already figured it out. She leaned her elbows on the table. "You have a plan?"

Derek sighed and slumped in his chair. "I have hope."

21

Solution

Eddies of dust whirled around them as the chopper kicked up loose grit. Robyn shielded her eyes and Lenti squinted to watch the metal beast fall from the sky. Behind them, Brock and Miranda stood guard by a stack of reinforced metal crates. As the chopper landed, the pulse of Eli's energy tether against her ribcage grew stronger.

The chopper had barely kissed the ground when Eli swung open the heavy door and leapt to the stone below. Robyn barely recognised the tall, muscular teen dressed in armour, but with Una attached to a padded strap on his shoulder, it could be no-one but Eli. He ran to Robyn and she pulled him into a hug, ignoring the reinforced chest plates digging into her ribs. This close, his energy tether almost overwhelmed her.

"I'm so glad to see you," Eli said, when they finally parted. He searched her face. "You're different."

Incredulous, Robyn stared back at the air walker. "Says you!"

Eli smiled and bowed to Lenti. "It is good to see you again, old friend."

Lenti returned the bow then reached out to fist bump the air walker. "I'm sorry it's not under better circumstances."

Eli's energy tether faltered. Robyn felt cold tendrils of fear and uncertainty displace the air walker's excitement. She grasped his forearm. "I never meant to leave you. I never knew that entering the spirit world on the mid-year solstice would lead me here."

Eli smiled at her. "It doesn't matter. You're here now." He looked over to where Brock and Miranda supervised a group of scientists loading the crates onto the chopper. "But it's time to get back to the others."

They waited for the rest of the metal crates to be loaded then, pulling on her backpack, Robyn followed Eli to the chopper, ducking low against the swirling blades. Lenti scrambled in behind them. Robyn scanned the cramped confines. This is what it came down to – the contents of her backpack, her mind and a few crates of MRI prototypes. It was all they had to defeat an ancient spirit and a madman bent on global domination. Was it enough? Only time would tell. She waved farewell to Brock and Miranda until the door slid shut and the chopper's blades whined.

Once they were airborne, Robyn perched on a crate opposite Eli. The air walker leaned forward and handed her and Lenti a slim earbud. Motioning her thanks, Robyn slipped hers on and Lenti followed suit. Una fidgeted, hopping from one crate to another trying to find a comfortable perch. For a creature built for flight, the osprey hated helicopters. Maybe it was a control thing.

"How's Ariana bearing up?" Robyn said, adjusting her earbud.

Eli shook his head. "She refused to leave Fletcher. Not now Nyx has him in her grasp." The air walker stared out the window at the blur of trees far below them.

Robyn felt Eli's tension rippling through his energy tether. She wanted to hug him but, under the circumstances, it seemed like a pretty futile gesture.

"Everything is happening so fast," Eli said. "I thought we had more time. What if it is impossible?"

Lenti helped Robyn carefully shrug off her backpack. She unzipped it and gently removed an insulated container. Eli watched her, head cocked to one side, just like his osprey. When she opened it, liquid nitrogen spilled over the sides. "I have been working on an inhibitor, a way to temporarily stop the induced convergence Vulcan is using in his armies."

Eli snapped to attention. "Really?"

Lenti grinned, holding up the Styrofoam container like it was a sacred offering.

Robyn's heart leapt. Seeing the air walker's eyes alight with hope made the past weeks of toil in the lab worth it. "Don't get too excited. It works on lab blood samples. I haven't tested it on an actual human-animal pair."

Una shrieked and spread her wings, startling poor Lenti who almost dropped the Styrofoam box. Oblivious, the osprey stretched, refolded her wings and preened her breast.

Robyn patted the boy monk's shoulder to reassure him. "It doesn't affect the walkers. I tested the MRI's blood samples from you and Ariana. The walker sequence is too complex for the inhibitor."

Eli turned and scrutinised the crates they sat on. "So if you're carrying the inhibitor, what the heck are in these?"

Robyn smiled. "A gift from the MRI."

Ariana heard the whir of blades and sprinted toward the barn. The helicopter touched down and soon after, Robyn ducked low and scrambled into clear space, a boy racing in her shadow. Ariana skidded to a stop on the slick grass and waved. Eli supervised the unloading of a stack of metal crates, pausing only long enough to wave back before manoeuvring another crate onto the pallets set up in the field.

Ariana walked over to where Robyn stood counting the crates. Her face lit up the moment she noticed Ariana. Robyn pulled Ariana close and enveloped her in a hug. "It's so good to see you, sea walker. My God, what are they feeding you? You've both grown so much!" Robyn chuckled, but as she looked to the farmhouse, her smile fell away. "Where's Fletcher?"

Ariana pulled free, the flicker of hope waning. "He's inside. The twins are watching him." Since the night they tried opening the boundary between the physical and the spirit worlds, they'd kept Fletcher under house arrest. Whenever she tried talking to him, Fletcher would withdraw into himself, eyes blazing, like a sulking child. Ariana wished she could tell him how much she hated seeing him bound to the physical world by the quartz collar, shackled like a dog. Wished she could tell him that she understood – how it reminded her of the MRI's monitoring wristband, the chip in her neck. Ariana knew Fletcher found their mistrust humiliating, but it was necessary. Even so, this constant internal war had left her drained and edgy; she didn't want Robyn to see her like this.

Robyn pressed a hand to her chest. She didn't need words to understand how Ariana felt – they were bound by the energy tether. "You know it's unavoidable."

All Ariana's emotions bubbled to the surface. Energy skittered across her skin, leaving behind a glimmer of blue light. "Nyx could have infected me or Eli just as easily. Fletcher was only trying to make it right."

"Hey," Robyn murmured, pulling her close again. "I promise I will do everything I can to save him. To save all of us."

Ariana shrugged off Robyn's embrace, fighting the despair rising readily in her gut. "You weren't here. You haven't seen how hard it's been. The whole world is falling apart and everything is on Eli and me."

Through the sea walker's energy tether, Robyn felt the crushing weight that Ariana bore. No sixteen-year-old should have to face such terror, such horror. First the loss of her brother, Terence, and now Fletcher. Robyn pointed to the teams of convergers training in the barn. "None of these people would be safe without you and Eli. It makes me proud seeing how strong you are, Ariana."

With a shaky sigh, Ariana straightened, blue light shimmering on her skin once more. "Thank you. But Fletcher?"

Robyn focused on her breathing, concentrating on the walkers' tethers until she felt the dull, dark energy linking her to the earth walker. "Take me to him."

Robyn left Ariana downstairs. Something told her it was best she confronted Fletcher alone. When she reached Ariana's bedroom, Robyn stopped in shock. The old wood-panelled door had been replaced by a thick sheet of reinforced steel. Opening it, she found

Fletcher sitting cross-legged on the floor in a patch of pale sunlight. The bars on the window cast a striped pattern across the floorboards. Behind him Eva sat in silence, her mournful expression matching Fletcher's own. Robyn faltered – Eva's blood had run across Robyn's hands. She'd seen the bear die.

Fletcher's energy tether flickered against her chest like the tongue of a lazy serpent. The connection felt weaker, as if Fletcher was deliberately closing himself off. Robyn sensed a dull, lingering anger. She walked into the room and chose to sit on the bed so she could gauge Fletcher's reactions. Eva shifted on her haunches so she sat square to Robyn. Goosebumps flared across Robyn's arms and she suppressed a shiver. The wrongness of this bear being here made Robyn want to flee. Tamping down her unease, Robyn focused on the dull energy linking her to the earth walker. He still hadn't even looked at her. His head was bowed as if whatever was on the floor was far more interesting than the appearance of the guide.

Robyn took a deep breath, preparing herself for whatever the earth walker might reveal. "Fletcher, it's me, Robyn."

Fletcher raised his head. His hair stuck out wildly from his scalp and his shirt was stained. When he looked at her, Robyn gasped. His eyes were no longer hazel; instead they were dark, bottomless pools.

The earth walker clawed at his throat. Beneath the collar, he had rubbed the skin raw. "You did this to me."

Robyn swallowed. This wasn't the Fletcher she remembered. "I'm sorry. It's for your own protection."

"My protection? I don't think so. You need all three walkers to open the portal." He hooked his fingers under the collar and yanked it hard. "This is a mistake."

His frustration surged against her ribcage. "I know you're upset," she said. "I'm going to find a way to fix this."

"I already have a way. Take this thing off me, and let me do what I'm meant to do."

"You know we can't do that, Fletcher." Robyn remembered the boy she'd met a year ago, frightened by his newfound powers, in awe of his connection to the animals that walked the earth, the trees that grew from it. Not this feral creature. "You tried to kill Eli and Ariana. That's not you, Fletcher."

All at once Fletcher transformed, shedding the snarling boy like a skin. He brought his knees to his chest, his eyes hazel and brimming with tears. "Please help me. I don't understand why I'm locked up in here. What have I done wrong?"

Fletcher's energy tether pulsed against her ribcage, transmitting vulnerability and fear. The force of it made Robyn reel, but her hopes soared. No matter how deep Nyx had sunk in her claws, Fletcher was still in there. Robyn rushed to embrace this fragile boy, ignoring the flicker of warning pulsing through Ariana's energy tether. Her fingers grazed Fletcher's. At first, all she registered was the churning mass of energy in his system. Then icy pinpricks exploded up her arm, tore across her chest, forcing the air from her lungs. Pressure crushed her chest. She could barely breathe.

Far away, Ariana screamed.

Robyn fought through the haze of pain and stumbled backwards onto the bed, taking huge gulps of air. As her breath slowed to normal, she looked over at Fletcher. His eyes were dark. Behind him, Eva growled, low and menacing.

Ariana bounded up the stairs and burst into the room. Fletcher shook his head. His eyes flickering from hazel to blackness to hazel again. His gaze jerked between

Ariana and Robyn's horrified faces. "What? What is it?" Without warning, he scrambled to his feet, arms raised defending his head from some unseen battering.

Nyx, Robyn realised. Fletcher was fighting the dark spirit within him.

Ariana grabbed Robyn's hand and pulled her toward the door just as Fletcher slumped to the floor. He buried his head in his hands. "You shouldn't be this close to me. I'm dangerous."

The earth walker's energy tether fluttered in Robyn's chest followed by dark energy oozing into every recess. "Fletcher …" Robyn began.

"Get out!" he shouted before sinking down onto the floor and curling into a ball. "I'm trying to fight Nyx, but it's hard," he whispered, "so very hard."

"I have a plan." Robyn swallowed back her own fears. "Hang in there, Fletcher." She'd give anything to make this right. To save Fletcher, to save Catherine, to destroy the MRI. She just hoped she could pull it off.

22

Back Door

The SCO has fallen. The tentative alliances that connected European nations have frayed and snapped. Country borders change by the day; humanity is scattered and ailing. A flood of refugees surges through the Mediterranean and Asia, with no safe refuge in sight. The MRI plague marches onwards, its appetite for destruction insatiable.

International Affiliated Press Syndicate, quoted in The Last Bastion of the Anthropocene, *Ester Akintola, the final UN Secretary General.*

Robyn stirred as sunlight slanted across her eyes. She pushed aside the blanket and sat up. It took her a moment to realise she had fallen asleep in the armchair in Bry's study and, despite the early hour, she wasn't alone. A strange man sat at the desk between Kate and Kara, his fingers skittering across his keyboard. Mugs of steaming coffee sat on piles of printouts. Even Aster had emerged from his tech lair in the barn, wearing a grin and his goggles pushed up over his hair.

"Morning sunshine," Kara said, without turning around. "You ready to join the party?"

"This is incredible," Kate said, pointing to the man's code-filled screen. "Is that a Turing sequence?"

The man turned around and Robyn couldn't believe her eyes. "Bohai?" Last time she'd seen him was in Beijing when he helped them rescue Eli, Sara and Jacob. "What are you doing here?"

"Eli picked him up on the last extraction," Kara explained, swivelling around in her chair. "He's been helping us access the MRI system."

"I don't understand." Robyn stared blankly at Bohai and her friends. She knew Bohai was good with computers – he'd been the twins' contact in Beijing – but how could he possibly help them crack the MRI's defences?

"I was helping the children escape from the

orphanage when the soldiers came. That's when I heard her name," said Bohai.

None of this made any sense. Robyn willed herself to fully wake up. "Whose name?"

"My sister. It's funny that she uses the nickname I gave her when I was little because I couldn't say her name properly."

"I still don't understand." Robyn stood and stretched. "Who are you talking about?"

Bohai looked at Kara, but she shook her head and said, "Uh-uh. She's your sister. You tell."

Bohai sighed and shot Robyn an apologetic smile. "Fang."

"No way," Robyn froze mid-stretch, her eyes wide. "Your sister is Fang?" How could this calm, measured man be related to such an ambitious, dangerous woman?

"We'd drifted apart, but when I heard her name, I knew there couldn't be two Fangs in the world." He rubbed the stubble on his chin, his expression sad. "She created the activation sequences that enabled Vulcan to create his army. Fang is the reason so many people have died."

Stunned, Robyn sank back into the armchair. Bohai

only knew half the truth. She had helped create the first activation sequence that became the foundation of Fang's work, making her equally responsible for all these deaths.

"I can't believe my sister is a killer," Bohai pressed, looking to each of them, pleading his case. "I think she's being forced to use her skills and knowledge by someone in the MRI." He pointed at the monitor filled with scrolling code. "That's why I'm here. My father's company designed the encryption software the MRI is using. I know I can help you get through to her."

Energy coursed through Robyn's system. She looked to Kara for an explanation.

Kate pulled up a complex-looking schematic on her screen. "In Bulgaria, we used hardware to infiltrate their system, but we can't do that now because they're in some goddamned fortress in Alaska and the solar flares render us blind."

"So while we have limited access to their systems," Kara explained, "the bad news is we can't actually *do* anything."

"Is this because of the solar flares?" Robyn asked, not wanting to admit that she was struggling to keep up.

"Electromagnetic shielding." Kate stretched her arms wide, miming a protective bubble. "HAARP has the biggest radio array in the world protecting the compound. Probably the safest place to be once the solar storm hits."

Bohai's screen beeped and a new sequence of code flashed across the monitor. He scrutinised the screen and smiled. "I always leave a back door in my coding. This means we are getting closer."

Aster peered at the code then clapped Bohai's shoulder. "Man, that really *is* a Turing sequence. I haven't seen one that complex before."

The jargon-fest washed over Robyn as she thought about Catherine trapped somewhere in that compound. She refreshed the screen on her tablet, bringing up Hypatia's blog. Last night, Robyn had read three months' worth of posts, catching up on world events. Hypatia, aka Kara, had documented the rapid collapse of international order. With growing horror, Robyn realised that this small contingent of convergers hiding out on a farm in the Welsh countryside were all that stood between Vulcan and world domination. They needed all the help they could get, and if Bohai could crack the MRI's encryption, then did it really matter that Fang was his sister?

Kate clapped her hands with glee, swivelling her chair a full three-sixty. "You bloody beauty! *We're in.*"

Bohai hunched over his keyboard, fingers tapping a mad dance. "Not completely. We can't change any of their primary operating systems, but if we remove the temporary cache files we can move through their network unseen."

"Baby, that's all we need," Kara said, cracking her knuckles. "Robyn? You ready?"

"Ready for what?" All Robyn wanted to do was pull the blanket tight around her shoulders and disappear, but everyone was looking at her as if the next move was hers.

Kate stood and indicated for Robyn to take her chair. She had no idea why, but Robyn figured the twins must have their reasons.

Kara plugged in code and slid the keyboard over to Robyn. "Let's do this."

23

Alliance

<<<Internal MRI message net>>>

sol.stice.bitch@mrinet.com: Fang. I can't believe I'm freaking doing this.

fisherxiaofang@mrinet.com: Who is this?

<Username abbreviation protocol active >

sol.stice.bitch: Okay, here goes. This is Robyn. You know, one of the other MRI PhD students? The one you tried to kill in Bulgaria?

fisherxiaofang: Derek, if this is you, this is a shitty prank. Your username – seriously?

sol.stice.bitch: No prank. I'll even add Derek in, if that helps.

<smithderek@mrinet.com has now joined

the conversation>

smithderek: Fang? Are we still on for the gym later?

sol.stice.bitch: Hi, Derek.

fisherxiaofang: Derek — I don't know who this is.

smithderek: Well, not just anyone can add users to a net convo. It's encrypted, right?

sol.stice.bitch: Right. Everyone's here. Except Catherine, of course, because she's locked in a cell. Okay. Fang. Your brother Bohai is here with us. Don't bother asking where *here* is.

smithderek: ... Robyn?

sol.stice.bitch: Bingo!

fisherxiaofang: Prove it. Prove he's there with you.

sol.stice.bitch: Bohai insists on including these facts as proof of identity.

1. Your favourite colour is aquamarine (I was expecting blood red, personally).

2. When you were eleven, you took cheek swabs and cultured them to prove to your

parents that Bohai wasn't brushing his teeth (I mean, I'm impressed if this is true).

3. When you broke your arm practising parkour (prohibited by your parents), you dosed yourself with whisky and set it yourself, and your parents never found out (hardcore, even for you).

fisherxiaofang: ... shit.

sol.stice.bitch: Happy now? Thanks to Bohai, we've unencrypted the MRI's system, so this message chain technically doesn't exist. You can say whatever you want.

smithderek: I want to say sorry.

sol.stice.bitch: Great! That fixes everything, doesn't it? Not like Vulcan's still got his animal-human armies and is killing teenagers in the streets, thanks to our research. Not like he's about to take over the goddamn world. How could you betray us, Derek?

fisherxiaofang: We've been trying to figure out a way to stop Vulcan, but he has soldiers, resources, and this damn radio array ...

smithderek: I never wanted this to happen. I'll do whatever I can to make it right. We can work together. If you've cracked the internal system, you could take down the radio array, expose the base to the solar flare activity. It would ground operations, at least temporarily.

sol.stice.bitch: Already tried that. Radio array has physical on-site failsafes that need to be deactivated. Plus, primary servers are a no-go, even with Bohai's magic touch. We have a plan, but there isn't much time left. Will you help?

smithderek: Anything.

sol.stice.bitch: Fang?

fisherxiaofang: Me too. Where do we start?

sol.stice.bitch: Get my girlfriend out of that DAMN CELL.

fisherxiaofang: We've already done that.

sol.stice.bitch: … what?

fisherxiaofang: I'll show you.

<heathercatherine@mrinet.com has now entered the conversation>

heathercatherine: Derek? Fang? What's going on? I thought we were meeting in Derek's room to go over Miranda's files – has there been a change of plan?

sol.stice.bitch: CATHERINE. Are you ok?

heathercatherine: I'm fine. Guys, who's the new recruit? Is that a good idea? We have to avoid drawing suspicion, remember?

sol.stice.bitch: It's Robyn.

heathercatherine: ... really? I thought ... I don't know what I thought. What I think.

sol.stice.bitch: I've been ... away for a long time. I only just got back. I'm so sorry, Catherine. For everything.

heathercatherine: There's so much I want to say to you, but not like this, not over the message net ...

sol.stice.bitch: I'm going to get you out of there.

heathercatherine: I knew you'd come back. It kept me sane. I miss you.

fisherxiaofang: Uh, we're still here. Kinda awkward.

<u>sol.stice.bitch</u>: Sorry. Okay. Here's the plan.

<File shared>

< *f**kthemri*>

<download complete>

<u>sol.stice.bitch</u>: Read it, it'll be deleted from the server in five minutes. See you real soon. Catherine – I love you.

<Conversation terminated>

Robyn buried her face in her hands, pressing her fingertips over her eyelids. "Catherine is all right. They're going to help us."

Kara gave her a quick thumbs-up and resumed tapping away at her computer.

"Ahem, may I?"

Robyn looked over her shoulder. Aster was clearly itching to claim the second computer. She vacated the seat and returned to the armchair out of everyone's way.

Kate joined her, perching on the coffee table, nursing her coffee. "I'm still not sure we can trust them. After everything Fang and Derek have done …"

"We have to work with what we've got," Robyn said, running a finger along the birthmark slashing her right eye. It tingled. "And we can't wait for the solstice. We have to move now. Where are Eli and the others?"

Eli used a crowbar to wrench open the crates then heaved the metal lids onto the floor of the barn. The circle of waiting convergers stepped closer. Ariana and Sara reached inside and pulled out sleek launchers.

Sara's eyes lit up. "Oh, I like this present," she murmured, running her fingers along the weapon.

"They look like the same blasters Mikey and the others used." Eli dropped the crowbar and, in dismay, turned to Robyn. "They won't work without the implant chips."

"Now that Vulcan's made upgrades, this model is obsolete, so ..." Robyn reached into the second crate. She withdrew a hunk of glittering quartz and held it up for all to see. "We're going to make some alterations."

Catherine and Derek rode the lift down in silence. The doors opened onto a world of sandstone and fluorescent strip lighting. Derek nodded at the guards as Catherine pushed the medical trolley over the rough floor. The smell reminded her of Robyn's earth ship.

Once they were out of hearing distance, Catherine paused and looked around nervously. "This is the convergers' gym?" As if in response, thuds and muffled voices drifted up the hallway. Once they reached the end of the hallway, Derek swung open the door and revealed the cavernous space beyond. The enormous gym had been hewn into the rock itself, with cathedral-height ceilings and thick sandstone walls. Convergers in active wear emblazoned with the white MRI stripe sparred on mats, lifted weights or sprinted the length of the gym, which was easily as long as a football field.

"Wow," Catherine said. "The scale of this place is unbelievable." She took a steadying breath and swiped open her tablet. Catherine pulled up a file and stared at the photo of a girl with a blonde ponytail. Spencer.

Derek surveyed the room. He pointed toward a line of punching bags, all still except for one. A girl with a blonde ponytail was laying into it like her life depended on it.

Derek stared at Spencer. In Bulgaria, she'd been the captain of Ariana's team in the battle games. Since then, the converger had been to hell and back. Spencer had insisted on staying behind to fight the MRI troops, allowing Ariana and the rest of her team to escape. In the process, she lost her partner animal, an orca. Now she was just one of Vulcan's pawns.

He shook off the memories. They had a job to do. "We have to be smart about this. Vulcan took some convincing that blood samples taken during intense aerobic activity would be beneficial for the main analysis. So, we'll have to take multiple samples." Derek counted the sterile syringes. "At least fifteen."

"Then we'd better get started." Catherine grabbed the trolley and began pushing it across the main floor. Hundreds of heads turned in her direction, but she ignored them and kept her eyes on Spencer.

As they approached, the blonde converger stilled and raised her eyebrows in greeting.

Derek launched into his official spiel. "We're monitoring ATP levels during aerobic exercise for a multifaceted analysis approach. We require you to submit a blood sample."

"Whatever," Spencer replied and ripped off her gloves with her teeth. "Let's get this over with." She extended her arm and looked intently at Catherine.

Catherine tied a rubber tourniquet around Spencer's arm and tapped for a vein inside her elbow. This close, she could see the glint of the implant chip at the base of Spencer's neck.

Spencer turned and watched as Catherine inserted a catheter and drew out a vial of blood. "I haven't seen you before."

Derek wheeled the trolley behind Catherine to shield them from the main floor. Distracted by Catherine, Spencer didn't notice him pull out a scalpel.

Catherine pressed a cotton ball over the puncture wound and taped a band-aid over the top. She leaned closer and whispered, "I have a message from Ariana."

Spencer turned and stared at Catherine. "She's alive?"

"And she's coming back for you. For all of us."

"I'm sorry," Derek said, raising the scalpel. "This is going to hurt like a bitch."

Fang flopped back onto Derek's bed. "We still don't know exactly when this attack will happen. What if Vulcan discovers our meddling before then? We're no good to anyone in a cell."

"I trust Robyn. You should too."

Fang sat up and gestured at Catherine, who sat on the floor going through the contents of Miranda's folder. "She's barely been out for a week, Derek! Vulcan won't just throw her in a cell next time."

"What choice did we have?" Derek said. "She had to know."

Catherine ignored them as she skimmed through the notebooks, thumbing the stack of photographs, waiting for the meaning of it all to drop into place. Robyn had dreamed of a temple for months, whispering in her sleep, and here it was; the crumbling temple, the mosaics, all of it.

"We can't afford for Vulcan to become suspicious," Fang said, cradling her face in her hands. "Clandestine meetings in your bedroom at the crack of dawn aren't exactly subtle, you know?"

Catherine smoothed out a photo of a ruined temple on the side of a mountain. "Robyn was trying to find this place."

Fang looked at the photo over Catherine's shoulder. "My ex-supervisor, Miranda, found it and was utterly obsessed with it."

"The way Robyn described it, it was beautiful. Gold ceiling, swirling mosaics glittering on the walls, not a ruin like this. But then, she only visited it in the spirit world."

Derek crouched beside Catherine and plucked another photo from the mess on the floor. It showed a dirt-smeared woman laughing beside a tanned young man in a bamboo rice hat.

Fang shook her head with a sigh. "See? Miranda. It doesn't tell us anything."

Derek switched on the desk lamp to better study the photo. "Look at the man beside her."

"It's probably just some poor PhD student helping with the dig," Fang said, returning to her position on the bed. "I've been through every single photo in excruciating detail, Derek. There is nothing to find that we don't already know."

Derek continued staring at the picture, his eyes glazed. Catherine watched him, hoping he might have stumbled across a vital piece of the puzzle. Fang sat ramrod straight, watching them both, a thin line of sweat beading her lip.

Derek snapped to attention and grabbed the photo from Catherine. "This is Brock." He held the picture right up to Fang's face so she could not look away. "And I remember what you did to me in Bulgaria."

24

Fortress

Earth's governments fell like dominoes. The increasing solar flare activity rendered any means of defence useless. The powers of East and West fell and the invisible lines separating nations disappeared. Around the world, houses of parliament became garrisons, curfews were enforced, and the people's suffering increased tenfold. Without a unifying governing presence, disorder reigned. A dark shadow fell across the planet. Its name? The Mitochondrial Research Institute. Its leader? The self-proclaimed polemarch, Professor Vulcan Manning.

Extract from The Last Bastion of the Anthropocene, *Ester Akintola, the final UN Secretary General.*

Robyn checked her launcher for the sixth time. A thick ridge of quartz was inlaid into the sleek metal barrel of the weapon, a glittering intrusion. She focused on the mineral and felt the quartz vibrate slightly at her touch, the weapon lighting up in her hands.

"Whoa, careful there," Ariana said, pulling the launcher from Robyn's hands. With a low whine, the weapon went dark.

"Sorry. Just checking," Robyn said with a small smile.

Ariana studied the launcher for a moment then handed it back. "It's beautiful, in a way."

The sea walker adjusted her carbon polymer armour and sat back down. Across the cabin, Eli spoke softly, issuing instructions to Sara and Chris as they strapped on their armour. Behind them, Ming and Iki lay curled up asleep.

Robyn glanced over to where Fletcher lay wrapped in a blanket, unconscious. They'd had to sedate him and Eva to get them on board. It hadn't been pretty. When Robyn had activated Fletcher's collar, it had sparked and the earth walker fell to his knees, eyes rolling into the back of his head as Ariana jabbed him with the syringe.

Ariana noticed Robyn staring at Fletcher. "Why does the quartz listen to us and not Nyx?"

It was a good question. Robyn thought about her meditations at the temple, the surety she'd felt amongst the ancient crystal mosaics that seemed to whisper to her. Ariana had described it exactly – it was like the crystals listened to them. All living things from every branch of life depended upon energy. Each organism interacted with the cosmic electromagnetic radiation that flowed through them, but only some could actively channel it – the walkers.

"Our DNA," Robyn said. "The walkers' unique convergence sequence allows us to interact with the cosmic energy field around us and manipulate it. Its power is what we harness to cross over to the spirit world and access the walker state."

Robyn ran a finger along the opaque crystal surface, thinking back to her time at the temple, the peace she'd felt there. "That's why the temple was built on a bedrock of quartz. When Liro fought Nyx in the temple, white energy had risen around him and pushed the spirit back, entombing her deep within the Earth. The quartz must have helped. It seems to amplify the walkers' capabilities."

"But not Nyx," Ariana completed the thought. She

looked at Fletcher with a glum smile. "I hope it's enough."

A surge of uneasy energy pulsed through Robyn's limbs. She felt Ariana and Eli's uncertainty and trepidation and it made her sick to her stomach. This was her plan. Her research. If it all went wrong, it would also be her fault.

Robyn shivered as something crawled across her neck and up to her earlobe. It drew her back to the present. "Poppy," she murmured. "That tickles." Jacob, the bee's human partner, remained in Wales helping the tech heads. Yet through Poppy, he was also on this mission. The pair had spent long months of training to expand Poppy's reach in her hive form, harnessing the energy of the spirit world.

The helicopter flew on through the night. Soon snow arced through the helicopter's lights. They were getting closer. Robyn found a spot on the floor to settle down and closed her eyes to meditate.

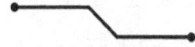

Jacob sat cross-legged on the armchair in Bry's study, electrodes plastered to his scalp. Poppy flickered on his ear, her russet fur glowing. "This is harder than it looks, you know," Jacob said to Kate, furrowing his brow in concentration.

Beside him, Kate sat on the floor where she was monitoring the electrodes' output. "I know, but it's pretty cool how you and Poppy can skim the spirit world and use its energy to keep Poppy in her hive form and our comms working."

Kara spun her chair around, first clockwise then anticlockwise. "But it's weird how it kinda looks like you're just sitting there."

"Cut it out, Kara, some of us are trying to work here," Aster said, glancing over his shoulder from the second monitor. At his laptop, Bohai grinned.

All of a sudden, Kara stopped treating Bry's antique office chair like a fairground ride. "Jesus! His brainwave activity is through the roof."

Kara tossed Jacob another chocolate chip biscuit. "Better keep your strength up. You're the only reason our comms are working through these erratic solar flares. I wish we'd thought of this weeks ago."

Kate cleared her throat. Kara shoved a biscuit in her mouth and threw her sister another.

"No pressure," Jacob mumbled through a mouthful.

Kate fist bumped his leg. "You're freaking killing it."

"Don't I deserve a biscuit too?" Aster said, holding his hands like paws and adopting a pitiful expression. "I've been a good boy too."

"They're supposed to be for Jacob," Kara mumbled, begrudgingly sharing the box around.

Bohai raised his hand. "Ssssh. They've just touched down. It's game on."

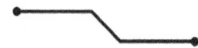

Robyn pressed flat against the snow. The chill crept through her jacket and sank into her bones. Around them, the forest was quiet, still, as if holding its breath. She edged forward, bringing her binoculars to her eyes. HAARP was clearly visible past the forest edge; a jagged burst of buildings and bitumen. The deep hum of the radio array thudded against her chest, making the air as thick as soup. Electricity crackled along the wires, sparking high into the air, and Robyn felt the answering surge of energy in her limbs.

Mindful of Poppy, Robyn gently brought her hand to her ear. "Kara? You with me?"

"Roger that. You're good to go. Parade ground is

clear. We'll deactivate the perimeter security once you reach the compound. Video feeds are already on a static loop of the forest recycled from yesterday. I'll be with you every step of the way."

"Yeah, me too." Kate joined in.

"Uh, forgetting someone?" Aster added, sending a band of static trilling across the connection. Someone snorted – Robyn guessed it must be Bohai.

Kara's exasperated sigh echoed in Robyn's earbud. "Guys, we talked about this. I'm in charge of relaying information. It's confusing otherwise, comprendez?"

Robyn shook her head. What a crack unit. "Would you all please shut up? We have a fortress to storm."

She stashed her binoculars in her backpack and turned to Eli and Ariana lying flat beside her. Ariana tapped her earbud and grinned.

Robyn pushed up into a squat and the launcher shifted against her spine. The weight of the weapon still felt foreign, unnerving. Eli and Ariana's energy tethers pulsed against her ribcage, calm and ready. She glanced at the pair. Gone were the normal teenagers they once were. Now they were warriors.

Fletcher sat in the snow, his closed eyelids twitching,

the quartz collar a rippling disc of pure energy. His tether pulsated against Robyn's ribcage in a barrage of darkness and icy cold. Beside him, Eva stood unnaturally still, her fur radiating with wisps of darkness. As if she sensed the danger, Chris' polar bear, Iki, stood between Eva and Ming, Sara's leopard, flanking the convergers.

Robyn steadied herself. They were out of time. This plan had to work. She slung her launcher off her back and brought it up to her shoulder. With a nod to the others, she led the team through the deep snow and away from the relative safety of the forest.

Robyn hovered her hand against the thick metal fence surrounding the compound and felt the answering thrum of energy.

"Deactivating perimeter security now," Kara said in her ear.

The pull of the electrified fence faded. Robyn touched the wires to confirm the fence was dead before allowing Eli within range. Red light flaring on his arms, the walker slashed a line through the metal. Sara gripped Fletcher's shoulder and propelled him through the gap. Robyn went to follow then paused as Fletcher stared at the radio array and smiled. She felt the answering tug of something stirring deep within him. Suppressing a shudder, Robyn stepped onto the bitumen. The plan would never work without him here, but they were taking a huge risk.

"Time to take down the radio array," Kara said in Robyn's ear.

By deactivating the radio array, the entire compound would be exposed to the ravaging bursts of electromagnetic energy from the solar flares, disrupting Vulcan's control of his human-animal armies around the world and rendering him, and them, helpless.

Gripping her launcher tight across her chest, Robyn signalled toward the towering, ominous array, ready to raise hell.

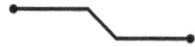

Derek crushed the photograph in his fist. "Now I remember everything – you *drugged* me, knocked me out." He couldn't believe it. This entire time, Fang had been manipulating him, steering him toward her own goals. "I'm nothing to you, am I? Catherine is nothing to you. You can't see past your own lust for power."

Fang held up her hands and stepped away from Derek. "I can explain."

Catherine gathered up the remaining photographs and notebooks and put them in a neat pile on the desk. "Do you two want to explain what this is about?"

Derek snorted and glared at Fang. "Yeah, Fang. Why don't you explain to Catherine why you tried to kill me?"

"It wasn't you I was trying to kill, Derek." Fang wrung her hands. Over the past few months, she'd had fifty versions of this conversation in her head. "It was *Vulcan*, damn it. Obviously, that was an epic fail. I was actually trying to keep you safe."

Derek laughed, a deep ugly sound. Fang appealed to Catherine. "You were there. Remember?"

Catherine nodded slowly, recalling their attack on the MRI base in Bulgaria. After the battle in the arena, Fang had appeared in the MRI laboratory right when Vulcan had a gun aimed at Catherine's head. "You saved me from Vulcan."

"With a syringe in the neck?" Derek shook his head in disgust.

"Yes, but—"

"Don't bother. I've heard enough." Derek grabbed his

tablet and headed for the door. "You're right, Fang. This is stupid and *I* was stupid to trust you. Stupid enough to believe you cared about anyone other than yourself."

Fang followed Derek, grabbing at his sleeve. Her heart thudded in her chest. She couldn't lose him as a friend, she just couldn't. "Derek, that's not true …"

The room plunged into darkness. Derek froze and Fang bumped into him.

"What the hell?" Catherine said, fumbling for the cord to the blind and opening it manually. Gentle sunlight filled the room.

Derek tapped at the keypad by the door. "Damn it," he yelled and punched the wall.

Fang joined Catherine at the window. She surveyed the compound. All was still and quiet. Not a soul was on the grounds. The crackling electricity that always arced between the enormous pylons was absent. "The radio array is down."

Out of the corner of her eye, Catherine saw a faint glimmer of blue and red light. She snapped the blind back down and took Fang by the arm, forcing her to turn away from the window. "Whatever is going on between you two, I think you need to process your feelings. The tension in this room is unbearable."

"What?" Derek blushed and folded his arms across his chest. "That's not what this is. I think you're ignoring the part where she *roofied* me and left me to potentially die."

"Screw both of you." Fang shook off Catherine and opened the blind, letting the morning light shine in. "We don't have time for this. They're here."

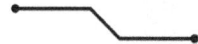

As the radio array went dead, Robyn felt the collective sigh from the trees rustling in relief under their snowy blankets. The air cleared and Robyn took a moment to revel in the peace. Before her, Ariana and Eli glowed with blue and red light as they destroyed the main power station controls.

"The compound is in lockdown mode. You have five minutes before soldiers are mobilised." Kara's voice crackled in Robyn's ear, spurring her forward. The walkers ran alongside her, while Sara and Chris flanked Fletcher and Eva behind them.

"Vulcan's armies are controlled from the main hub in the centre of the compound. Even though the radio array is down, in between solar flares he will still have intermittent control over his armies via the implant chips. You need to destroy the command centre to terminate the link."

"Roger that." Robyn skirted the perimeter of the main building. Eli and Ariana kicked open the door as easily as if it were made of paper.

"We're in," Robyn relayed to base. She scoped the corridor. Behind the string of closed doors came yelling and the sound of fists hammering. "You sure we're safe?" she said to Kara.

"Positive. All internal doors are locked down. Head straight. Take the first left. The command centre will be on your right. You can't miss it."

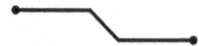

"Well, isn't this great? Trapped in here with a vacuous, cold-blooded, power-hungry villain," Derek snapped, nursing his throbbing hand. "Are you planning on killing Catherine too?"

"Oh for God's sake, Derek, get over it!" Fang balled her hands into fists and shoved them in her pockets to stop herself doing anything else she might regret.

"Did you die? No. Right now, I think we have more important issues to deal with."

Catherine placed herself between Fang and Derek. "I hate to say it, but Derek has a point. You did save me in Bulgaria but a couple of minutes later, you also threatened to kill me. In fact, if it weren't for you, I wouldn't be here in the first place." Catherine stepped toward Fang, her voice laced with steel. "Can we trust you now? Robyn needs to trust you for this to work."

"If you mean, do I want to control the MRI, then no. At least, not anymore." Fang appealed to Catherine and Derek. "Vulcan has gone too far. He's taken my research – *our* research – far beyond the realm of ethics and morality. Coercion, loss of free will, the use of this incredible bond for war, for dictatorship of the planet. I can't stand by and watch that happen. We have to do something."

Fang slumped against the desk. Catherine saw her defences crumbling, her exhaustion showing now the mask had slipped. How hard must it have been to keep pretending to be somebody that you weren't? Beneath the façade, Fang was just like them – trying to do the best with what she had. "You're right. We all want the same thing – to stop Vulcan and save the planet." Catherine shook her head with a wry grin. "I never thought I'd say this, but I believe you. Jesus, what's the world coming to?"

"Complete and utter destruction, if we don't hurry up," Derek said. He turned to Fang and exhaled sharply, his face grave. "Promise not to stab me with any more needles?"

A pained expression flashed across Fang's face as she realised she might never win Derek's forgiveness. "Promise. If you behave yourself," she added in an attempt to lighten the mood, but Derek just shook his head and turned away.

Catherine grabbed a pen off the desk and jimmied it into the door panel. It prised free with a *clunk*, exposing thick cords of coloured wires. She removed her cardigan, balled it into a glove and yanked at the wires.

"Stop!" Fang cried, pushing Catherine aside. "Lockdown protocol has been activated. We can't just start ripping the wires out of the wall – the secondary door will seal us in even tighter." She pulled out her tablet and plugged it into the panel. The smell of singed wool filled the room. Catherine dropped her cardigan on the floor and stomped out the smouldering embers.

"With the radio array down, we're on backup power."
Fang explained. "The generators cycle every ten minutes,
with a thirty-second window during the changeover. If
I overload the circuit during that changeover, the panel
won't register the lockdown protocol." Code flashed
across Fang's tablet. She glanced at her watch.

The panel lit up and with a *ding* the door sprang open.
Fang unplugged her tablet and turned to Catherine and
Derek. "I thought you said we were in a hurry?"

25

Nightmare

An arc of electricity slammed into the wall above Robyn's head. She ducked as chips of plaster rained over her. The flickering lights illuminated the hallway in a staggered burst of fluorescents. At the other end of the hallway stood a group of convergers wearing the distinctive dark bodysuits of the MRI, including a familiar face. "Shit," Robyn said.

"Back again?" Mikey asked, reloading his blaster. His lion pawed the ground and snarled.

Blue light flashed over Ariana's skin. She went to run forward but Eli grabbed her arm. The walkers' unease sat deep in Robyn's stomach. She sensed a movement behind her and turned to see a second group of convergers had blocked the other end of the hallway.

They were trapped.

"Screw you, asshole," Sara shouted, dropping to one knee. She flicked off the safety catch, cocked her head, and fired.

The inhibitor sphere collided with the boy beside Mikey. He grimaced and clutched at his torso. Confused, he studied his sticky fingers. "I'm not hurt," he said.

Robyn began counting down. *One.*

With a grin, Mikey raised his primed blaster. "Oh dear. It looks like you brought the wrong toys."

Two.

"Uh-uh," Sara smirked, balancing her launcher on her shoulder.

It took three seconds for the skin to absorb the inhibitor. Once it entered the bloodstream, the deactivation sequence rapidly cycled through the body, targeting the mitochondria.

Three.

Screaming, the boy stumbled to his knees, clutching his head in agony. His mastiff froze, its eyes filling with fear and confusion.

Mikey's cockiness wavered. He lowered his blaster. "What the hell did you do to him?"

Electrified, the mastiff surged forward and bit the boy's calf before hurtling down the hallway.

"Mika," the boy cried weakly. "She's gone. I can't … feel her anymore."

The temperature plummeted and Fletcher smiled. Dark energy rippled off Eva. Beside the earth walker, Chris grew pale. It was as if Nyx was feeding off the malice and terror.

Fear then rage flashed across Mikey's face. He fired at Robyn, yellow electricity arcing from his weapon. As the bolt skated through the air, Ariana and Eli pivoted and stood back-to-back. Mikey's blaster shot ricocheted harmlessly off their combined energy shield and hit the wall, kicking up a shower of dust.

Then the hallway erupted with a deafening barrage as Ariana, Eli and Sara fired on the gathered convergers. Electricity spiked through the air. Chris ducked low to protect Fletcher, Iki beside Eva. As the inhibitor spheres found their marks, screams echoed from either end of the hallway. Convergers dropped in pain, clutching their skulls.

Robyn aimed her launcher. The quartz vibrated under her palm as it lit up. *Time to stop these convergers in their tracks.* Her first shot clipped a girl in the shoulder. "No," the girl cried as she fell. Her snow leopard ducked away, its nostrils flaring. Robyn kept firing inhibitor spheres, pivoting as they hit their marks. In her ear, she heard Jacob. "It's us or them, Robyn."

Her earbud bled static, despite Poppy's frantic figure eights. "Shit," Robyn muttered, pressing a finger to her ear. No response. Without directions from the crew back in the farmhouse, Robyn was flying blind. Squinting through the dust, she tried to gauge their position. They'd been close to the command centre when they were ambushed. Then she spotted it; a heavyset steel door right behind Mikey.

The unharmed convergers formed up behind Mikey and began marching toward Robyn and her team.

"We have to get to that door," she yelled, pointing to the door. Ariana gave her the thumbs-up and blue light expanded around them in a rush, deflecting a barrage of blaster fire. Most of the electroshocks ricocheted off the energy sphere, all except one. Ariana spun, clutching her shoulder with a hiss of pain.

"... elevator," Robyn caught as her earbud sparked into life then died again. Poppy buzzed desperately against her earlobe. Robyn gasped as the stainless-steel doors ahead of them slid open: a bank of elevators filled the entire length of the hallway in the space separating them from the MRI convergers. Dozens of convergers poured out into the hallway between them and Mikey. Blasters raised.

"Damn it."

How the hell did they mobilise this quickly? She had to get her crew out of here and fast. "Change of plan – into the elevators." Blaster fire rained down on them. Robyn shivered as the temperature continued to plummet and the walkers' auras flickered in and out. She ducked another blaster shot.

"Watch out," Chris shouted, pushing Sara out of Mikey's line of fire in the nick of time.

Then Robyn saw Fletcher. He was walking straight toward the MRI convergers, a beatific grin spread across his face. Eva rolled alongside him, her fur thrumming with dark light. Swearing, Robyn fumbled in her pocket for the electromagnetic receiver that amped up the earth walker's piezoelectric collar. She pointed it at the earth walker and pressed the button. Nothing. Fletcher kept walking. Somehow Nyx was overriding the quartz inhibitor, growing stronger in the conflict.

Eli and Ariana rushed to grab Fletcher. He simply pushed them aside like toys, their red and blue auras dissipating at his touch. Robyn gasped as sharp pain shot through their energy tethers. Thanks to Eva's dark energy aura, the electromagnetic blasts ricocheted off the earth walker. Steeling herself, Robyn nodded at Chris and Sara. Chris' polar bear, Iki, launched herself at Eva, surprising the brown bear who stumbled back toward the elevator. Robyn grabbed Fletcher, hissed in pain. The walker's skin was like ice, but she didn't let go. White light flickered on her skin as she dragged Fletcher toward the elevators, Sara and Chris covering them with inhibitor fire. A blast clipped Robyn's shoulder. She reeled as pain exploded down her arm. Ariana was leaning against the elevator doors to keep them open. As Robyn and Fletcher fell inside, she slapped a sedative patch on his arm. The walker sagged and Eva slumped at his side.

Ariana released the doors and the last thing Robyn saw was Mikey's grinning face.

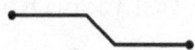

"I repeat, *do not* get into that elevator," Kara yelled,

thumping her monitor. "No, no no! It's a damn trap."
She turned to Jacob in desperation. "Anything?"

Sweat streaked Jacob's forehead. "I'm trying." Poppy
flickered in a haze of pixellated light at the crown of
his head as the pair struggled to repair the spirit world
energy relay that kept their comms working.

Kate peered at his bio readouts, shooting Bohai a
worried glance. Aster pulled up the schematics of the
MRI compound. "Shit. That elevator only has one
destination."

Kara swore under her breath. "I know."

Robyn pushed open the elevator doors, launcher
primed, and gestured for the walkers and convergers to
stay behind her.

The enormous sandstone cavern seemed to go on
forever, fluorescent lights and humming fans the only
modern intrusions. It felt like a cathedral, a sacred
space built in worship of an ancient power. Hundreds of
convergers filled the vast room. Row upon row, at least
twenty deep. Vulcan's disciples, his warriors. At their
head stood Daniel, his bear by his side. He waved his

blaster in greeting. "Welcome. I think this reunion is long overdue, don't you?"

"Oh hell no," Sara said.

Ariana stepped in front of Robyn, moving her arms rapidly though the ancient moves to summon her aura. "You have to get to the command centre. We'll hold them off."

Robyn shook her head, fear twisting in her gut. "No. There's too many. I'm not leaving you."

Derek stopped dead, arms swung wide to halt Catherine and Fang. "Did you hear that?"

Catherine looked up and down the hallway, searching for the direction the sound came from. "It sounds like ... gunfire." *Where the hell were Robyn and the walkers.* "Fang?"

"I'm on it," Fang replied, fingers skimming across her tablet. "The base is definitely under assault. The main skirmish seems to be near the bank of elevators and the command centre."

A burst of static flared over the emergency intercom and Vulcan's gravelly voice filled the air. "Attention all staff. Return to your rooms immediately. The radio array is temporarily down. Backup power will be used to maintain essential systems. Direct any questions to your supervisors. Military personnel will be conducting a sweep of the area as a safety precaution."

Derek took off down the hallway, yelling, "We have to get to the command centre!" Catherine and Fang jogged behind him. "This has to be it. Robyn must be here," Fang murmured.

As they rounded the corner, they nearly collided with a troop of soldiers.

Immediately, the commander braced her weapon across her chest, the safety catch off. "Dr Smith. Dr Fisher. Kindly return to your rooms and take your associate with you."

Derek's eyes darted between the three soldiers and the door that separated them from the main wing of the compound and the command centre.

Fang rolled her shoulders back and straightened to her full height. "We're required in the command centre to oversee re-activation of the radio array," she said, glaring at the commander.

"No, you're not."

The *clack clack* of a cane was unmistakeable. Fang turned, her face carefully blank. "With all due respect, sir, if the array is down, we are the most qualified …"

Vulcan thumped his cane on the floor to silence her. "It's not just the radio array. The compound has been compromised." Vulcan turned to the commander. "Stand down. These three are coming with me."

The soldiers snapped to attention and saluted Vulcan, moving aside to let them pass.

Catherine followed behind Derek and Fang, keeping as far away from Vulcan as humanly possible. The closer they got to the main wing, the more evident the damage became. A lingering cloud of dust blurred the fluorescent lights into a dull haze. Outside the command centre, the acrid smell of blaster fire hung in the air. Vulcan pressed his hand to his ear and spoke into the earpiece. "Secure the command centre while we deal with the insurgents. The major video feeds are down, but I'm confident I know who we're dealing with."

Catherine risked a glance at Derek and Fang and found the same question written on their faces; did Vulcan already know it was Robyn?

Vulcan palmed open the door. Inside, technicians

worked furiously to get systems back online, guarded by a team of convergers. Mikey saluted Vulcan. "I can confirm it is the same group as Bulgaria, sir."

Vulcan grunted. "As I suspected. Hold this position. No-one comes in or out. And if any of these three try anything, you have my permission to shoot."

Derek flinched. "Sir?"

Vulcan narrowed his eyes at his former student. "You must think me an idiot. Your little meetings in your quarters? Removing Catherine from her cell? I've been watching you."

At Derek's shocked expression, Vulcan smiled. "Robyn and her band of rebels will be taken care of."

Catherine stepped forward, ready to tell Vulcan to stick it, but Fang put a hand on her shoulder to stop her.

"We're loyal to the MRI," Fang said. "Our work is the foundation of everything you have accomplished. This is utterly ridiculous."

Vulcan simply looked amused. "The only person you're loyal to is yourself. I don't trust any of you."

Mikey watched Vulcan leave the command centre then turned and sneered down the barrel of his blaster. "Well, *doctors,* if you'd be so kind as to sit down."

"Oh, shut the hell up, Mikey," Fang snapped. "You thick-headed wannabee alpha."

"Fang," Catherine cautioned, "please don't get us all killed."

"Don't tempt me," Mikey snarled.

Derek, Fang and Catherine slowly sat down on the stairs. "Shit," Derek muttered.

Mikey waved his blaster at Derek. "And no talking."

Spencer hated the convergers' gym, hewn deep into the rock like a tomb. She longed for water, for freedom. Standing at the back of the ranks of restless convergers, she went unnoticed. Without Flint, she wasn't one of them. Spencer recalled sitting with her orca, the pain as Flint exhaled her last breath, torn and bloodied on the destroyed arena floor in Bulgaria. Thanks to her orca's sacrifice, Ariana and her teammates had escaped, but without Flint, life was empty.

The MRI tried to pair her with another orca by injecting her with their artificial sequences, but it had failed. Spencer was glad. There would never be another Flint. Not that it stopped the MRI trying; new dosages every week, forced visits to the compound aquarium where the poor animals were kept penned in five metres of water. *No more.* Spencer ran a hand over the bandage at the base of her skull, feeling the rough edges of the new scar she'd carry for life. Derek was no surgeon, but thanks to him, she was one step closer to freedom. Now she was going to give the MRI hell.

Spencer pulled the cobbled-together device from her pocket and twisted it open to standby. The circuits trilled softly. She'd stolen parts from air conditioning panels, tablets and lights around the compound. The convergers around her were completely focused on Daniel, waiting for his signal. No-one noticed her step away and pretend to check her launcher. As the elevator doors dinged open, Ariana and her friends started pouring out. They did notice – too late – when she sprinted toward the rebels.

Despite the circumstances, Ariana smiled when she recognised the familiar blonde ponytail and ferocious expression. Leaving Chris and Sara to support the semi-conscious Fletcher, Ariana unclipped an inhibitor sphere from her belt and hurled it across the gym. Hundreds of convergers watched it sail through the air.

Spencer caught it and slammed it into her homemade bomb. Eli whirled his arms through the energy forms, wreathing Robyn and the others in a protective shield of red energy. Daniel turned to bark orders, and the convergers closest to Spencer pivoted toward her, blasters at the ready.

"This is for Flint," Spencer whispered and lobbed the bomb into the middle of the neat military lines of convergers. It detonated in mid-air, sending a mushroom cloud of pale-white mist cascading over the convergers. She counted her heartbeats as the mist descended. *One. Two. Three.*

Screams filled the room. Animals backed away from their former partners, shrieking and howling in terror. Some convergers raised their blasters but the weapons were inert in their hands, their energy source gone. Daniel stumbled backwards trying to escape his advancing bear, but he was trapped. The bear snarled, bone crunched and Daniel lay still.

Ariana winced and looked away. She scanned the gym for Spencer and found her on the sidelines, staring at the havoc. Leaving the protective embrace of Eli's energy sphere, Ariana sprinted toward her old friend. "Spencer."

The spell broken, Spencer turned and clapped Ariana on the back. "I've missed you, rook." White mist from the inhibitor bomb hung in the air, the veil pierced by unearthly cries.

"Time to go, guys!" Robyn yelled from behind them. "We need to find somewhere safe to keep Fletcher." Chris and Iki stood beside her, Fletcher's limp form draped over Chris' shoulder. Sara stood at the ready with her launcher, covering Chris' exposed flank.

Ariana scanned the gym, looking for an alternate escape route. The elevators were a no-go; dazed convergers were already swarming toward them.

"There's an emergency staircase this way," Spencer said to Ariana, leading her over to a heavy metal door that seemed to blend into the wall itself, partially hidden by a rim of sandstone. Ariana alerted Robyn and Eli, and Sara and Chris followed. Iki shepherded Eva as Chris carried the sedated earth walker.

"Where does it lead?' asked Robyn.

"It'll take us out up the top, near the cafeteria. It's the safest route."

"I hope you're right," Ariana replied.

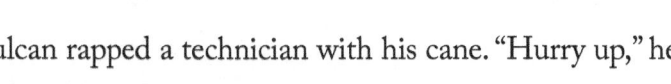

Vulcan rapped a technician with his cane. "Hurry up," he commanded. "I want the system fully operational, *now*."

There were half a dozen technicians crowded into Vulcan's office. A harried-looking man typed code on a laptop connected by a bundle of cables to the backup systems generator. Between them and the door, ten soldiers stood guard.

The video feed flickered on Vulcan's tablet then stabilised. "Show me the convergers' gym."

The man nodded and a new screen flashed up, but all Vulcan could see was white mist. "Fix it," he ordered.

The technician licked his lips and stammered, "That's the live feed, sir."

Vulcan pointed his cane at the screen. "The elevators, this floor. *Now*."

The tablet flickered again, resolving into a view of the elevator doors and the contingent of waiting soldiers. Vulcan smiled. If the convergers had somehow failed to deal with Robyn and the walkers, the soldiers would crush any resistance. Permanently.

The elevator lights lit up. Except, when the doors slid open, crazed animals sprung free, trampling the surprised soldiers in their desperate flight to safety and leaving their convergers cowering in the rear of the cabin. A bear rose up on its hind legs and hurled a soldier against the wall, shattering the video camera into a million pieces.

The technician cowered at his terminal. "Sir? Your orders?"

Vulcan snatched up his tablet and hurled it at him, howling, "To the hub, you idiot! Hurry!"

Robyn peered into the corridor. Empty. Spencer stuck her head around the doorway and pointed. "This way."

Human screams and animal howls bounced off the corridor walls, contorting into a symphony of pain and fear.

"Wedge formation," Robyn murmured, nodding to Sara and Chris. "Protect Fletcher. We need to get to that command centre – together."

On her order, they bolted down the corridor, toward the growing volume of agonised screams. The floor outside the elevator was covered in blood and the metal walls were etched with claw marks. Robyn had to step over the bodies of the MRI soldiers to reach the door panel. After several long seconds trying to get it open, she beckoned for Eli.

Eli brought his hands to the panel and closed his eyes. Una flickered red on his shoulder as light funnelled down his arm. With a hiss, the door slid open.

Inside, operators hunched over their terminals. They turned and stared at Robyn. "Is there a problem?" one managed, her voice strained.

"Change of ownership," Robyn snapped. Eli and Ariana surged past her, rippling with red and blue light. The operators froze. "Up against the wall. Don't move."

Chris and Sara barricaded the door with the vacated desks. Sara jabbed her launcher into the control panel, frying it. The overhead lights flickered but held.

Robyn took a deep breath and studied the enormous screen. Hundreds of video feeds. Hundreds of enslaved animal-human pairs. A complete aberration of the natural link of convergence.

The door shuddered and sparks arced through the middle of the door. "They're cutting their way in," Sara warned. "We don't have much time."

"No, you really don't."

Robyn spun around. Ariana and Eli quickly moved to flank her.

Out of the shadows emerged dozens of convergers. Mikey slowly descended the stairs. "But you just locked yourself into your worst nightmare."

26

Пчх

Mikey calmly raised his blaster and issued the order; "Fire."

The command centre filled with electroshock blasts. Ariana and Eli's auras blossomed from their skin, but even they could not withstand the relentless barrage. Hit, Eli stumbled. Before he could recover, Mikey had him in his sights. Yellow electricity raked Eli's frame and the air filled with the smell of scorched flesh.

Ariana growled and expanded her energy field to encapsulate Eli. Dropping to one knee, Sara kept up a steady return fire, but it was hard to know where to aim as the MRI convergers disappeared in and out of the darkness. Robyn couldn't tell whether she'd hit any of the shadowy figures hiding behind the rear terminals.

Chris pushed Fletcher roughly behind him and tossed Spencer a spare launcher.

"Thanks." Spencer grinned, already sighting down the weapon.

"It's good to have you back, Captain," Chris said, ducking low beside his polar bear. Iki stood beside Eva, huffing nervously and watching the quiet brown bear at her flank. Eva's eyes were dark and her fur rippled with black energy as electroshocks flashed around them. Fletcher sat unmoving, eyes closed, a whisper of a smile on his face.

"Robyn!"

At the sound of her name, Robyn turned. Further along the wall near the door, Catherine stood wedged between Derek and a thin Asian woman. *Fang*, she realised. It had to be. A knot of six convergers surrounded them, blasters raised, but all Robyn felt was relief. *Catherine's all right. She's alive.* For a moment, the rest of the command centre faded away and all that remained was Catherine's face.

Robyn forced herself to look away, to make sense of what was happening. She surveyed the command centre. Above the main terminals sat a larger terminal.

It stood unattended, in the no-man's land between them and Mikey's convergers. And Catherine.

"Cover me," she yelled and sprinted for the stairs. Robyn ducked under an electroshock blast and skidded sideways as another brushed her shoulder. With a silent scream, she dived behind the central terminal. Around her, electroshocks ricocheted off metal like lightning.

Commotion erupted behind her as Fletcher twisted free from Chris' grip and dashed the converger's head against the floor. Iki growled a challenge, but Eva snarled at the polar bear and rose on her hind legs. Iki stepped back to protect Chris, who lay unmoving on the floor, his forehead a bloodied mess. Without a second glance at the wounded converger, Fletcher walked across the battlefield of the command centre, trailing his hand across the row of terminals.

At the sudden wrench of Fletcher's tether, Robyn scanned the room. Chris lay unconscious on the floor. Iki and Eva sidestepped each other, neither ready to make the first move. But when the earth walker turned in her direction, his eyes dark, her stomach lurched.

Fletcher pressed a hand against one of the computer

terminals. Tremors of black light danced across his skin and the computer screen flickered.

"This is beyond even what I imagined," Fletcher said and released a deep, maniacal laugh.

"Get back!" Spencer yelled, moments before the door exploded inwards and the screech of cleaving metal filled the air.

Soldiers in MRI fatigues poured through the door, their footsteps echoed by the powerful thuds of dozens of paws.

Robyn stared in horror at the lions and bears beside the soldiers, at the heavy-duty armour on both humans and animals. She could see the implant chips glinting at the base of their skulls. Robyn drew a shuddery breath. *So many. They needed more time, damn it!*

Spencer crouched beside Chris, shaking him and urging the converger to his feet. Iki, a low growl in her throat, pushed them toward Robyn and the others.

The soldiers parted to make way for a stooped man with a cane who shuffled through the melee to the centre of the room. "This is completely unnecessary," Vulcan declared, waving his cane at the operators cowering against the wall. "Get back to your stations." Casting nervous glances toward the soldiers and their animals and Robyn and the walkers, they resumed their seats. Out of the gloom strode Mikey and his team. With a crisp salute at Vulcan, they joined the other soldiers.

Robyn motioned to Eli and Ariana to desist. The walkers' skin flickered with their energy auras, their faces lit with determination, but there was only one guide. One chosen to wield a power borne of millennia of evolution and bring balance to the world. Against her was one who believed that snatching power and bending people to his will justified death and terror. Robyn stood tall as she met the polemarch face to face for the first time.

"Drop your weapons," Vulcan ordered.

His gaze pierced Robyn like a knife. When Sara sought her confirmation, Robyn hesitated before pulling her own launcher from her shoulder and placing it on the ground.

The smallest smile, no more than a twitch of muscle on Vulcan's face, told Robyn what she wanted to know. Vulcan believed he had the upper hand.

"Step away from the hub, that way nobody gets hurt," he barked.

Robyn looked to Catherine and, in response, her girlfriend raised an eyebrow. *He's lying. He'll say anything to protect his control over his converger armies.* Robyn regarded the enormous terminal, spreading her hands across the screen. *The hub.* They were supposed to have more time. Kara was supposed to be in her ear, talking her through the takedown process. And now she had run out of options.

Robyn looked at the control room filled with convergers. Then she turned her gaze towards the head of the MRI, so certain he was the man in control. This is what Robyn had come here to do. *I have to destroy the implant chip connection.* She studied the images playing out on the enormous wall screen. *Every single one of them around the world.*

Robyn closed her eyes and tuned into the energy coursing through her limbs and looping through her chest. White light blazed beneath her eyelids then energy cascaded through her fingers and surged into the hub terminal.

"No." Fletcher's confident voice carried across the command centre.

Robyn met his resistance, his dark energy unfurling against her own, stopping her efforts. Gasping, she released her grip on the hub terminal.

Fletcher stood calmly at the front of the room, his hands behind his back. Eva swayed beside him, her eyes lost in a gleaming mass of shadows.

"Stand down, boy," one of the soldiers spat. The lion by his side snarled, shaking its mane.

Fletcher smiled and the white light on Robyn's skin dulled. Ariana and Eli yanked her away from the terminal. Eyes watering with pain, she heard Chris swear under his breath as he sagged against Spencer's shoulder.

The soldier's lion roared, the sound reverberating against Robyn's chest. Fletcher's tether thinned to a wispy cord of energy connecting her to the earth walker. The main screen flickered as hyphae of dark energy spiralled across hundreds of video feeds.

With a desperate glance at Catherine, Robyn slowly reached for her launcher. *Run. Get away*, she wanted to scream. The air crackled with energy. The ranks of bears and lions froze and went unnaturally quiet. Silence blanketed the command centre. As one, the animals turned to face the soldiers.

Vulcan rapped his cane against the nearest desk. "What is going on?"

The operators threw up their hands. "It's not us, sir. The system is glitching."

A soldier went to give his lion a reassuring pat. Fletcher tipped his head and the lion snarled then crushed the soldier's arm in its jaws.

As one, the lions and bears advanced. The room filled with agonising screams as claws slashed skin and sliced muscle. The operators rushed toward the door, trampling over one another, desperate to escape, but the crazed animals struck them down. The very animals they'd been monitoring and controlling for months.

Fear froze the scream in Catherine's throat. The bravest of the convergers guarding them raised their blasters, although their arms trembled. Mikey screamed as his lion lunged, its powerful jaws latching onto his arm and flinging the converger across the room.

He landed with a sickening thud and did not move. Catherine slipped between the two convergers directly behind her. Fang pivoted, slamming an elbow into one converger's throat and sent him reeling. The remaining convergers scattered in horror.

Catherine ran through the carnage. A soldier dropped beside her, deep bloody gashes gouged into his chest. She stumbled when a lion pounced on another man's ribcage, splintering bone as it ripped out his throat. The animal raised its bloody maw and growled, defending its kill. Catherine backed into a body and desperately scrabbled for a weapon. Legs, hips, holster … The lion advanced, blood dripping from its jaws as it bared its teeth. With trembling fingers, Catherine raised the rifle. The lion lunged. *Crack*. The recoil jarred her shoulder, sent her head spinning. With a low whine, the lion dropped, eyes rolling back in its head. She fought the urge to vomit, clutching the rifle to her chest. *I have to get out of here.* A hand grabbed her shoulder. Catherine yelped and spun around. It was Fang, a rifle in her hands and brains smattered across her shirt.

"Let's go," Fang cried, pointing upstairs.

Ahead of them, Derek sprinted through the battle, leaping over fallen desks, intent on only one thing – reaching the hub. Numb, Catherine followed Fang.

"Fire!" Robyn yelled. Her heart hammered in her ears, displacing all sense of time as she focused on the fighting around Catherine and Fang. She picked out targets, sending down a barrage of inhibitor spheres. The animals roared as the dye splattered them, shaking their heads to get rid of it. Fletcher's tether pulsed against her ribcage. She spotted him standing by the terminals, hands outstretched, dark energy rippling over his arms. With rising horror, Robyn watched as, one by one, the animals recovered. *Nyx is using the MRI system to control the implant chips.*

Ariana pushed Robyn's blaster down. "It's no use."

A man bounded up the steps and stopped in front of them. *Derek.* Beside her, Ariana's skin flared with blue energy.

Derek held up his hands. "Please. I can help."

Blue light expanded around Ariana in a rush. "Can we trust you?"

He appealed to Robyn. "The hub. I know my way

around the system. I can help you. Please, believe me," Derek pleaded.

Robyn refused to look at him. She turned to Ariana. "Watch him."

Derek leapt over the desk and booted up the hub.

Catherine and Fang ran side by side, skirting around fallen soldiers. "What the hell is happening?" Catherine yelled.

"All I know is that the MRI no longer controls its assets." Fang paused and glanced around the room, then turned her attention back to the bloody obstacle course at their feet. "Can you see Vulcan anywhere?"

"No," Catherine replied, feeling stronger with the weapon in her hand and the hope that Vulcan was no longer in control.

"He's either dead or he's escaped. My money's on him escaping. That man has nine lives." Fang pointed at the stairs, dropping to one knee in front of Catherine. "Derek's at the hub. He should be able to reign this in. Go – I'll cover you."

The moment Catherine saw an opening, she took it, racing up the stairs to where Robyn stood, launcher raised, streaked in blood. A goddess. She ran headlong into Robyn's strong embrace and pulled her in for a desperate kiss: wet, crushing, exhilarating. With a sigh, Catherine released her girlfriend and raised her rifle. "About bloody time, babe."

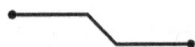

It was dark, all dark. Fletcher floated in the void, adrift. Visual flashes blazed across his mind, gone as readily as they appeared.

Through the blackness a girl appeared. Ana. She flickered like a video-game glitch, her expression sorrowful. "Don't do this, Fletcher. You can fight this."

Fletcher tried to answer, but his body was no longer his. He was just a vessel, trapped inside his mind, the in-between, fading away.

"I know you can," floated Ana's voice.

Fletcher desperately tried to focus on Ana. "How," he managed before an invisible force slammed into him. Cold tendrils spiralled through his limbs, locking his body in a terrifying spasm. His entire world contracted to the pain coursing through his body. "How do I fight something I can't even see?"

But there was no answer; Ana had gone.

A section of darkness lifted like cinema curtains retracting to reveal the main show. Eva roared, spittle flying from her jaw, defending her position in a sea of chaos. *We're at the MRI compound in Alaska.* There was a trek through the snow, a skirmish with Mikey in the hallway then nothing.

Fletcher focused on the flickering images. A room, filled with computers. Fallen bodies barricaded the doorway. A wall of flesh. A reinforced internal glass window shook as animals hurled themselves against it. He felt the brush of their minds, heard their single purpose. *Kill them.* No! It was his voice, hurled back at him in a chorus of death. *Kill them. Kill them. Kill. Them.* Lions and bears with bloody jaws and froth at their lips. The mauled bodies of convergers littered the command centre. Animals heaved shuddering final breaths. *This is my fault. It's all my fault.* Despair filled Fletcher as he realised he was powerless to stop Nyx's puppetry of his own body. A black aura blossomed inside his body like a disease.

Horrified, Fletcher watched it spread. He pushed all his strength into a single thought. *Stop this.*

Through the blackness surged another voice that

seemed to come from nowhere and everywhere all at once. *You are my vessel, earth walker.*

The animals continued hurtling against the glass. Tiny cracks whispered across its surface.

You will all be removed from this Earth and I shall be free once more.

Fletcher saw Ariana and Eli by Robyn's side, Sara, Spencer and Chris behind them.

Desperation filled his mind. *But it's not yet the solstice.*

Yes, but you have delivered to me something so much stronger.

Fletcher saw an image of the radio array. *But we destroyed it.*

Not for long. A small sun, yet powerful enough.

Then crippling pain, as if he'd grabbed hold of a live wire. Fletcher shuddered, trying to maintain a grip on his mind. The quartz collar around his neck cleaved in two and clanked to the floor. A moment of relief before Nyx's dark energy surged through his system and choked him.

It is time to reclaim this planet. Remove the scourge of humanity and the feeble spirits who chose you.

Whoomp! The window shattered and tiny shards

of glass rained down. Oblivious to the razor-sharp fragments lacerating their paws, the animals leapt into the room: wolves, coyotes, bears, tigers and jaguars. Trailing bloody footprints, they stalked the group huddled in the centre of the room. Around and around they circled, closing in on their prey. Through the thick haze of pain, Fletcher saw it was his friends. Blackness tightened its grip around his throat.

27

Attack

"Robyn! Robyn, can you hear me?" Kara screamed in her ear.

"Oh thank God, yes!" Robyn yelled over the chaos. "Fletcher's up to something, I don't know what ..."

A deep hum filled the command centre.

"What the ... I'm getting abnormal energy readings here," Kara said. "Oh, shit."

"The radio array is back online," Fang called out over the cacophony of terror and pain. She dropped to one knee and shot an advancing bear. With a bleating wail, the animal collapsed.

"I recognise them," Spencer whispered. "These animals are from the convergers' gym, or at least, the ones that used to be paired with convergers."

A cold chill ran down Robyn's spine as Fletcher's tether warped, and the world teetered around her.

Catherine grabbed her arm to steady her. "What's happening?"

"Fletcher," Robyn forced out, eyes locked on the earth walker. "Nyx."

A chorus of howls echoed around the command centre.

"Iki, what's wrong?" Chris' polar bear shook her head from side to side, her shoulders tensed. Chris moved to comfort her, but the polar bear reared and knocked him to the ground.

Ming squirmed in pain then turned to Sara with dispassionate, savage eyes.

"Please, Ming, I know you're still in there."

The leopard pounced. Sara desperately tried to fend her off, but Ming managed to sink her teeth into Sara's leg. She screamed in agony. Blue light flared on Ariana's skin and she used her aura to force Ming to retreat. The leopard hissed and prowled to a safer distance.

Just as Iki lunged, Eli's energy aura pushed Chris sideways.

Robyn realised what was happening. Nyx, via Fletcher,

had co-opted the MRI's implant chip system to control the animals. Except why were Iki and Ming no longer responding to Chris and Sara? Then she understood: *because they're both terrestrial animals.* Somehow, Nyx had used Fletcher to control every earth-bound animal. *Whether they had a chip or not.*

Pain ripped through Robyn's flesh like jagged wire. She gasped and fell to her knees. Fletcher's energy tether had connected to something powerful – the radio array.

Ariana watched Robyn collapse. She grabbed Eli's sleeve. "We have to do something. I know you're not going to like it, but we need to—"

"Return to the void. I know." Eli sat cross-legged, red light glimmering against his skin.

Ripples of fear coursed through Ariana's mind. "Last time we tried to enter the void, it nearly ended in disaster."

"Nyx has given us no option."

Ignoring the gunshots and screams, the fatigue, the blood on her armour, Ariana shut her eyes. Her skin hummed with blue light and the battle faded away. Jericho's tail tickled her ear and energy whispered through her limbs.

Her mind cleared. Ariana opened her eyes and found herself in complete darkness, her body weightless, surrounded by the familiar blue light of her energy aura. Jericho swirled through the vacuum beside her.

I am here with you. Atlantis' voice echoed through the blackness.

A whisper grew around Ariana, building into a chanting harmony. People appeared in the darkness, extending outwards in a spiral. In the centre stood Yves, hands outstretched, his eyes kind. "It is time, young sea walker. You must open the portal between the worlds and destroy Nyx's hold over the planet and the earth walker."

The flickering visions of past sea walkers never wavered. They gazed at her with such intensity that it kindled her courage. A deep thudding reverberated in her chest, sending a wave of energy cascading through her system, buoying her up.

Robyn blinked several times, but it wasn't a trick of the light, or the smoke, or the pain. Eli and Ariana hovered above the floor, encased in their energy auras. The strength of their energy tethers eased the pain of her connection to Fletcher. She managed several rasping breaths, braced herself on her forearms and pushed herself up. Catherine helped her to her feet.

Derek turned away from the console, his face grim. "It's not working. Fletcher — or whatever he is — has locked me out."

As if he had heard his name mentioned, Fletcher looked up at Robyn and sent her a smile. His eyes were completely black.

"Ariana?" Eli's question pierced the darkness.

The blue visions of her past selves faded away, except for Yves. Ariana sent her mind spinning in the direction of the air walker's voice. "Can you hear me?"

"I'm with Clara. She says it's time."

"I know."

The void reverberated, contracting with power not of their making. Dark energy swirled around Ariana, permeating the very fabric of the void.

"The dark spirit is strong here, even without the power of the solstice. She is drawing power from another source." Fists clenched, Yves stepped in front of Ariana as if to protect her from the undulating dark energy.

"Nyx must be using the radio array." Ariana's heart sank. The ancient spirit had discovered a mini-sun right here at HAARP.

"Concentrate," Yves urged. He pressed his palm against his heart. "We are all within you. Our strengths, our memories, our courage. Now you must go further than any of us ever did."

Eli burst through the darkness, Una gliding behind him. Ariana swore she caught a glimpse of a slender girl in a sari by Eli's shoulder. *Clara.*

Red tendrils of energy snaked outwards from his body. Ariana lifted her hands and sent out an arc of blue energy to meet it.

"Now!" Eli said.

Ariana's entire world contracted to the push and pull of energy in her body. She dived deeper and deeper within herself, dancing slowly through the transitions Atlantis had taught her many, many months ago, aware of Eli mirroring her movements. The void thrummed, drawing on their energy, churning, turning in on itself, re-folding into something new, something long forgotten. Ariana felt stronger than she ever had. Surrendering to the reservoir of energy within, she moved; thinking body, dancing mind. The void embraced her, the humming like an ancient chant building in volume. It permeated every atom of her being.

Abruptly, a discordant note. Icy cold crept up her spine and dulled the energy flow. Pain cleaved her skull and Ariana hung motionless, like a puppet whose strings had been cut. The enormous reservoir of energy went still.

Ariana watched in terror as her energy aura began to dissipate. In her peripheral vision she saw the thick tendrils of Eli's red energy contract inwards, his energy aura reduced to a dull sheen coating his limbs. Yves had gone. Clara had gone. They were alone.

An invisible hand curled around her skull and, out of the darkness, Fletcher emerged. "Goodbye, walkers."

Not Fletcher. Nyx. Her worst fears realised. Nyx via Fletcher planned to stop them opening the portal. The vice around her skull tightened. Ariana's mind became hazy and her vision blurred.

Ariana focused all her energy into moving her hand. Ever so slowly, her fingers trembled, rebelling against the invisible force that had her in its grip. With all her will, she reached out to Eli.

No tricks this time, sea walker, Nyx warned.

"Fletcher, please fight this," Ariana forced out through her locked jaw, her heart aching for the sweet boy trapped within the dark spirit's merciless grip.

Fletcher is no longer here. Only I remain, and before Ariana could respond, pain exploded through every bone, muscle and tendon. The void swallowed her screams.

Robyn stumbled backwards as the animals weaved between computer monitors, under desks, advancing on her and her team. They were everywhere at once, co-ordinated and deadly. She felt the smooth wall behind her. Nowhere to go. Through the jagged remains of the internal window came the sounds of battle as more animals roamed the corridors beyond. A wolf slunk behind the central hub and disappeared. Robyn searched for Catherine's hand, entwined their fingers. "I'm so sorry for everything."

"It's not your fault."

Robyn wasn't so sure about that. But, if this was it, she had one thing she had to say. "I love you."

Catherine's thumb pressed into the soft skin of Robyn's wrist. "Me too."

A wolf leapt at Derek and latched onto his arm. Screaming, he defended himself with his free arm just as a bear seized his leg. Sara ripped a monitor free from its cables and hurled it at the wolf. The animal squealed and dropped to the floor, scurrying away. Now free, Derek pushed the bear away with one hand and repeatedly punched it in the snout until it released him. He stumbled away, blood running freely down his arm and legs. Fang pushed in front of him and emptied her stolen rifle across the desks and abandoned monitors. Animals fell with strangled cries.

Iki roared and charged toward them. Sweat and tears mixed on Chris' cheeks as he raised his launcher. "Come on, girl," he sobbed. "It's me."

"Don't be stupid, Chris," Sara hissed, trying to push through the pain and get to her feet. "It's not her anymore!"

He didn't answer her. Raising his weapon, Chris brought it crashing down against the polar bear's skull. Iki dropped to the ground, unconscious.

A wolf grabbed Sara by the ankle and pulled her to the floor. Without her willing them, Robyn's arms glided through the air. Energy hummed through her fingertips and released a flash of white light. The wolf yelped and slunk away.

Sara scrambled to her feet and limped over to Chris. The boy stood frozen, staring down at his polar bear.

Sara pulled him into a hug. "We'll get them back, I know we will."

Robyn surveyed the semi-darkness. Illuminated with each glitch of the fluorescent lights, she saw fur and blood and still bodies. And, in the middle of it all, like some triumphant ancient god on a battlefield, stood Fletcher. He, the seething source of electromagnetic energy, linked to satellites beaming power across the world.

"What the hell is going on?" Fang said, lowering her rifle and looking around for answers.

Derek tore the remnants of his shirt into strips and tried his best to bandage the worst of his wounds. He paused long enough to look over to Fletcher, lit up by the enormous flickering screen. "The spirit Nyx is controlling Fletcher."

Fang knelt down to help him. "This is what Miranda's notebooks were trying to warn us about."

Robyn turned back to the walkers. Eli and Ariana

still hovered above the floor, encased in their energy auras. Hopefully, this was a good sign. It was up to them now. Her job was to protect them. They had to survive. Robyn steadied her launcher. Beside her, Catherine raised a jagged plank of wood, the remains of a shattered desk. Derek looked at his blood-soaked arm. His bare chest heaved as he picked up a discarded rifle with his good arm, Fang by his side.

Robyn looked at the slight woman, smeared in blood. A gash stretched from her eye to her lip. Robyn touched it with her fingertip. "That promises to leave a nasty scar."

Fang just smiled. "It will give me a good story to tell when I'm old."

Robyn chuckled. "Provided we live that long."

"Eva?" Catherine whispered.

Robyn turned to ask what she meant. Then she saw the brown bear had left Fletcher's side. The other animals moved aside as Eva approached the stairs to the hub. The broken steps reverberated beneath her paws as she slowly made her way toward Robyn.

Memories flashed through Robyn's mind. Travelling on the bear's solid, warm back through the forest.

Sleeping pillowed against her stomach, falling asleep to her heartbeat. "Eva," she called. "We're your friends, your family. Fletcher wouldn't want this."

Eva turned her gaze on Robyn; her eyes were vacant. The rich green of the forest had gone. No. Eva had gone. This animal was merely a vessel for Nyx. Eva died months ago in Bulgaria. Robyn stepped away from the advancing bear and tightened her grip on her launcher.

Then Eva did the unthinkable. She pivoted away from Robyn and lunged sideways. Catherine barely had time to raise her arms in a desperate attempt to defend herself. Robyn braced for an attack that never happened, losing crucial seconds before she processed what the bear was doing. Her legs sluggish, as if wading through molasses. *Not Catherine. Please, not Catherine.* Too late, energy welled in her limbs. Eva was already sailing through the air.

Derek dived at Catherine and shoved her aside. In the split second before the bear slammed into him, Derek turned to Robyn. She registered the thin smile, the sorrow in his eyes. The unspoken apology. Then Eva roared and connected with Derek, crushing him against the wall.

Catherine crawled toward Robyn. Robyn pulled her to her feet. "You're alive. Thank God."

The bear huffed and sniffed at Derek, who lay slumped on the floor.

"Derek!" Fang yelled, smothering her face with her hands.

Eva swung around. She flicked her head between Fang and Robyn and Catherine, as if she couldn't decide who would be her next victim.

Dark energy rippled across Eva's flanks. The bear huffed and Eli and Ariana fell to the ground. Their bodies convulsed, their pain ricocheting through their energy tethers straight into Robyn's ribcage. With a stifled shriek, she crouched beside them.

Eva roared again and the remaining animals heeded her call. They formed a tight ring around Robyn and the others, their bright eyes flashing in the semi-darkness.

28

Sacrifice

"Fletcher. Fight this. You have to," Ariana managed to splutter through the paralysing pain. She clutched the threads of her aura as darkness snaked around her hands, her feet, her head. Ariana screamed.

Ariana?

Fletcher, his presence embedded deep in her consciousness. Ariana reached for him and pulled Eli into the connection.

I'm scared. I don't know how to stop this.

Ariana focused on their tethered minds, pushing aside the pain. *We can do this together. It's why we're here. To open the portal, destroy Nyx.*

I can't. I'm not in control of my own body anymore. I can't stop killing them.

Fletcher, please.

Part of me ... wants to.

I'm sorry ...

Ariana focused on every memory she had of Fletcher: meditating together in the forest, the joy when they entered the spirit world for the first time, just the two of them. Eli added his memories to the stream of consciousness. Training, feeling the push and pull of their energy auras, running through the forest, the warmth and love of the strange little family at the earthship. The darkness wavered, began to recede, and her aura surged.

Eva shook her head in confusion. The other animals also paused. Eli and Ariana twitched then lay still.

Robyn took advantage of the bear's momentary distraction to check on the walkers. She felt for their pulses; sluggish, their breathing shallow. *I can't lose them.* Helpless, Robyn scanned the faces looking back at her; Catherine, Fang, Sara, Spencer and Chris against the wall, next to the motionless walkers and Derek. Everyone trusting that she could do something about this. Robyn froze. *Wait – maybe there is.*

Focusing, she willed the white light on her skin to bloom. A faint glimmer answered her call. She'd been able to help the walkers in the void last time – maybe she could again. It was worth a shot. What was her one life, when compared to the vast interconnected world, the millions of life forms on this planet that she could save? A speck of cosmic dust, destined to be part of the living, breathing ecosystem forevermore.

"I have to help them. It's our only chance," Robyn whispered to Catherine then took her place between the two walkers and gripped their hands.

Catherine knelt in front of her and pressed her forehead to Robyn's. "I'll be here when you get back." Catherine closed her eyes, her lashes wet with tears, lips trembling.

Robyn stilled Catherine's quivering lips with a kiss, wishing she had time to express all she felt. Gratitude. Apology. Goodbye. Then she plunged into darkness, colours dancing beneath her eyelids. Red and blue.

Concentrating on Eli and Ariana's energy tethers, Robyn hurtled through the darkness. Flashes of light skittered past like stars. She felt weightless, composed only of atoms, breaking down into light itself. Abruptly, she stopped. White light flared on her skin. Before her hung Eli and Ariana, surrounded by red and blue light. From the darkness between them emerged the faintest glimmer of green. *Fletcher.* Robyn felt the gentle tug of his energy tether.

Ariana's expression was calm despite the turmoil ravaging through her energy tether. *We're getting through to him.*

Robyn dipped into the shared pool of memories, added her own. Embracing Fletcher in front of the earthship in the early hours of the morning, absorbing his despair, his fear. How she loved him as if he were her own brother. How strong, how good, how brave he was. Fletcher's energy tether swelled and green light pulsed around him.

The darkness receded. Ariana felt more alive than she ever had. Pulsating with white light, Robyn fed her energy to the walkers. Ariana opened herself up, acting as a conduit for something bigger.

Yes. Atlantis' voice resonated in her mind. Beyond that, Ariana heard the faint echo of another spirit through her connection to Eli; Notos, the air spirit. The layered inflections created a calming harmony. *Together, you must open the portal.*

Light burst outwards from her aura then accelerated and penetrated the very fabric of the void. Red light overlapped the blue, strengthening and gaining momentum.

Catherine shielded her eyes against the blinding white light shining from Robyn. Beside her, Eli and Ariana glimmered red and blue. Green light crept along Fletcher's slumped form. The room began pulsating with a strange brightness. Debris whirled through the air as if funnelled by the walkers. The remaining glass shattered, pulverised into glittering dust. Sara went to protect Ariana and Eli, but Catherine grabbed her. "Don't. I think this is something only they can do."

Red light from Eli's chest surged toward Fletcher, followed by blue light from Ariana. At the contact, Fletcher bucked and jerked but then green light on his chest brightened and spread over his limbs. Wreathed in white light, Robyn sat motionless, gripping the hands of the air and sea walkers.

You are the earth walker. You are connected to the earth spirit, to this planet, to us, Ariana urged. Visions of her past selves flickered into being, faint but present.

Fletcher's voice was choked and ragged. *I'm not like you. I've never been half the walker you and Eli are.*

Ariana and Eli felt his despair, his suffering.

We're so close. I know you can stop this, Fletcher, projected Eli.

I've already destroyed so much … I don't know if I can. Fletcher's green energy began to fade.

No! That was Nyx, not you. You are strong, kind and brave. Come back to us, Fletcher. Together we are strong. We can destroy Nyx and restore balance to our world.

Green light exploded from Fletcher and coalesced into a vibrant helix.

Ariana gasped as energy swelled within her, racing through her limbs, through her blood, through the very atoms that made her. She felt as if she had burst apart and was being re-made. For an instant, she was at one with the universe, with energy, and the light.

Sacrifice. Eli's voice, calm in her mind. What was her body, her life, in the face of this? To long for a particular collection of atoms, a temporary body, when beyond the self was this boundless, eternal space? To give up her one small life didn't seem like a sacrifice.

Ariana embraced the void and their three auras fused into one; a searing sphere of bright white light.

Together, the earth spirit sang, suddenly free.

Together, the air and sea spirits chimed.

Robyn came back into herself with a yelp of pain. She'd barely opened her eyes when Catherine pulled her into a hug.

"You're all right," Catherine said, tears glazing her cheeks.

"They did it." Robyn held Catherine tight, watching the white light recede from the room.

Fang crouched down beside the walkers. "They're not waking up."

She was right. Eli and Ariana hadn't moved. Robyn gently shook the walkers. When they didn't respond, panic bubbled up inside her. *No.* This couldn't be happening. She'd been there. They'd reached Fletcher and restored his energy aura. They'd saved him.

She scrambled to her feet and slid over the smashed desks, landing next to the earth walker. He lay slumped on the floor, but when Robyn gently shook him, he stirred. He was alive! Fletcher groaned, and green light flickered over his skin, free from the contaminant darkness. Robyn crushed him to her chest. "It's over. You're safe."

Bewildered, Fletcher looked around the command centre, taking in the destruction. "But I can still feel Nyx."

"That's not possible ..." Robyn began to explain but she was drowned out by the roar of a bear.

Eva reared up on her hind legs. She roared again, the sound reverberating around the room. Her dark eyes were fixed on the inert forms of Ariana and Eli slumped on the floor.

Fletcher's eyes filled with sorrow. "She's not really Eva. She's a manifestation of Nyx's dark energy, but somehow I can still feel her."

Robyn released her hold on Fletcher and sprinted toward Eva, hurdling desks and fallen bodies. With an otherworldly snarl, Eva charged the walkers. "No!" Robyn screamed. Eli and Ariana were still adrift in the in-between. If Nyx reached them while they were undefended, she'd kill them and destroy the walker lineages forever.

Fang fired, emptying her rifle into Eva's chest, but the bear kept coming. She scrabbled backwards toward Catherine and the convergers, who formed a guard in front of Ariana and Eli. Eva simply barged through them, but not before Robyn managed to twist her fingers through the bear's fur.

Robyn yanked hard and the bear swerved, howling in rage. Rolling onto her side, Robyn leapt to her feet, ignoring the fear racing through her blood. Claws bit into her flesh, sliced cleanly through muscle, and Robyn fell. The bear loomed over her. She struggled to pull herself upright, but a jagged edge of bone penetrated her shin. In desperation, Robyn tried to summon energy from her body, but it was impossible to focus. She couldn't move, couldn't escape.

"No. More." Fletcher's voice cut through the chaos. He climbed onto a broken desk and surveyed the command centre. Green light surged from his limbs and a ring of figures flickered around him. "This ends now."

A sudden explosion of green light. An inhuman shriek of pain.

With a splutter, Ariana and Eli awoke. Robyn

shielded her eyes with her forearm against the impossible brightness of the walkers' combined auras. White light blossomed across her skin and her aura joined forces with those of Ariana, Eli and Fletcher.

Eva crumpled. The dark light coalesced like a black hole and imploded into nothingness, sending a blast of energy shooting across the command centre.

Silence. Sunlight filtered through the rain of powdered glass and metal. It was almost beautiful, in a nightmarish hellscape kind of way. Robyn's vision clouded, bright lights dancing beneath her eyelids. Red, green, blue.

29

Resilience

"The MRI has fallen. Today we can confirm reports of a skirmish at a military compound in Alaska involving members of a resistance group backed by former UN Secretary General Ester Akintola. The resistance group is responsible for the global takedown of the converger armies that have occupied all major centres throughout Europe, Asia and the Americas ... The number of casualties remains uncertain but the global yoke of oppression has been lifted ... around the world, celebrations continue."

"Extraordinary discovery ... convergers on all continents ... scientists are confirming the activation of an ancient gene sequence located on the mitochondria in the wake

of a tremendous energy surge ..."

"Recently acquired a partner animal? Drop in to your local vet for a check up!"

"Solar energy levels are off the charts! According to cosmic energy specialists, the intensity of cosmic radiation is responsible for the spectacular auroras we have witnessed over the past week. We can expect an even more dramatic lightshow next month with the coming solar storm ..."

Extracts from global news providers in the aftermath of the fall of the MRI, as quoted in Equilibrium, *by Ester Akintola, first elected Polemarch of Earth.*

Robyn woke to the warm embrace of sunlight. She sat up and waited for the dizziness to subside, revelling in the breeze blowing through the open window. Memories surfaced. She regarded her right leg, heavy and useless, wrapped in a cast bearing an array of signatures. She recognised Sara's loopy handwriting, Jacob's pensive scrawl, but there were many others she couldn't place.

She stretched out slowly to read them all, hitting a mound of blankets at the end of the bed. "Ow," the blankets said. Robyn chuckled as Lenti emerged from his nest. "It's good to see you, monk."

"And you, guide." Lenti jumped down from the bed and bowed. "I am so very honoured to have served you, Robyn. Your bravery will go down in history." The monk peered out of the privacy curtain and then stuck his head back in. "But right now, I'm going to go find you some decent food."

After Lenti disappeared, Robyn settled back against the headboard and looked across at Catherine asleep in the chair by the bed. Robyn stroked her hair and the sleeping figure stirred.

"Robyn?" Catherine murmured, her voice heavy with sleep. Then she snapped upright. "You're awake!"

A flash of red darted onto Catherine's lap, startling Robyn and sending a fresh wave of pain through her system. "What is that?" she groaned, rubbing her head where she'd banged it against the headboard.

Catherine smiled, patting the little red fuzz ball as it rearranged itself into a comfortable position.

Robyn caught a glimpse of a damp snout. "A fox?"

"Well, when you and the walkers destroyed Nyx, the portal between our world and the spirit world opened." Catherine stood, the fox snuggled into her arms, and kissed Robyn's forehead. "There are more convergers now than I could ever have dreamed."

Robyn stared at the fox cub. If what Catherine said was true, then this was more amazing than she had ever imagined. She pulled Catherine into a hug. "And how are Eli and Ariana?" she said into Catherine's shoulder.

Catherine let her go and pulled her phone from her jeans pocket. She tapped out a quick text and smiled. "See for yourself. There's a line of people desperate to visit. Anyone would think you have been here four weeks, not four days."

She passed Robyn a glass of water. "Drink up. A lot has changed while you've been slothing about. The MRI is history. All evidence of their operation at HAARP has gone. It's a whole new world."

The privacy curtain flung open and people flooded in. Kate and Kara squeezed in alongside her good leg. Sara and Jacob jumped on the end of the bed, nearly pushing the mattress off and Robyn with it. Jacob passed Robyn a jar of golden honey, murmuring that it was a thank you gift from him and Poppy.

Ariana and Eli arrived last. Eli deposited a bouquet of wildflowers on the bedside table. Ariana threw her arms around Robyn. "We missed you so much."

Tears rolled down Robyn's cheeks. "I didn't know if you were going to make it back."

"We almost didn't," Eli murmured.

Ariana took Robyn's hands in hers. Memories of the maelstrom of death that had greeted them at the MRI compound came rushing back.

"Hey, I'm here too, you know," floated a voice from the other side of the privacy curtain. "How about sharing some of the sympathy?"

With a theatrical flourish, Ariana opened the curtain to reveal Fletcher lying in the next bed. He waved at Robyn, his eyes filled with familiar warmth. Robyn squealed with joy and gestured for the boy to come and give her a hug. But now he was back to his old self, Fletcher settled for giving her hand a squeeze. His energy tether thrummed against Robyn's ribcage. She had never felt anything quite so good. This was how the guide was supposed to feel – whole.

"I'm not meant to be up yet," he said with a shrug,

"But I'm feeling much better."

"He needs rest," Catherine said, pushing him back into his own bed like a mother hen. Kate took the opportunity to grab a bag of chocolates off the bedside table and dump the treats onto Robyn's bed.

"I'll sit with you," Ariana said, perching next to Fletcher. She tidied a lock of hair that had fallen across his eyes, stroking his cheek as she did so. "We did it. The world is finally in balance."

Fletcher grinned and sank into his pillows with a contented sigh.

"I'd hardly call this … balance," said a familiar voice.

Kate and Kara shifted aside. Fang lay propped up in the opposite bed. She looked pale and an array of monitors beeped by her shoulder. An older man sat on one side, a frog peeping out of his coat pocket. On the other chair, Bohai snored gently in his sleep. A tight little ball moved across Fang's chest and the head of a baby panda peeked out from its sanctuary in Fang's hospital gown. Fang stroked its soft fur.

"It's good to see you." Robyn grinned at her enemy-turned-friend, but her smile faltered as Fang's face dissolved into tears.

"Derek is dead."

The twins froze, chocolate in their hands. Kara pushed the treats aside and turned to Robyn. "We were planning to tell you once you were better," she said.

"By the time the backup team got to you, he was already gone," Kate added. "I'm so sorry."

Robyn tried to assimilate the news. She'd hated Derek for so long for betraying them, yet in the confines of that command centre, Derek had revealed his bravery.

Catherine squeezed her hand. "He saved my life."

"I never got to thank him; to forgive him," Robyn choked out. She remembered meeting Derek when she'd arrived on his doorstep with Fletcher and Eva and he'd taken them in. The stoic Derek who'd spent long hours in the lab by her side. Yes, he'd made mistakes but ultimately, Derek had proved to be a true friend.

"I'm sure he knows, Robyn," Brock said from the open doorway, one arm slung over Miranda's shoulder, the other holding a paper bag.

"I hope we're not intruding," Miranda asked, edging into the room.

Fang managed to turn an even paler shade of white. "No, it's not possible. You're dead."

Brock nudged Miranda toward Fang's bed. She fiddled with an earring, clasped then unclasped her hands. "I'm sorry, Fang. Vulcan didn't understand. I had to find a way to avert the solar storm, to help the walkers destroy Nyx. It was the only way."

Fang pulled herself upright. Her panda squeaked and disappeared further inside the folds of her hospital gown. "You made me believe in the work I was doing, when all I was doing was helping Vulcan."

Miranda sat on the corner of Fang's bed and regarded her with a soft smile. Her hand slid along the bed covers until their fingers were almost touching. "I also left you my notebooks. I'm proud of you, Fang. When it counted, you made the right choices."

Fang stared at their hands. No-one said anything. Catherine mouthed, what's going on? Robyn shrugged. She had no idea what Fang was thinking. Whatever emotions she had were buried deep.

Fang snapped to attention. Rummaging around inside the chest of drawers beside her bed, she produced a ring bound lecture pad. "I've been working on a theory that unifies the energy and thermodynamic potential of the physical and spirit world."

Fang's father stood and gestured to his chair. "Please, take mine. I need to stretch my legs."

Miranda smiled and pulled the chair closer to the bed. "Show me where you're up to."

Brock sauntered over to the throng surrounding Robyn and thrust the paper bag at her. "Grapes. Apparently, that's what you give someone when they're in hospital."

Robyn smiled and peeked inside the bag. Red ones, her favourite, but Brock already knew that.

"I'm glad to see you're all right. All of you." Brock bowed lightly toward Eli, Fletcher and Ariana. "It's an honour to meet you properly, young walkers."

"You, uh, don't really need to bow," Eli mumbled, turning a bright shade of crimson.

Ariana smirked. "I don't know, I kinda like it."

"Yeah, I could get used to it," Fletcher added.

"Uh, what about me?" Jacob ran a hand through his hair, dislodging Poppy. With a buzz, she coasted down to his shoulder.

Sara punched his other arm. "You did good. Thanks for having our backs." She bent down and stroked Ming. The leopard purred and nuzzled her hand.

Robyn swallowed past the lump in her throat. They'd lost friends but she felt whole, at peace. It was hard to believe that the MRI was gone and the world was safe. Harmony had been restored.

"Make way, coming through," Lenti called as he held a tray aloft with one hand and swatted Kara's hand away with the other. "This is Robyn's breakfast."

"Geez, I wish I had a personal monk attendant," Kara said, rolling her eyes as she reached for another one of Robyn's chocolates on the bed.

Brock chuckled, then reached into his pocket. With a flourish, he produced a cluster of glittering quartz crystals hanging on leather thongs. "I've brought each of you a present."

Robyn rubbed the smooth crystal between her fingers and leaned forward so Catherine could drape it over her head. Instantly, the walkers' energy tethers clarified. "Oh," she whispered.

"Temple crystal. We've been working to improve its conduction capability. The leather has been soaked in a chlorophyll-mycelial solution to enhance its range of frequencies." Brock winked at her. "Thanks to your research, Dr Greene."

"An electromagnetic energy conductor," Catherine murmured approvingly.

"This is kind of cool," Jacob said, slipping the leather thong around his neck. Poppy clung to the crystal, flickering in and out of her hive form. "Poppy likes it."

Ariana pulled her own necklace out of her shirt with a sheepish grin. "Eli and I have been trialling the temple crystal necklaces with Brock and Lenti."

Robyn raised her eyebrows. "Trialling them how?"

Red light flickered on Eli's skin and Robyn felt his excitement through his energy tether. "With meditation and practice, anyone can enter the spirit world now."

"Thousands of people are finding their partner animals every day," Brock added. "Thanks to you, Robyn, it's a whole new world." He swept his arms wide. "Thanks to all of you."

Robyn squeezed the crystal in her hand and choked back a sob. Around her, heartbeats chorused in a steady thrum. Energy flowed freely through her veins. *A whole new world.*

30

New World

To: Hypatia

From: <u>polemarch@earthcouncil.org</u>

Subject: Thank you

Thank you, friend. You and your group of resistance fighters accomplished what the world's military and judicial might could not. I am honoured to have played a small part in your victory over the MRI and the dictator-to-be, Vulcan.

No doubt you already know that the people of Earth have elected me their first Polemarch. I do not take on this title lightly and have no intention of becoming another Vulcan.

The fledgling Earth Council has the full support of the former members of NATO and the SCO. This new world was forged by solar fire, by energy, and our kinship with all living creatures. I intend to honour life in all its forms, wherever it is found. Today, we chart a new course for humanity.

Ester Akintola, first elected Polemarch of Earth

P.S. A strategic meeting of the Council passed your Earth Protection Act — congratulations! I look forward to seeing you on the Council in the coming year. We have much to accomplish.

P.P.S. Please congratulate Dr Fisher on her recent Nobel Prize for the Fisher–Smith Theory of Quantum Displacement. I don't quite understand it, but I am eternally grateful for its application in creating clean energy sources.

Robyn stood facing the valley, the wind whipping at her shirt. Behind her, the sunlight caught on the newly restored golden ceiling of the temple and reflected light through the open door. Just as it had for millennia.

Thanks to Lenti, and Miranda and Brock's meticulous work, the temple had at last been returned to its former glory.

Hundreds of pilgrims also stood on the rocky outcrop, some clutching rough quartz charms. By their sides were sturdy yak, horses, dogs and all manner of creatures. Many now made the pilgrimage to the temple, to sit in contemplation and find solutions to their problems. Today, the mountain top hosted many more pilgrims than usual. The atmosphere crackled with anticipation.

"Coming through!"

Robyn instinctively ducked as Ariana swooped down on Jericho's back, the dragon's scales glimmering with blue light.

Eli jogged over from the newly built monastery to join her. "You're late." Una, his osprey, landed on his shoulder and riffled her feathers.

"Perfectly punctual, thank you," Ariana replied, sliding off Jericho's back. In a flash the dragon was once again a tiny salamander. He immediately clambered up to his favourite spot and curled on the top of Ariana's head.

"Hurry up, you two!" Fletcher called from the temple steps, Lenti almost unrecognisable in his fancy new robes by his side. The crowd parted, clearing a path for the walkers. Their energy auras blossomed as the quartz called to them. Lenti bowed deeply in greeting. In the temple behind him was assembled his new order of monks, all grinning with excitement. Many had answered the call of the temple, learning the histories of the walkers, eager to serve the ancient spirits.

"Are you sure you want to stay here with me? You should be up there with the others – the solstice ceremony is about to start," Catherine murmured in Robyn's ear.

Robyn turned and smiled. White light flickered on her skin as she tenderly kissed Catherine's forehead. "This is exactly where I'm meant to be."

The monks began to chant. The chorus rose into the sky and the trees beyond the temple sighed. The humming of the quartz beneath Robyn's feet intensified into a gentle harmonious melody, and the crowd of pilgrims gently swayed to its rhythms.

Beneath her bare feet, Robyn felt the deep rumbling of an enormous amount of energy vibrating through the quartz, calling to her. The trees responded, shaking their branches. The solar storm struck the ionosphere and the sky exploded in a network of red, green and blue flashes.

The walkers' auras swelled to encompass the mountain top. Robyn pulled Catherine close, the energy within her at peace, the walkers' energy tethers humming at the same resonant frequency as the quartz. Robyn drank in the sight of the crowd, her gaze skimming the bright faces, the hope and joy in the smiles around her. Brock and Miranda stood by the side of the temple. Her former supervisor waved and Robyn acknowledged him with a grin. The walkers' auras merged and pure white light bathed the mountain in its soft glow, a baptism of this new and wondrous world. For the first time in a thousand years, the Earth was in balance, and Robyn had never been more ready to face the future.

About the Author

Marita Smith is a freelance editor and gourmet mushroom grower based on the South Coast of NSW. She has a PhB (Hons) in Science from the Australian National University and considers chemistry a language in its own right. She spent several years as a paleo-biogeochemist, splitting her time between Australia and the Netherlands, before travelling through Europe to work on small farms. The first story she can remember writing involved being able to speak to her donkey, Mindy.

@ @maritasmithauthor
maritasmithauthor
www.maritasmithauthor.com

An ancient secret, a genetic key, a planet in peril

For scientist Robyn Greene, her laboratory is a second home. Here she searches for the ancient gene that is supposed to enable humans to communicate with animals. After years of failure, she's beginning to wonder if the gene is a myth. But when she stumbles across a strange genetic mutation, Robyn's world turns upside down. The man posing as her boss is, in fact, an operative of the mysterious international organisation, the MRI. Worse, they have dark plans to exploit her discovery.

In a race against time, Robyn must track down the individuals with this rare gene before the MRI turns them into lab rats. But when she meets the three teenagers, she realises that protecting them from the MRI is not only about saving their lives. Fletcher, Ariana and Eli are capable of more than anyone realises; they are part of an ancient cycle designed to keep the Earth in balance. A terrible future awaits the planet if the MRI gains control of Robyn and her research before she's figured out the kindred ties that bind these teenagers.

The fight for order has only just begun…

Fletcher, Ariana and Eli are walkers: carriers of a rare gene that enables them to communicate with animals and bridge our world and the spirit world. It is up to them to avert a catastrophic solar storm that threatens to release a dangerous dark spirit. Yet they're hunted by a powerful genetics organisation, the MRI, which will stop at nothing to control their powers.

Reeling from loss and betrayal, scientist Robyn Greene must protect the walkers at all costs. Can she figure out the MRI's plans and help the walkers bring Earth back into balance before it's too late?